"Unique, heart-wrenchin[...]
Tamora Pierce, *author of* Alanna: The First
Adventure *and other* Tortall *novels*

"Its fluid prose, naturalistic dialogue and pace make
The Assassin's Curse supremely readable. And in
Ananna, the young offspring of pirate stock, we have
a heroine both spirited and memorable."
Stan Nicholls, author of the Orcs: First Blood *trilogy*

"An inventive debut with a strong narrative voice, a
glimpse of an intriguing new world."
Adrian Tchaikovsky, author of the Shadows
of the Apt *series*

"Ananna of Tanarau is a delightfully irascible heroine,
inhabiting a fascinating and fresh new world that I
would love to spend more time in. Pirate ships? Camels?
Shadow dwelling assassins? Yes please! Can I have
some more?"
Celine Kiernan, author of the Moorhawke *trilogy*

"Inventive and individual storytelling about engaging
and intriguing characters."
Juliet E McKenna, author of the Hadrumal Crisis
novels

CASSANDRA ROSE CLARKE

The Assassin's Curse

STRANGE CHEMISTRY

An Angry Robot imprint
and a member of the Osprey Group

Lace Market House
54-56 High Pavement
Nottingham NG1 1HW
UK

44-02 23rd Street, Suite 219,
Long Island City,
NY 11101
USA

www.strangechemistrybooks.com
Strange Chemistry #4

A Strange Chemistry paperback original 2012
1

Cover art and design by Sarah J Coleman.
Set in Sabon by THL Design.

Distributed in the United States by Random House, Inc., New York.

ISBN 978-1-908844-01-9
eBook ISBN: 978-1-908844-02-6

Printed in the United States of America

9 8 7 6 5 4 3 2 1

This book is dedicated to my parents,
for all their years of love and support.

CHAPTER ONE

I ain't never been one to trust beautiful people, and Tarrin of the Hariri was the most beautiful man I ever saw. You know how in the temples they got those paintings of all the gods and goddesses hanging on the wall above the row of prayer-candles? And you're supposed to meditate on them so as the gods can hear your request better? Tarrin of the Hariri looked just like one of those paintings. Golden skin and huge black eyes and this smile that probably worked on every girl from here to the ice-islands. I hated him on sight.

We were standing in the Hariris' garden, Mama and Papa flanking me on either side like a couple of armed guards. The sea crashed against the big marble wall, spray misting soft and salty across my face. I licked it away and Mama jabbed me in the side with the butt of her sword.

"So I take it all the arrangements are in order?" asked Captain Hariri, Tarrin's father. "You're ready to finalize our agreement?"

"Soon as we make the trade," Papa said.

I glowered at the word trade and squirmed around in my too-tight silk dress. My breasts squeezed out the top of it, not on purpose. I know that sort of thing is supposed to be appealing to men but you wouldn't know it talking to me. At least the dress was a real pretty one, the color of cinnamon and draped the way the court ladies wore 'em a couple of seasons ago. We'd nicked it off a merchant ship a few months back. Mama had said it suited me when we were on board Papa's boat and she was lining my eyes with kohl and pinning my hair on top of my head, trying to turn me into a beauty. I could tell by the expression on Mistress Hariri's face that it hadn't worked.

"Tarrin!" Captain Hariri lifted his hand and Tarrin slunk out of the shadow of the gazebo where he'd been standing alongside his mother. The air was full up with these tiny white flowers from the trees nearby, and a couple of blossoms caught in Tarrin's hair. He was dressed like his father, in dusty old aristocratic clothes, and that was the only sign either of 'em were pirates like me and my parents.

"It's nice to meet you, Ananna of the Tanarau." He bowed, hinging at the waist. He said my name wrong.

Mama shoved me forward, and I stumbled over the hem of my dress, stained first with seawater from clomping around on the boat and then with sand from walking through Lisirra to get to this stupid garden. The Hariris were the only clan in the whole Confederation that spent more time on land than they did at sea.

Tarrin and I stared at each other for a few seconds, until Mama jabbed me in the back again, and I spat out one of the questions she made me memorize: "Have you got a ship yet?"

Tarrin beamed. "A sleek little frigate, plucked out of the Emperor's own fleet. Fastest ship on the water."

"Yeah?" I said. "You got a crew for that ship or we just gonna look at her from the wall over there?"

"Ananna," Mama hissed, even as Papa tried to stifle a laugh.

Tarrin's face crumpled up and he looked at me like a little kid that knows you're teasing him but doesn't get the joke. "Finest crew out of the western islands." It sounded rehearsed. "I got great plans for her, Mistress Tanarau." He opened his eyes up real wide and his face glowed. "I want to take her out to the Isles of the Sky."

I about choked on my own spit. "You sure that's a good idea?"

"Surely a girl raised on the Tanarau doesn't fear the Isles of the Sky."

I glared at him. The air in the garden was hot and still, like pure sunlight, and even though the horrors I'd heard about the Isles of the Sky seemed distant and made-up here, Tarrin's little plan set my nerves on edge. Even if he probably wasn't talking truth: nobody makes a path for the Isles of the Sky, on account of folks going mad from visiting that little chain of islands. They'll change you and change you until you ain't even human no more. They're pure magic, that's what Mama told me. They're the place where magic comes from.

"I know the difference between bravery and stupidity," I said. Tarrin laughed, but he looked uncomfortable, and his father was glowering and squinting into the sunlight.

"She's joking," Mama said.

"No, I ain't."

Mama cuffed me hard on the back of the head. I stumbled forward and bumped right up against Tarrin. Under the gazebo, his mother scowled in her fancy silks.

"It does sound like a nice ship, though," I muttered, rubbing at my head.

Captain Hariri puffed out his chest and coughed. "Why don't you show Mistress Tanarau your ship, boy?"

Tarrin gave him this real withering look, with enough nastiness in it to poison Lisirra's main water-well, then turned back to me and flashed me one of his lady-slaying smiles. I sighed, but my head still stung from where Mama'd smacked me, and I figured anything was better than fidgeting around in my dress while Papa and Captain Hariri yammered about the best way for the Tanarau clan to sack along the Jokja coast, now that the Tanarau had all the power of the Hariri and her rich-man's armada behind them. Thanks to me, Papa would've said, even though I ain't had no say in it.

Tarrin led me down this narrow staircase that took us away from the garden and up to the water's edge. Sure enough, a frigate bobbed in the ocean, the wood polished and waxed, the sails dyed pale blue – wedding sails.

"You ain't flying colors yet," I said.

Tarrin's face got dark and stormy. "Father hasn't given me the right. Said I have to prove myself first."

"So if we get married, we gotta sail colorless?" I frowned.

"If we get married?" Tarrin turned to me. "I thought it was a done deal! Father and Captain Tanarau have been discussing it for months." He paused. "This better not be some Tanarau trick."

"Trust me, it ain't."

"Cause I'll tell you now, my father isn't afraid to send the assassins after his enemies."

"Oh, how old do you think I am? Five?" I walked up to the edge of the pier and thumped the boat's side with my palm. The wood was sturdy beneath my touch and smooth as silk. "I ain't afraid of assassin stories no more." I glanced over my shoulder at him. "But the Isles of the Sky, that's another matter." I paused. "That's why you want to go north, ain't it? Cause of your father?"

Tarrin didn't answer at first. Then he pushed his hair back away from his forehead and kind of smiled at me and said, "How did you know?"

"Any fool could see it."

Tarrin looked at me, his eyes big and dark. "Do you really think it's stupid?"

"Yeah."

He smiled. "I like how honest you are with me."

I almost felt sorry for him then, cause I figured, with a face like that, ain't no girl ever been honest to him in his whole life.

"We could always fly Tanarau colors," I suggested. "Stead of Hariri ones. That way you don't have to wor—"

Tarrin laughed. "Please. That would be even worse."

The wrong answer. I spun away from him, tripped on my damn dress hem again, and followed the path around the side of the cliff that headed back to the front of the Hariris' manor. Tarrin trailed behind me, spitting out apologies – as if it mattered. We were getting married whether or not I hated him, whether or not Mistress Hariri thought I was too ugly to join in with her clan. See, Captain Hariri was low-ranked among the loose assortment of cutthroats and thieves that formed the Confederation. Papa wasn't.

There are three ways of bettering yourself in the Pirates' Confederation, Mama told me once: murder, mutiny, and marriage. Figures the Hariri clan would be the sort to choose the most outwardly respectable of the three.

I was up at street level by now, surrounded by fruit trees and vines hanging with bright flowers. The air in Lisirra always smells like cardamom and rosewater, especially in the garden district, which was where Captain Hariri kept his manor. It was built on a busy street, near a day market, and merchant camels paraded past its front garden, stirring up great clouds of dust. An idea swirled around in my head, not quite fully formed: a way out of the fix of arranged marriage.

"Mistress Tanarau!" Tarrin ran up beside me. "There's nothing interesting up here. The market's terrible." He pouted. "Don't you want to go aboard my ship?"

"Be aboard it plenty soon enough." I kept watching those camels. The merchants always tied them off at their street-stalls, loose, lazy knots that weren't nothing a pirate princess couldn't untangle in five seconds flat.

Papa told me once that you should never let a door slam shut on you. "Even if you can't quite figure out how to work it in the moment," he'd said. He wasn't never one to miss an opportunity, and I am nothing if not my father's daughter. Even if the bastard did want to marry me off.

I took off down the street, hoisting my skirt up over my boots – none of the proper ladies shoes we'd had on the boat had been in my size – so I wouldn't trip on it. Tarrin followed close behind, whining about his boat and then asking why I wanted to go to the day market.

"Cause," I snapped, skirt flaring out as I faced him. "I'm thirsty, and I ain't had a sweet lime drink in half a year. Can only get 'em in Lisirra."

"Oh," said Tarrin. "Well, you should have said something–"

I turned away from him and stalked toward the market's entrance, all festooned with vines from the nearby gardens. The market was small, like Tarrin said, the vendors selling mostly cut flowers and food. I breezed past a sign advertising sweet lime drinks, not letting myself look back at Tarrin. I love sweet lime drinks, to be sure, but that ain't what I was after.

It didn't take me long to find a vendor that would suit my needs. He actually found me, shouting the Lisirran slang for Empire nobility. I'm pretty sure he used it as a joke. Still, I glanced at him when he called it out, and his hands sparked and shone like he'd found a way to catch sunlight. He sold jewelry, most of it fake but some of it pretty valuable – I figured he must not be able to tell the difference.

But most important of all, he had a camel, tied to a wooden pole with some thin, fraying rope, the knot already starting to come undone in the heat.

Tarrin caught up with me and squinted at the vendor.

"You want to apologize for laughing at me," I said, "buy me a necklace."

"To wear at our wedding?"

"Sure." I fixed my eyes on the camel. It snorted and pawed at the ground. I've always liked camels, all hunchbacked and threadbare like a well-loved blanket.

Tarrin sauntered up to the vendor, grin fixed in place. The vendor asked him if he wanted something for the lady.

I didn't hear Tarrin's response. By then, I was already at the camel, my hands yanking at the knot. It dissolved quick as salt in water, sliding to the bottom of the pole.

I used that same pole to vault myself up on the saddle nestled between the two humps on the camel's back, hiking the skirt of my dress up around my waist. I leaned forward and went "Tt tt tt" into his ear like I'd seen the stall-vendors do a thousand times. The camel trotted forward. I dug the heels of my boots into his side and we shot off, the camel kicking up great clouds of golden dirt, me clinging to his neck in my silk dress, the pretty braids of hairstyle coming unraveled in the wind.

The vendor shouted behind me, angry curses that would've made a real lady blush. Then Tarrin joined in, screaming at me to come back, hollering that he hadn't been joking about the assassins. I squeezed my eyes shut and tugged hard on the camel's reins and listened to the gusts of air shoving out of his nostrils. He smelled awful, like dung and the too-hot-sun, but I didn't care: We were wound up together, me and that camel.

I slapped his reins against his neck like he was a horse and willed him to take me away, away from my marriage and my double-crossing parents. And he did.

All of Tarrin's hollering aside, we galloped out of the garden district without much trouble. I didn't know how to direct the camel – as Papa always told me, my people ride on boats, not animals – but the camel seemed less keen on going back to that vendor than I did. He turned down one street and then another, threading deeper and deeper into the crush of white clay buildings. Eventually he slowed to a walk, and together we ambled along a wide, sunny street lined with drying laundry.

I didn't recognize this part of the city.

There weren't as many people out, no vendors or bright-colored shop signs painted on the building walls.

Women stuck their heads out of windows as we rode past, eyebrows cocked up like we were the funniest thing they'd seen all day. I might have waved at them under different circumstances, but right now I had to figure out how to lay low for a while. Escaping's always easy, Papa taught me (he'd been talking about jail, not marriage, but still). Staying escaped is the hard part.

I found this sliver of an alley and pushed at the camel's neck to get him to turn. He snorted and shook his big shaggy head, then trudged forward.

"Thanks, camel." The air was cooler here: A breeze streamed between the two buildings and their roofs blocked out the sun. I slid off the camel's back and straightened out my dress. The fabric was coated with dust and golden camel hairs in addition to the mud-and-saltwater stains at the hem, and I imagined it probably smelled like camel now, too.

I patted the camel on the head and he blinked at me, his eyes dark and gleaming and intelligent.

"Thanks," I told him again. I wasn't used to getting around on the backs of animals, and it seemed improper not to let him know I appreciated his help. "You just got me out of a marriage."

The camel tilted his head a little like he understood.

"And you're free now," I added. "You don't have to haul around all that fake jewelry." I scratched at the side of his face. "Find somebody who'll give you a bath this time, you understand?"

He blinked at me but didn't move. I gave him a gentle shove, and he turned and trotted out into the open street. Myself, I just slumped down in the dust and tried to decide what to do next. I figured I had to let the camel go cause I was too conspicuous on him. Together we'd wound pretty deeply into Lisirra's residential mazes, but most people, when they see a girl in a fancy dress on a camel – that's something they're going to remember. Which meant I needed to get rid of the dress next, ideally for money. Not that I have any qualms about thievery, but it's always easier to do things on the up and up when you can.

I stood and swiped my hands over the dress a few times, trying to get rid of the dust and the camel hairs. I pulled my hair down so it fell thick and frizzy and black around my bare shoulders. Then I followed the alley away from the triangle of light where I'd entered, emerging on another sun-filled street, this one more bustling than the other. A group of kids chased each other around, shrieking and laughing. Women in airy cream-colored dresses and lacy scarves carried baskets of figs and dates and nuts, or dead chickens trussed up in strings, or jars of water. I needed one of those dresses.

One of the first lessons Papa ever taught me, back when I could barely totter around belowdeck, was how to sneak around. "One of the most important aspects of our work," he always said. "Don't underestimate it." And sneaking around in public is actually the easiest thing in the whole world, cause all you have to do is stride purposefully ahead like you own the place, which was easy given my silk dress. I jutted my chin out a little bit and kept my shoulders straight, and people just stepped out of the way for me, their eyes lowered. I went on like this until I found a laundry line strung up between two buildings, white fabric flapping on it like the sails of our boat.

Our boat.

The thought stopped me dead. She wasn't my boat no more. Never would be. I'd every intention of finishing what I started, like Papa always taught me. But finishing what I started meant I'd never get to see that boat again. I'd spent all my seventeen years aboard her, and now I'd never get to climb up to the top of her rigging and gaze out at the gray-lined horizon drawn like a loop around us. Hell, I'd probably never even go back to the pirates' islands in the west, or dance the Confederation dances again, or listen to some old cutthroat tell his war stories while I drifted off to sleep in a rope hammock I'd tied myself.

A cart rolled by then, kicking up a great cloud of dust that set me to coughing. The sand stung my eyes, and I told myself it was the sand drawing out my tears as I rubbed them away with the palm of my hand. There was no point dwelling on the past. I couldn't marry Tarrin and I couldn't go home. If I wanted to let myself get morose, I could do it after I had money and a plan.

I ducked into the alley. The laundry wasn't hung up too high, and I could tell that if I jumped I'd be able to grab a few pieces before I hit the ground again. I pressed myself against the side of the building and waited until the street was clear, then I tucked my skirts around my waist, ran, jumped, spread my arms out wide, and grabbed hold of as much fabric as I could. The line sagged beneath my weight; I gave a good strong tug and the clothes came free. I balled them up and took off running down the alleyway. Not that it mattered; no one saw me.

At the next street over I strode regally along again till I found a dark empty corner where I could change. I'd managed to nick two scarves in addition to the dress, so I draped one over my head in the Lisirran style and folded my silk dress up in the other. I figured I could pass for a Lisirran even though I've a darker complexion than most of the folks in Lisirra. Hopefully no one would notice I was still wearing my clunky black sea-boots underneath the airy dress – those would mark me as a pirate for sure. The dress was a bit tight across my chest and hips, too, but most dresses are, and the fabric was at least thick enough to hide the lines of the Pirates' Confederation tattoo arching across my stomach.

I knew the next step was to find a day market where I could sell my marriage dress. I couldn't go back to the one where I stole the camel, of course, but fortunately for me there are day markets scattered all over the city. Of course, Lisirra is a sprawling crawling tricky place, like all civilized places, full of so many happenings and people and strange little buildings that it's easy to get lost. I only knew my way around certain districts – those close to the water and those known to shelter crooks and others of my ilk. That is to say, the places where my parents and the Hariri clan would be first to look. And I had no idea where the closest day market was.

I strolled along the street for a while, long enough that my throat started to ache from thirst. It was hotter here than it had been in the garden district, I guess cause it was later in the day, and everyone seemed to have retreated into the cool shade of the houses. I walked close to the buildings, trying to stay beneath the thin line of their cast shadows. Didn't do me much good.

After a while I slouched down in another shady alley to rest, sticking the marriage dress behind my head like a pillow. The heat made me drowsy, and I could barely keep my eyes open...

Voices.

It was a couple of women, speaking the Lisirran dialect of the Empire tongue. I peeked around the edge of the building. Both a little older than me, both with water pitchers tucked against the outward swell of their hips. One of the women laughed and a bit of water splashed out of her pitcher and sank into the sand.

"Excuse me!" My throat scratched when I talked, spitting out perfect Empire. The two women fell silent and stared at me. "Excuse me, is there a market nearby? I have a dress to sell."

"A market?" The taller of the women frowned. "No, the closest is in the garden district." I must have looked crestfallen, cause she added, "There's another near the desert wall. Biggest in the city. You can sell anything there."

The other woman glanced at the sky. "It'll close before you get there, though," she said. She was right; I must have fallen asleep in the alley after all, cause the light had changed, turned gilded and thick. I was supposed to have been married by now.

"Do you need water?" the taller woman asked me.

I nodded, making my eyes big. Figured the kohl had probably spread over half my face by now, which could only help.

The taller woman smiled. She had a kind-looking face, soft and unlined, and I figured her for a mother who hadn't had more than one kid yet. The other scowled at her, probably hating the idea of showing kindness to a beggar.

"There's a public fountain nearby," she said. "Cut through the alleys, two streets over to the west." She reached into her dress pocket and pulled out a piece of pressed copper and tossed it to me. Enough to buy a skein plus water to fill it. I bowed to thank her, rattling off some temple blessing Mama had taught me back when I was learning proper thieving. Begging ain't thieving, of course, but I ain't so proud I'm gonna turn down free money.

The two women shuffled away, and I followed their directions to the fountain, which sparkled clean and fresh in the light of the setting sun. Took every ounce of willpower not to race forward and shove my whole face into it.

I reined myself in, though, and I got the skein and the water no problem. The sun had disappeared behind the line of buildings, and magic-cast lamps were twinkling on one by one, bathing the streets in a soft hazy glow. I could smell food drifting out of the open windows and my stomach grumbled something fierce. I managed to snatch a couple of meat-and-mint pies cooling on a windowsill, and I ate them in an out-of-the-way public courtyard, tucking myself under a fig tree. They were the best pies I'd ever tasted, the crust flaky and golden, the meat tender. I licked the grease off my fingers and took a couple of swigs of water.

I didn't much want to sleep outside – it's tough to get any real sleep, cause you wake up at the littlest noise, thinking it's an attack – but I also figured I didn't have much choice in the matter. I curled up next to the fig tree and used the marriage dress as a pillow again, although this time I yanked my knife out of my boot and kept it tucked in my hand while I slept. It helps.

I had trouble falling asleep. Not so much cause of being outside, though, but cause I kept thinking about the Tanarau and my traitorous parents: Mama smoking her pipe up on deck, shouting insults at the crew, Papa teaching me how to swing a sword all proper. It's funny, cause all my life I've loved Lisirra and the desert, so much so that I used to sleep belowdeck, nestled up among the silks and rugs we'd plundered from the merchant ships, and now that it looked like I'd be whiling away the rest of my days here in civilization, all I wanted was to go back to the ocean.

Figures that when I finally fell asleep, I dreamt I was in the desert. Only it wasn't the Empire desert. In my dream, all the sand had melted into black glass like it had been scorched, and lightning ripped the sky into pieces. I was lost, and I wanted somebody to find me, cause I knew I was gonna die, though it wasn't clear to me if my being found would save me or kill me.

I woke up with a pounding heart. It was still night out, the shadows cold without the heat of the sun, and I could feel 'em on my skin, this prickling crawling up my arm like a bug.

My dress was damp with sweat, but the knife was a reassuring weight in the palm of my hand. I pushed myself up to standing. Ain't nobody out, just the shadows and the stars, and for a few minutes I stood there breathing and wishing the last remnants of the dream would fade. But that weird feeling of wanting to be found and not wanting to be found stuck with me.

Maybe the dream was the gods telling me I wasn't sure about leaving home. Well, I wasn't gonna listen to 'em.

I took a couple more drinks from the skein then tucked my knife in the sash of my dress and headed toward the desert wall. I was still shaky from the dream and figured I wasn't going to be sleeping much more tonight, so I might as well take advantage of the night's coolness and get to the day market right as it opened.

CHAPTER TWO

The woman from yesterday hadn't lied; the day market was the biggest I ever saw, merchant carts and permanent shops twisting together to create this labyrinth that jutted up against the desert wall. I wandered through the market with my dress tucked under my arm, the early morning light gray and pink. The food vendors were already out, thrusting bouquets of meat skewers at me as I walked by. My stomach growled, and after ten minutes of passing through the fragrant wood-smoke of the food carts, I sidled up to a particularly busy vendor and grabbed two of his goat-meat skewers, even though I do feel bad about thieving from the food vendors, who ain't proper rich like the merchants we pirate from. I ate it as I walked down to the garment division, licking the grease from my fingers. Tender and fatty and perfect. You get sick of fish and dried salted meats when you're out on the ocean.

The garment division was an impressive one, with shop after shop selling bolts of fabric and ready-made gowns and scarves and sand masks. Tailors taking measurements out on the street. Carts piled high with tiny pots of makeup and bottles of perfumes.

It was a lot of options. I knew that I wanted a merchant who wouldn't ask me no questions, but I also couldn't use someone who was the sort to traffic in stolen goods, since I didn't want anyone who might have gotten word from the Hariris to be on the lookout for their missing bride. I decided it was probably safer going the slightly more respectable route, and that meant cleaning up my appearance some.

I snatched a pot of eye-powder and a looking glass from one of the makeup carts and darted off into a corner, where I wiped the kohl off my face with the edge of my scarf – a mistake I realized too late, when I saw I'd stained it with black streaks. I flipped the scarf around and tried to tuck the stained ends around my neck. Then I smeared some of the eye-powder on my lids the way I'd seen Mama do it, a pair of gold streaks that made my eyes look big and surprised. Good enough.

The market was starting to get busy, people walking in clumps from vendor to vendor. I kept my head down and my feet quick, scanning each dress-shop as I passed. None seemed right. One I almost ducked into – it was large, a couple of rooms at least, and full of people, which meant my face would be easily forgotten. But something nagged at me to walk on by, and I did, sure as if I had seen my own parents leaning up against the doorway.

I was nearly to the desert wall when a shop – the

shop, I thought – appeared out of the crush of people. It was tucked away in the corner of an alley, and I only noticed it cause someone had propped up a sign on the street with an arrow and the words We buy gowns written out neat and proper.

The shop was small, but a pair of fancy gowns fluttered from hooks outside the door, like sea-ghosts trapped on land. I went inside. More gowns, some only half-finished. The light was dim and cool and smelled of jasmine. No other customers but me.

"Can I help you?" A woman stepped out from behind some thin gauzy curtains. She wore a dress like the one I'd stolen, only it was dyed pomegranate red and edged with spangles that threw dots of light into my eyes. As she walked across the room, the sun splashed across her face. She was beautiful, which set me on edge, but there was something off about her features, something I couldn't quite place–

"Oh, I apologize," she said in Ein'a, which was the language of the far-off island where I'd been born, the language my parents had spoken to me when I was a baby. "We don't normally get foreigners."

Maybe I wasn't as inconspicuous as I thought.

"I speak Empire," I said, not wanting to stutter my way through Ein'a.

The shopkeeper smiled thinly, and I realized what it was that bothered me about her face – her eyes were pale gray, the same color as the sky before a typhoon. I ain't never seen eyes that color before, not even up among the ice-islands.

Something jarred inside of me. I wanted out of that shop. But even so, I unwrapped my silk dress and laid it out on the counter, the movements easy, like I was acting by rote. "I was hoping to sell this," I said.

The woman ran her hands over the dress, idly examining the seams, rubbing the fabric between her thumb and forefinger. She looked up at me.

"It's dirty."

I bit my lower lip, too unnerved to make a joke.

"And it reeks of camel." She glanced back down at the dress, tilted her head. "I recognize the cut, though. It's from court. Last season. How'd you come across it?"

"My mother gave it to me." Avoid lying whenever possible. Always leave out information when you can. Another one of Papa's lessons.

"Hmm," she said. "Looks like it's been through quite the adventure. I suppose I can use it as a guide. Merchant wives tend to be a bit behind on things." She folded the dress up. "I'll pay you one hundred pressed copper for it," she said.

"Two hundred."

"One fifty."

"One seventy."

She paused. Her lips curled up into a faint smile. "That's fair," she said. "One seventy."

Kaol, I wanted out of that store. The haggling went way too easy, and that smile chilled me to the bone. It was like a shark's smile, mean and cold.

She glided off to the back of the store, carrying the

dress with her. When she came back out she handed me a bag filled with thin sheets of pressed copper. I slid the bag into the hidden pocket in my dress and turned to leave. Didn't bother to count. Felt heavy enough.

"Wait," said the shopkeeper.

I stopped.

"Be careful," she said. "I don't normally do this for free, but I like the look of you. They're coming. Well, one of them. Him."

I stared at her. She said him like it was the proper name of somebody she hated.

"What are you talking about?"

"Oh, you know. Your dream last night."

All the air just whooshed out of my body like I'd been in a drunkard's fight.

"I ain't had no dream last night."

She laughed. "Fine, you didn't have a dream. But you know the stories. I can tell. I can smell them on you."

"The stories," I said. "What stories?" All I could see was the gray in her eyes, looming in close around me. And then something flickered in the room, like a candle winking out. And I knew. The assassins. That bogeyman story Papa used to tell me whenever I didn't mind him or Mama.

"Ah, I see you've remembered." The shark's smile came out again. I took a step backwards toward the door. "You're going to need my help. I live above the shop. When the time comes, don't delay."

I tried to smirk at her like I thought she was full of it, but in truth my whole body was shaking, and I was

thinking about Tarrin yelling at me yesterday afternoon, trying to get me to come back. My father isn't
afraid to send the assassins after his enemies. But
men'll say anything to get you to do what they want.
If Tarrin couldn't charm me onto his ship, he'd try to
scare me. Well, it wasn't gonna work.

The shopkeeper tilted her head at me and then
turned around, back toward the curtains. I darted out
into the sunny street and took a deep breath. The eeri-
ness of the shop faded into the background; out here
there was just heat and sand and sun. Normal, com-
forting. Plus I had money hanging heavy in my pocket.
I reached down to pat it. Enough to pay for a room at
a cheap inn.

Fear still niggled at the back of my head, though.
I hadn't thought about the assassins in years and
years.

Papa talked about them like they were ghouls or
ghosts, monsters come to take me away in the night.
The stories always ended in the death of the intended
victim. "They're relentless," he had said, one night
when I was ten or eleven, my face red and itchy with
anger. I'd sassed him or Mama or both, and probably
spent some time down in the brig for it too, but by
then we were in the captain's quarters. The lanterns
swung back and forth above our heads, the lights sliding across the rough features of Papa's face. "You can't
escape an assassin." He leaned forward, shadows swallowing his eyes. "Hangings, bumbling bureaucrats,
dishonest crewman, jail – those you can talk your way

out of, you try hard enough. But this kind of death is the only kind of death."

He always said that when he told me assassin stories – the only kind of death. It was this refrain I'd get in my head whenever I did something bad, like playing tricks on the navigator or trying to read one of Mama's spell-books without permission. The assassins were blood magicians in addition to skilled fighters. They lived in dark lairs hidden in plain sight, like crocodiles. They were the last refuge of a coward, of a man too afraid to fight you himself – and that was why they were so dangerous. They gave power to cowards.

As I got older I realized, for all the stories, I ain't never heard of a pirate's out-of-battle death that couldn't be explained away by drink or stupidity. And at some point, I decided the assassins weren't real, or if they were, they weren't interested in tracking down a captain's daughter as punishment for not minding her elders. Or refusing marriage, for that matter.

So that's what I told myself as I cut through the sunlight, back toward the food vendors to buy myself a sweet lime drink. The woman was probably a witch in her spare time, trying to drum up business for her cut-rate protection spells, and the only thing stalking me in the night was some memory from my child-hood. A story.

I paid for a room at an inn on the edge of town, not far from the day market. It was built into the desert wall, and my room had a window that looked out over the desert, which reminded me a bit of the ocean, the sand cresting and falling in the night wind. The room was small and bright and filled with dust, although clean otherwise – cleaner than my quarters on Papa's boat anyway.

I stayed in the inn for four days, and for four days nothing happened but dreams. They were the same one as the first night, me wandering around the black glass desert, waiting for somebody to find me, knowing I was going to die. I took to sleeping during the day – though that didn't stop the dreaming none – and went out as the sun dropped low and orange across the horizon, wasting my nights at the night market that was conjured up by sweet-smelling magic a few streets over from the day market's husk. The vendors at the night market hawked enchantments and magic supplies instead of food and clothing, spellbooks and charms and probably curses if you knew who to ask. It was a dangerous place for me to go: not cause I'd started believing in the assassins, but because you get a lot of scum hanging around the night markets, and the chance of somebody spotting me and turning me into the Hariri clan or my parents was pretty high.

But I went anyway, wearing my scarf even though the sun was down so I could pull it low over my eyes. I liked to listen in on the sandcharmers who worked magic from the strength of the desert. Mama could do the same thing but with the waters of the ocean, and it occurred to me, as I listened to the singing and the chanting, that I missed her. The most I'd ever been away from her – and from Papa too – was the three weeks I spent failing to learn magic with this sea witch named Old Ceria a couple years back. But that had been different, cause I knew Papa's boat would pick me up when the three weeks were up, and Mama'd be waiting for me on deck.

That wasn't going to happen now.

I spent a lot of my time daydreaming during those four nights, too, letting my mind wander off to what I was gonna do now that I wasn't tied to a Confederation ship no more. I knew I had to hide out till the Hariris got over the slight of me running away from the marriage, but once that all settled I'd be free to set out from Lisirra and make my fortune, as Mama used to say of all the young men who set sail with ships of their own. A ship of my own was what I really wanted, of course – what Confederation child doesn't? Course, the Confederation won't let women captain, and the Empire ain't nothing but navy boats and merchant ships, but I could always make my way south, where the pirates don't take the Confederation tattoo and don't adhere to Confederation rules, neither.

It was a nice thought to have, and there was something pleasant about spending the early mornings before I fell asleep planning out a way to get first to one of the pirates' islands – probably Bone Island, it's the biggest, which makes it easier to go unnoticed – and then down to the southern coast. The daydreams took my mind off the Hariris, at any rate, and most of the time they kept me from feeling that sharp pang of sadness over my parents.

On the fourth night, I woke up the way I always did, after the sun set, but my head felt heavy and thick, like someone'd filled it up with rose jam. I skipped eating and walked down to the night market, thinking the cool air would clear my thoughts. It didn't. The lights at the night market blurred and trembled. The calls and chatter of the vendors amplified and faded and then thrummed like a struck chord.

I'd barely made it through the entrance gate when out of nowhere I got stuck. I couldn't move. I stood at the entrance to the market, and my feet seemed screwed to the ground. My arms hung useless at my sides. I smelled a whiff of scent on the air, sharp and medicinal, like spider mint. It burned the back of my throat.

And then, quick as that, I was released.

The whole world solidified like nothing'd happened, and I collapsed to the ground in a cloud of dry dust, coughing, my eyes streaming. I could hear whispers, people telling one another to keep a wide berth and muttering about curses and ill omens. I pushed myself up to sitting. Onlookers stared at me from out of the shadows, and I did my best to ignore 'em.

This wasn't Mama's magic, sent out to bring me home: that I knew. Her magic had too much of the ocean in it, all rough and tumble, crashing and falling. You plunged into her magic. This – this was calculated.

I stood up. A nearby vendor had one eye on me like he thought me about to steal his vials of love potion. I stumbled backward a little, coughed, wiped at my mouth. My hand left a streak of mud across my face.

"Hey," said the vendor. He leaned over the side of his cart. I didn't meet his eye. "Hey, you. Don't even try it."

My head was still thick. I stared at him, blinking.

"Go on," he said. "You think I've never seen this trick before? Whoever your little partner is, he's gonna get blasted with my protection spell."

"I don't have a–"

The vendor glared at me. I gave up trying to explain. Besides, I kept thinking the word assassin over and over again in spite of myself. The vendor turned toward a customer, his face breaking into a smile, but he kept glancing over his shoulder as he filled the order. Keeping his eye out for thieves, like any vendor.

I coughed again, turned, wanting to get back to the inn, with its coating of dust and its view of the desert. The street leading away from the night market was emptier than it should've been, and quiet too. Halfway down I stopped and eased my knife out of my boot, and then I hobbled along, wishing I could walk faster, or run – but something had my joints stiff and creaking as an old woman's.

The shadows moved.

I froze.

So did the shadows.

I stood there for a few seconds listening to my heart beat and to the distant strains of music floating out of the night market. Papa's old assassin stories worked their way into my head – that old detail about how they moved through darkness and shadows the way a fish moved through water. I loosened my grip on the knife, holding it proper, the way you're supposed to, and dreaded the moment when the shadows would move again.

Nothing.

I slid forward, just a couple of steps in the direction of the inn. That stirred the shadows up. They slid along the buildings like snakes. My body ached worse and worse or else I would've taken off running; instead, all I could do was creep along, my heart hammering and my breath short and my skin cold and hot all at once.

My head cleared.

It happened real sudden, as if a latch had been sprung, and I saw the whole world as clear and crystalline as if I were still at sea beneath a shining blue sky. A man was following me. I whirled around and caught sight of his robes, dyed the color of the night sky, fluttering back into the liquid shadows. I'd no idea what had broken the spell, but I was grateful for it.

"You want to fight me? Come out and fight me!"

My voice bounced off the buildings. Eyes glowed pale blue in the darkness.

My head started going thick and fogged again. The magic crept in. The eyes burned on and on. My fear was a thick coil in the pit of my stomach holding me in place.

It was an assassin.

"Fight me!" I shrieked, and I could feel the hysteria in my voice, like my words were splintering into pieces.

The assassin glided forward, black on black except

for the strip of silver at his side. He didn't seem to be in much of a hurry. I forced myself forward, through the magic, and it gave me a pain in my spine that set me screaming, and my scream amplified up out into the starry night, rising up over the buildings, transforming into an explosion of white light that showered sparks and brightness down upon us both.

No one was as surprised as me.

I collapsed onto the ground, but for a second I saw the assassin like it was daytime: the grain in the fabric of his robes, the bump of his nose beneath his dark desert mask, the carvings etched into his armor. He was glaring at me.

"You're from the Mists?" he hissed. The bastard spoke perfect Empire.

"The what?"

The assassin jerked his head around like he was looking for somebody. I wanted to see where he was looking but I also didn't dare take my eyes off him.

"Who are you?" he said, though before I could answer he spat out a word in a language like dead flowers, beautiful and terrible all at once. Then he darted out of the glow of the light and melted into the shadows, all too quick for me to see.

For a few minutes I waited to die.

It didn't happen. The light I'd somehow screamed into existence burned away. I sat there in the street and remembered Papa's stories: they always kill their victims. But he hadn't killed me. He'd just melted into the shadows.

I didn't let myself get too cocky about that, though. Cockiness is useful to fake on occasion, but it'll only get you killed if you believe it. Maybe the man hadn't been an assassin assassin, just some hired knife sent by Captain Hariri. But then what about the moving shadows and the fog in my head and his eyes? Ain't no crewman on the Hariri able to pull off that trick with the eyes.

And my voice turning into light… Ain't no way that was me. That sort of protection spell was basic magic, and I couldn't even get the hang of basic magic back when Mama was trying to teach me.

I shuffled toward the inn, working things over in my head, clutching the knife to my breasts like I was some scared merchant's wife who had no clue how to use the damn thing. Everything was so dark. It took me a minute to realize none of the magic-cast lanterns were burning, and that sent another quake of chills vibrating through my spine.

It wasn't until I was dragging past the empty day market that I remembered the shopkeeper. The woman who bought my dress.

You're going to need my help. Don't delay.

I stopped. The night was quiet and still. I couldn't even hear the night market anymore.

I don't trust beautiful people. But Papa always told me you sometimes got to trust the one person you don't want to trust. "Just be smart about it," he'd say.

Well. I'd managed to avoid the only kind of death. I

figured I could be smart about the woman at the dress shop, too.

Mama tried to teach me magic, meeting with me down in the belly of the ship after my first menses showed up, but it turned out that I took more after Papa, who's completely untouched: better adept at stealing and sneaking and charming and fighting, all talents borne of the natural world. But unlike Papa, I can at least recognize magic when I see it and when I feel it, and I know better than to mess around with it.

I went to the woman's dress shop straight away, climbing over the day market fence and skittering through the empty streets till I found the sign with the arrow. The woman sat outside the shop eating a honey pastry, a lantern illuminating the lines of her face. She looked tired.

"Good," she said when she saw me. "You didn't delay."

"It was you, right? That's my thinking right now and I want to know for sure." I paused, rubbed at my dry eyes. The woman took a bite of pastry. "Earlier tonight," I said. "When the assassin attacked me."

The woman set her pastry in her lap. "You know that by all rights you should be dead."

"I know it. But you helped me."

She blinked at me.

"Though I can't figure out why."

The woman shrugged. She plucked the pastry out of her lap and finished it off. "Why don't you come inside?" she said. "I can prepare some coffee. I think we both need it."

She stood up and went into the shop. I hesitated. It still seemed too easy to me, her helping me with the assassin. Easy the way it had with the haggling. The woman stuck her head back out into the street.

"You come from pirate stock, don't you?"

I frowned. "How do you know that?"

"Because I looked at you. Don't worry, I won't hand you over to whoever it is you're running from."

"I ain't running from nothing."

"A pirate in the desert? You're obviously running from something." She smiled. "The reason I asked is because the pirates I deal with are so wary, but always over the wrong things. You look at my shop door like it's booby-trapped, but you go traipsing through the night market when you've got an assassin tracking you."

I didn't have nothing to say to that, cause I knew she had a point.

"Come inside," the woman said. "And I'll help you."

She took me to the back of the store, behind the curtains, and set some water to boiling in the hearth. Steam curled up into the dusty moonlight. I sat down at a low table in the corner and watched her. She didn't spend a lot of time getting the coffee all perfect, the way they do in drink houses, and she didn't ask me how sweet I wanted it neither.

She sat down at the table across from me. I waited until she drank from her own cup before drinking from mine.

"What do you know about them?" she said.

I looked down at the little swirls of foam in my coffee. "They're hired," I said. "They know blood magic." I closed my eyes. "They're the only kind of death." I felt weirdly safe in this small back room. I wanted to fall asleep.

"Ananna," she said, and at the sound of my name my eyes flew open. My hands turned to fists. The woman gazed at me with heavy-lidded eyes.

"How'd you know my name?"

The woman smiled. "How'd I know you were targeted? I know things."

"Yeah, I wouldn't mind knowing how you knew the assassin was after me, too."

She gave me a demure smile.

I scowled, took another sip of coffee, and glanced around the room, trying to find something that I could use to get the woman to talk to me. But there were just dresses and bangles and bolts of fabric. The shop could have belonged to anyone.

"I've fought one of them before," she said. "I won."

That got my attention. I stared at her, trying to figure out if she was lying or not, if she really was a woman who had escaped the only kind of death.

"Don't look so impressed," she said. "Contrary to what you may have heard, they are human."

"What happened?" I asked. "Why would anyone try to kill you?"

"Why would anyone try to kill you?" she shot back. "It doesn't matter, really. All that matters is one of them is after you."

"You ain't gonna tell me anything, are you?"

"Of course not. That sort of knowledge is more precious than gold. But I will help you. I'm not going to risk my life to save yours, mind, but I can offer aid."

I hadn't quite decided if I trusted this offer or not when she pushed her coffee cup aside and slid her hands over the tabletop. Figures rose out of the wood. A little man in a long robe, a girl in a courtier's dress.

"I'm no good at magic," I said. "So don't think I'm facing him down alone."

"But you already did face him down alone." The woman didn't look at me. "And besides, you've got enough magic," she said. "I can see it in you."

"You sure about that? Cause believe me, I've tried–"

She lifted her eyes to mine, and I got swallowed up by gray and couldn't talk no more. My ears buzzed and my lungs closed up.

"Quite sure," she said.

"Alright. You're sure." My voice came out small and weak, but the woman smiled and the gray all disappeared. The room fell back to normal.

"Tomorrow night," she said. "Go out to the desert. It'll make things easier, to be out in the open."

On the table, the two figures began to move. The assassin's robe fluttered out behind him. The girl – I couldn't think of it as me – took small hesitant steps backwards, her hair swirling around her face.

"This is how it's going to go without me," the woman said.

And in one movement, the assassin lashed out with

a tiny sword and the girl collapsed on the ground.

I jumped in my seat, my blood pushing violently through my veins. I cursed in the secret language of the Confederation. The woman raised an eyebrow.

"That's not going to happen," she said. "I'm going to give you something. A few things, actually. What they are isn't important."

She raised her hand over the figures. They reset themselves. This time the girl carried four tiny vials in the palm of her hand. When the assassin's robes began to flutter, the girl hurled the vials, small as grains of rice, in his direction. A flash of green light. The assassin was gone.

"Where he'd go?" I asked.

"Elsewhere," the woman said. "A place where he'll never be able to track you." She waved her hand over the table and the figures slid back down into the wood.

"So he'll die?"

The woman stood up, walked to a counter on the other side of the room. She pulled out four narrow vials.

"No," she said. "Don't ask so many questions." She set the vials on the table. "Four ingredients," she said. "Equal parts each. Throw them all at once. Say the invocation. That opens up the doorway. They'll pull him through."

"Who's 'they'?"

The woman didn't answer.

"So why can't you do it?"

She scooped up the four vials and handed them to me. All four fit in the palm of my hand.

"Practice," she said.

"What? You can't do it cause of practice?"

The woman glared at me. "I've better things to do than follow you out to the desert. It's enough of a favor giving you the vials at all, let alone two sets. Their contents are rare and very expensive."

I scowled.

She pointed to a clear stretch of wall, empty of any dresses or jars of enchantments. "Throw them there. I want to see if you can open up the portal; the invocation is tailored only for the assassin, so no threat of getting pulled in ourselves. Oh, and I suppose you'll be needing the invocation, won't you." She stood up and glided over to the counter and wrote something down on a scrap of paper, folded it over, handed it to me.

I opened it up.

"I can't read this," I said. I assumed it was another language, cause even though I knew the alphabet the words looked like gibberish. "Sound it out a few times," she said. "I used the Empire spelling."

There was no way this was going to work. Trying to work magic in an unfamiliar language? Taking advice from a beautiful woman with weird gray eyes? But if I didn't, I'd be dead. The only kind of death.

I stumbled over the words a few times, until the woman said, "That's good enough. They'll know what you're saying."

"There's that *they* again. Any reason you ain't telling me who they are?" I didn't like that she wouldn't.

"That's not what you need to worry about." She

jerked her head toward the blank wall. "Now say the invocation and throw the charms. Do it all at once."

I took a deep breath. I recited the incantation in my head once for good measure. Then I drew my arm back, stammered out the words, and threw the vials into the air.

They exploded into a corridor of glass-green light, powerful enough that I staggered backward. The air swirled around me, and I thought I could hear a hum, deep and reverberating, coming from the slash of green. Light scattered across the floor of the shop. That corridor of light darkened and widened until it became a doorway. On the other side I saw mist.

Then, slowly, the light faded, growing dimmer and dimmer until there was nothing left but the doorway, and then that faded away too. I shuffled over to the table and collapsed in the chair. I felt like I'd just been through a thousand sea-battles.

"Now you know why I don't want to do it," the woman said. "It takes all your energy to open a portal like that."

I dropped my forehead to the table. The wood was cool against my skin.

"I have to do that again." The thought left me unsettled. "You sure this is going to work?"

"As sure as I'm standing here before you," she said. "You send him away, and he won't ever come back."

I felt my heart beating in my chest, reminding me I was still alive.

"I suggest you go somewhere to sleep," she said.

"Rest. I've got a protection spell on you that'll last until sundown, but I'm not staving him off for another night."

I lifted my head and drained the rest of my coffee, then dumped my cup upside down so I could look at the dregs. Not that I ever remember what they mean. This time wasn't no different.

"Satisfied?" the woman asked. I didn't like the way she asked that. Almost like she was making fun of me.

"Maybe," I snapped.

She laughed. And then she handed me a fresh set of vials and sent me on my way.

CHAPTER THREE

I left the inn at sunset. The four vials were tucked away in my pocket, but I kept my knife out. Even though Papa had partially gotten me into this mess, I hated to think what he would say if I went out there completely unprepared.

I walked across the sand for a long time, long enough that the sun melted into the horizon line and the stars began to twinkle in the unending blackness overhead. The wind pushed my hair away from face, tangled my dress up in my legs. And I was so scared I kept choking on my own empty breaths. I'd been in battle before. Battles with weapons, though. Battles against people, not ghouls. And even in those battles my skin turned clammy and numb beforehand, even then I had to remind myself to breathe.

I walked long enough that Lisirra was just a chain of lights in the distance. For a minute I wanted to turn back, just drop the vials and run straight to the garden district and beg my apologies.

Suddenly that medicine scent, the one from the night before, saturated the air.

I stopped walking. The wind howled, blowing my hair into my eyes. I clutched my knife in one hand and stuck my other hand in my pocket and waited.

The shadows lengthened, curled, expanded. I whirled around, looking for a pair of glowing eyes, a flick of dark fabric. Nothing.

I wrapped my hand around the vials.

The world was suddenly too big.

And then he was there. I didn't see him, but I felt him, a shiver of cold breath on the back of my neck. I spun around, kicking up a spray of moonlit sand, and shoved the knife into my dress sash.

A flash of skin.

I pulled the vials out, broke them between my palms, and threw the whole thing, blood and magic and glass, in the direction of that skin. I screamed the invocation, the words still clumsy on my tongue.

The light erupted clean and bright. In the desert darkness it was the exact same color as the southern seas. It shot up like a fountain toward the sky. For a few seconds the entire desert glowed green.

And then something happened. The light didn't shower across the sand as it should. It didn't change into a doorway and disappear. It simply blinked out, like a candle between Mama's thumb and forefinger as she said goodnight, and I was plunged back into darkness and there was the assassin standing in front of me, his eyes – dark tonight, normal, not blue at all

– narrowed above his desert mask.

I screamed. I didn't have time to think about the failure of the woman's magic. I didn't have time to think about anything. I just screamed and screamed, and the assassin stared at me with a sword glinting like starlight at his side.

I stumbled away. The sword flashed, sang, cut a long gash in my right forearm. I fell down into the sand. He darted toward me, and I drew up Papa's strength and in one movement yanked my knife out from my sash and implanted it squarely in the assassin's thigh. He stumbled backward, dragging the knife from my grasp, and I thought he looked a little stunned.

No time for thinking, though. I dove forward, grabbed the knife again. He swung his sword down at me and I was able to roll away, sand coating my face, stinging my eyes. I skittered backward across the desert like a crab. I thought the assassin was moving kind of slow for an assassin. Maybe the magic had done something after all. Or maybe he felt sorry for me. That sort of thing happens among cutthroats more often than you'd expect.

The assassin reached into some dark place in his armor and I flung the knife at him, in my panic not taking care to throw it properly. The hilt bounced off his chest. He stopped and looked at me. All I could see were his eyes, but they had a lightness in them that made me think he was laughing, which got me angry instead of scared. I reached over and grabbed the knife, jumped up to my feet, swung my head around, looking for something to use as a weapon or something to use as a trick. Nothing.

Nothing except a weird slithery motion through the sand, black against the black night. Then a pair of narrow white fangs. It was coming up behind the assassin, creeping up close to his ankles, but he didn't take no mind of it. Too busy pulling some murderous enchantment out of his cloak.

I ain't never liked snakes. You don't see enough of 'em on the water to get used to 'em, really, and when I saw this one I shrieked without meaning to and stuck my knife clean through it, cause my fear had turned me into a fool who only acted on reflex. Darkness pooled out onto the sand, and the snake flopped a few times and then died.

The whole night went still. I swear it was like the assassin and me were the only two people left in the world.

The assassin said something in that beautiful-terrible language of his. But he didn't try to kill me, which was what I expected. I pulled the knife out of the snake and wiped the blood off on the hem of my dress. The assassin kept staring at the snake like he'd never seen one before. I took this opportunity to attempt an escape, and began creeping back over the sand on my hands and knees.

"Stop," the assassin said, and I froze, sure I was about to die.

Footsteps thudded on the sand. He came and stood beside me, and when I looked up at him, half-forcing myself to meet his eyes, he pulled the mask away from his face.

He wasn't a ghoul at all, just a man, like the shop-keeper had said, and younger than I would've expected, though still a bit older than me, maybe by about five or so years. His entire left cheek was scarred, ripples and folds in the flesh as if from a fire or maybe magic. Beneath the scar he was handsome, though, almost as handsome as Tarrin of the Hariri, so I didn't exactly relax.

"Did you save my life?" he asked.

"Maybe." I figured in a situation like this, ambivalence is always best.

"Why did you do that?"

I looked at the dead snake and back up at his scarred face. "Seemed like a good idea at the time."

The assassin frowned, and it twisted his face up in a way I found interesting. I waited for him to pull out his sword and slice my throat, but instead he sat down on the sand beside me. He draped his arms over his knees and stared morosely off in the distance.

"I wish you hadn't done that," he said.

"Um… I'm sorry?" I waited for a few minutes, watching him. Then I asked, "Are you going to kill me or what?" I figured I might as well get it out of the way.

He looked over at me, moonlight flashing across his dark eyes. I decided I rather liked the look of him, which was a bit of a problem, all things considered.

"No," he said, sounding glum.

"Oh." Relief flooded over me, and anybody with any

lick of sense would have picked up and ran back toward Lisirra. Instead, I opened my mouth. "Why not?"

He hesitated. "You saved my life." A pause. "From an asp, of all things."

"That's the dumbest reason I ever heard."

"I'd expect you'd be grateful for it."

"Oh, I'm plenty grateful," I said. "I'm just saying, that's a dumb reason."

"Yes, well, I'm afraid there's more."

I eyed him warily.

"I have to protect you now." The words came out in a rush, like he was embarrassed to say 'em. I woulda been.

"What? Why?"

"You saved my life. That's how it works."

"How what works?"

He didn't answer, just rubbed at his forehead, and I figured this must be some kind of honor thing, like he swore an oath or something. Pretty stupid oath for an assassin, but what did I know? I'd heard about ships in the Confederation with ridiculous rules of honor. Like this one captain who had his crew give a portion of gold to a temple every time they made port in Empire lands. More often than not the temple turned 'em in, so they spent half their time being chased by the Empire navy.

Fortunately, Mama and Papa never much went in for things like that. They always taught me that honor was best defined on a case-by-case basis.

"Well," I said. "I don't require your protective services. I'm a pirate."

"A bit far from the ocean," he said. He glanced at me out of the corner of his bad eye. "Besides, I'm afraid you do. The Hariri clan expects you dead. They'll send someone else."

"Or," I countered, feeling pleased with my cleverness, "you could just tell them you did it."

"They require proof."

"Oh, hell." I did shudder a little at that, though. Bad enough they hired someone to do their fighting for them. Demanding proof? Good thing I managed to avoid marrying into that family.

We sat side by side without speaking for a while. He went into some kind of trance, and the scent of mint was everywhere and his eyes glowed pale blue like before. Now that I wasn't scared out of my mind I realized they were the color of the glaciers in the northern seas.

While he was in his trance, I sat there and did some thinking of my own. I lucked out with that snake, no doubt about it. If they sent another assassin – and I figured they would, on account of this one screwing up the job – it might be handy to have a bodyguard around. Better still if that bodyguard was an assassin himself. I didn't much want to admit it, but he was probably right about me needing his help.

Sides, once the Hariris were taken care of, I could ditch him and head off to Bone Island or maybe straight to the southern port cities. His honor wasn't my problem.

After a while, he shook his head and blinked, and his eyes returned to normal, like his soul had come back from wherever he'd sent it. You never know with magic-users.

"How's your leg?" I asked him. Figured it might be good to play at making friends.

"What?"

"Your leg. I stabbed you."

He stared at me. Then he peered down at his leg, spread his hands over the dark fabric of his trousers. Blood on black is too dark to see in the best of times, and even with the moonlight I couldn't make anything out.

"A flesh wound," he said. "I'll be fine." He paused, tilted his head toward me. "How's your arm?"

"Oh." I glanced down at it. The blood had dried onto my skin, and the wound had stopped hurting sometime in the middle of the fight. "Nothing I haven't dealt with before." I paused. "My name's Ananna, by the way."

He hesitated. I was about to tell him he didn't have to give his name, but then he spoke up. "You can call me Naji."

"Glad I have something to call you," I said. He looked like he wanted to smile, and his eyes kind of brightened, but otherwise his face didn't move.

The wind picked up.

I didn't think much of it, except to duck my head to keep sand from blowing in my eyes. But Naji grabbed me by the wrist and pulled me roughly to my feet. When I looked up my heart started pounding something fierce, cause the desert was lit up like it was daytime, light coming from the swirls of sand slicing through the air.

When the sand struck against my skin it left a shimmery golden glow, like the pots of expensive body paint we sometimes stole from merchant ships.

"The Hariris?" I said, dazed. Sand stung the inside of my mouth. "Already?"

Naji yanked the mask back over his face, leaving just his eyes. "No," he said. "Find someplace to hide."

"It's the middle of the desert!"

He shoved me away from him, and I stumbled across the sand, almost losing my balance. My eyes watered and my nostrils burned. I pulled the knife out of my sash and clutched it tight, close to my hips, the way Papa taught me. I had no intention of slinking off behind some moonlit desert tree. My people do not hide.

A figure emerged from the swirl of sand and light: a woman dressed in long rippling skirts. Something about her, about the way she moved, seemed familiar–

It was the woman from the dress shop.

She looked a lot grander than I remembered, and even more beautiful. Her hair streamed out in dark ribbons behind her, and her skin glowed with the same light from the sand. Her pale eyes were stones in the middle of her face. I tried to find my voice, to tell her Naji wasn't no threat anymore, but she spotted me and I froze in place.

"You," she said. "Why aren't you dead?"

"What?" It came out barely a whisper. My heart thudded against my chest, anger and confusion spinning out through my body.

The woman scanned the desert. "I should have known better than to send a sea rat out here." Her gaze flicked over to me. "Though you seemed to have so much potential. I really did think it would work."

I realized then that the woman had used me – I didn't know the full of it, but I hated that I'd trusted her enough to let her do it. So I lunged forward, knife outstretched, but she picked up one hand and flicked her fingers and I went flying backward. I landed hard enough in the sand that all the breath slammed out of me, but then Naji was pulling me up to standing. He pressed his face close to my ear, his mask rippling as he spoke.

"If you insist on fighting, take this." And he slipped something into my hand, something rough and dry and so powerful that even I recognized the magic in it, before bounding off to face down the woman.

"Assassin," she hissed, drawing out the word, and Naji reached into his armor, pulled out the same satchel he'd almost used on me. He didn't throw it at her, though, just reached in and pulled out some dark dust, which he blew across the desert, cutting out all the light from the woman's incandescent sand. The desert plunged back into night. The woman's scream echoed through the darkness, and then her silhouette attacked his silhouette, and I blinked a couple times, willing my eyes to adjust.

When they did, Naji had drawn his sword, the blade flashing in the moonlight. And the woman had a sword of her own.

I held up the charm he had slipped me. It was a necklace, a ball of dusty dried-out vines and flower petals hanging off a piece of narrow leather. I slipped it over my neck and immediately I felt protected, impenetrable. Safe.

Damn him! He was sticking to that idiotic oath to protect me. Which meant he was in the middle of a magic-and-sword fight without protection. The charm must have stopped the magic from before, the magic intended to suck him through the portal – now if she tried anything, it would actually work.

I knew better than to jump into the middle of the fight, much as I wanted to. Instead, I looped around behind the woman, keeping myself low to the sand. The woman knocked Naji back with a burst of magic, and as she regrouped herself, I attacked. I shoved my knife into her shoulder blade. She howled, whirled around. Light seeped out of the wound, and a few droplets flung across my face. It was hot on my skin, and for a moment I faltered, not sure what to do about a beautiful lady who bleeds light.

But then she did that flicking motion with her hand again, only this time I stayed put, protected, and in the few seconds before she could realize the secret hanging around my neck, I stuck the knife into her belly. More light spurted out, landing on the sand, on the fabric of my dress.

There were hands on my shoulders, pulling me backward. Naji. He sang something in his language, and the sky ripped open, the stars streaming in the blackness. He wound one arm over my chest and pulled me close to him, close enough that I could feel his breath on the back of my neck. All the wind in the world blew into that gash in the sky. The woman screamed, and her feet lifted up off the earth, light pouring out of her wounds and turning into stars in the darkness, and then she tumbled head over feet through the air and was gone.

The gash sewed itself back up.

Naji let me go. I dropped down to the sand, exhausted, and rolled over onto my back to look up at the sky. The light from the stars was dazzling.

"Who was she?" I asked.

"Stand up," said Naji. "We shouldn't stay here. It's not safe."

"You didn't answer my question." But I got back up to my feet, shaking as I did. The woman's light was still on my clothes and skin and knife, although the glow was beginning to fade. Naji reached over and plucked the charm from my neck, and I felt his touch long after he'd slipped the charm back into his cloak.

"Well?" I said.

"She's from the Otherworld," said Naji. "She's been chasing after me for some time."

I stared at him. "Another world?" I asked. "What, like the ice-islands?"

Naji's head turned in the darkness. He still had on his mask.

"No," he said. "Not like the ice-islands."

I waited for an explanation.

He sighed. "It's a world layered on top of our world. Some call it the Mists."

"Oh, well that clears everything up." But I remembered the woman refusing to tell me where the green-light portal would send Naji. Elsewhere.

"I'll explain it to you later. We need to get out of the desert before the fallout takes effect."

I took fallout to mean the magic-sickness, since even I could feel that prickle in the air that always comes when you use too much magic at once. Mama'd told me stories about how it changes you, since that's all magic is anyway, pure change – she said she knew a dirt-witch who got turned into a pomegranate tree after trying to resurrect her dead husband. And I'd seen clams and ripples of sea-bone sprout out of the side of the Tanarau after Mama used magic in battle.

Naji turned, cloak swirling around him, and walked in the direction of the city. And cause the air was choking with magic, the sand twisting into figures in the darkness, my own skin crawling over my bones, I followed him.

CHAPTER FOUR

We walked for a long time, the city growing brighter and more distinct on the horizon. Naji didn't talk. I kept trying to think of things to say, and I kept coming up short. Fortunately all that walking warmed me up against the chill of the dusty night wind.

Naji stopped right outside the desert wall, his cloak rippling and casting slinky shadows across the sand. He pulled his mask away and then turned toward me. He looked like he had been in a fight: blood on his face, ragged cuts on his clothing, scratches in his armor. I realized I probably didn't look much better.

"Did you have any belongings in your room at the inn?" he said.

"What?"

"The Desert Light Inn." He jerked his chin toward the city. "Where you were staying."

"How did you... Oh." I frowned, wondering if he had ever watched me through the open window without me knowing. "Some spare clothes." I knew better than to tell him about the money. "Why?"

His face got all intense and he said, "I have to protect you. But I'm afraid you shouldn't stay at that inn any longer. We can find somewhere in the pleasure district."

I saw where he was going with this. We could rent a room in the pleasure district and the innkeeper would probably take me for a whore or a mistress and not think anything of it. Not that I look like anybody's mistress, but you know – there wouldn't be any questions. If I were just some runaway it'd be the perfect place to hide, because nobody ever looks anybody in the face down there. Unfortunately, the pleasure district was exactly the part of town I might expect to find my parents – or worse, a gang of Hariri crewman.

Assuming my parents were still in the city at all.

That thought made me sad. I turned away from Naji so he couldn't see that sadness washing across my face.

"Collect your things," he said. "I'll wait for you in the alley outside the inn." And he started to dissolve, turning into shadows like the ones I'd seen the first time he attacked me. Just like in the stories. He was halfway disappeared when he turned solid again.

"What do you want?" I snapped.

"A word of warning. Don't think you can slip out the back of the inn. I will know."

"What! I wasn't gonna slip out."

"I can track you," he said. "And I can bind you to me if necessary."

"Oh yeah?" I was a little pissed, cause I ain't done

nothing to make him think I had any intention of sneaking off. Not while the Hariris were still after me, at any rate. "Why didn't you just do that straightaway? Bind me to you?"

"Because it's cruel," he said.

That stunned me, ain't gonna lie. I dug the heel of my left foot into the ground, kicking up a spray of sand, and he gave me a look halfway between a glare and an eye-roll and took to dissolving again. I walked through the desert gate alone, although every now and then I caught a movement out of the corner of my eye, as though he was gliding along beside me.

My room was just how I left it, my spare dresses draped over the back of the divan, my money still shoved beneath the loose floorboard under the bed. It was like I'd only been out at the night market, not battling some creature from the Mists and picking up an assassin-protector for my trouble.

Naji was waiting for me in the alley like he said, not as a shadow but as a man, although he'd covered his face again. He looked sinister. At least his eyes weren't glowing.

"You're too conspicuous," I told him. I handed him one of my dresses, folded up to look like a package. "Here, take this."

He didn't. "I've been doing this much longer than you have—"

"I doubt it. Besides, I bet you always worked alone, didn't you? You could slink around in the shadows, no problem. But now that you got me you have to act like a normal person." I pressed the package against his stomach, and this time he touched his hands gingerly against its sides.

"What are you giving me?"

"It's one of my dresses. I don't want to carry it all the way to the pleasure district. Now take off your mask and act like you have a right to be here."

He stared at me. The glow from the street illuminated the little burst of scarring that peeked up from the top of his mask. Then he handed the dress back and turned into shadow.

I cursed under my breath. He had disappeared completely from the alley; all the surrounding shadows lay flat and still and unremarkable. I spent a few minutes juggling my dresses, finally tucking two under one arm and one under the other, before stepping out onto the street. Hardly anybody was out, just a few shopkeepers getting everything ready for the start of the day. I nodded at them like it was totally normal for me to be traipsing through the streets in the dark hours before dawn, heading in the direction of the ocean, alone.

I got to the pleasure district as the sky was turning gray with the day's new light. I ducked into an alley and waited.

Naji materialized a few moments later.

"Now what?" I said. "By the way, I should tell you, my parents might be down here. Wouldn't be up at this hour, but you know."

"Your parents?" He pulled the mask away from his face.

"Yeah, my parents. Kaol, don't you know?"

"I obviously don't."

"I mean, don't you know why you were hired – why the Hariris–"

"I'm not told the particulars," he said, interrupting me. "Only what's needed for my tracking spells. We need to find a place to stay before the sun comes up. You really should rest."

"Is that part of your protection deal? Making sure I get enough sleep?"

He didn't answer, just stepped out onto the street. I hoped he'd pay for the room and I could save my coins for later. That's what Papa would've told me.

Naji stuck his head back into the alley, looking all angry and put-upon, like I was some little kid he got saddled with. I shuffled out to join him. The pleasure district was mostly full of drunks stumbling home for the night. Nobody paid us any mind.

We'd been walking for about ten minutes when Naji spoke.

"Why would your parents be here?"

I glanced over at him. He had his eyes fixed straight ahead. It was like he didn't want anyone to know we were having a proper conversation.

"They're pirates," I said. "I told you."

"You said you were."

We were close enough to the waterfront that I could smell the salt in the sea, and my stomach twisted up with homesickness, not just for Papa's boat but for the ocean itself.

"I grew up on a pirate ship," I said. "Looting and pillaging's all I know."

"How charming. Would your parents take you back if they found you?"

He didn't sound hopeful when he asked it.

"What if they did?" I asked. "What would happen to you? Are you seriously telling me you'd have to tag along, just cause of some stupid oath–"

The expression on his face stopped me cold.

"You talk too much about things you don't understand," he told me, his voice low and dark. "Come along, the Snake Shade Inn's this way."

I knew the Snake Shade Inn, but I didn't say nothing. No place in the pleasure district's exactly high class, but the Snake Shade was lower than most of the places there, and my parents generally avoided it when I was in tow. I'd heard stories from the crew, though, mostly about whores they'd met up with there.

So I probably wasn't going to run into my parents, but if Captain Hariri had dispatched any of his men – maybe. A little shiver of fear eked up my spine, and I snuck a glance at Naji, with his mask and his armor and his black clothes, and wondered if I was gonna need his protection again.

All around us, the food vendors were opening up their carts for breakfast. Cause it was the pleasure district, there were still drunks dragging themselves around, trying to find a place to sleep off the drinking-sickness. Most of 'em shied away from us, crossing the street and turning their faces away, but I could still hear 'em whispering as me and Naji walked by. It was an uneasy feeling, the way their fear followed us down the street.

Abruptly, Naji reached up and yanked his mask over his face. He didn't falter or stop walking, but the suddenness of his movement set me on guard.

"What's wrong?" I asked.

He glanced at me out of the corner of his eye. "We're almost there."

"That don't answer my question."

"You're not in danger."

"Why'd you put your mask on?"

His eyes darkened and he turned away from me and started walking more quickly, his strides long and brisk. I sighed with irritation and then lagged a little behind him, ambling along, taking my time. He glared at me over his shoulder.

"What?" I asked. "You said I wasn't in any danger."

A peal of laughter broke out from the shadows of one of those narrow Lisirran alleys that run like glass-cracks between the buildings. A man spilled out of the alley, an old Empire sailor from the looks of the rags he wore. He leaned up against the building and guffawed and then said, "Now this is something I never thought I'd see. A little girl hassling an assassin." He laughed again, snorting like a camel, and then took a long drink from a rum bottle.

"I ain't a little girl," I said. Naji just glanced at him and kept walking, although I noticed he stuck his hand on the hilt of his sword. I followed after Naji, though

I wasn't too worried – it was just some drunk. What else do you expect down here?

"Why you wearing the mask?" The man tottered forward. "You know you ain't in the desert."

Naji didn't answer, just stared straight ahead. I found myself hanging back a little, watching the whole thing with interest. You live your whole life with pirates, you start smelling when a fight's brewing.

"You don't got an answer for me?" the man called out, stumbling after Naji. "Or are them stories true, that they cut out your tongues?" And then the man grabbed Naji by the upper arm. In one clean movement, Naji had the man laid out on the ground, his foot on the man's chest, the point of his sword at the man's throat. I was pretty impressed in spite of myself.

"No," Naji said, "They don't."

By this point a crowd had gathered, drunks and sailors and sleepy-looking whores. A few of 'em tittered nervously at that, and Naji looked up at 'em, his dark eyes glittering. They looked away.

Then the drunk rolled out from under Naji's foot, grabbed him by the ankle, and yanked hard. Naji stumbled a little but managed to catch himself at the last moment. Even though it was a good sight more elegant than most men could do, I was still surprised by that reminder that he really was just a man.

And then I felt something cold against the side of my neck.

"Oh, hell," I said, dropping my dresses to the ground.

"I'll cut your little friend's throat," the man said.

"How do you like that?" His hands were shaking and his breath stank, and I stood extremely still, my heart pounding. The giddiness of watching a fight got washed out by the fear of actually being in one. I wasn't aware of the gathered crowd no more – the only things I knew were Naji glowering at me and the coldness of the knife and the drunk pressing his body up against me

Naji took a step forward. The knife dug deeper into my skin.

"Don't move!" I shrieked. "Please, you'll get me killed!" I tried to make my voice sound as hysterical as I could so the drunk wouldn't notice my hand slipping into the sash of my dress.

"Aw, you ain't gonna help her?" the man said. "Hoping to find someone prettier?"

I jabbed my knife into his side. The man howled and fell away from me and I raced over to Naji.

"Told you I don't need your help."

Naji glared at me. Then he stalked over to the drunk, who was curled up on the street, one hand pressed against his stomach, redness seeping through his fingers. The crowd was whispering again. Naji reached down and dipped his fingers in the man's blood. The man let out a low, frightened moan.

Naji started chanting.

The crowd lurched away, their whispers turning into a terrified babble. Naji's eyes gleamed blue. The man gasped and keened and then his head dropped back and the entire street was full of silence.

Naji gathered up my dresses and my knife and

handed them to me. "Come," he said, yanking on my shoulder, pulling me away from the scene.

The crowd let us go.

"What did you do to that man?" I asked. I tried to pull away from his grip but he wouldn't let go. "Did you suck the soul of his body? Why didn't you just kill him normal?"

"I didn't kill him at all," Naji snapped. "He'll wake up in an hour."

We walked the rest of the way in silence. My neck was still bleeding a little from where the knife had pricked it, and I kept wiping at it and looking up at Naji and thinking about the drunk's blood staining his fingers.

When we arrived at the inn, its main room was mostly empty save for a couple of bedraggled-looking whores and a man I pegged as another pirate by the way he was dressed up in aristocrat's clothes. When Naji walked in, all three of them got to their feet and filed out without saying a word. And the innkeeper got the shakes when Naji told him he wanted a room. He kept glancing over at me, eyes all wide with fear. I wondered if it was cause he'd heard about the fight or cause the innkeep was just terrified of assassins generally.

"And… and the lady?" he said, stammering. "Will she have her own room?" I wanted to laugh, him calling me a lady when I had blood on my arms and my dress.

"No," Naji said. "She'll stay with me."

The innkeeper went pale, like Naji had just produced the ghost of his dead mother or something. He tried to hand over the key to the room and dropped it on the counter instead. I didn't want to laugh anymore. It occurred to me that if this was how people were gonna act every time me and Naji came into a place – well, I could see that getting to be a problem. Maybe Tarrin would meet some pretty Saelini girl and the Hariris would just forget the whole thing and I could slip off when Naji was in one of his trances. Not that I thought any of that would happen.

Naji finished the transaction and glided over to the stairs. I went up to the counter, leaned over it, and said to the innkeep, "Don't worry, you'll see me again."

The innkeep's eyes twitched from me to Naji, who was leaning against the doorway and looking annoyed.

"He won't do nothing," I said, but the innkeeper shook his head.

"Run," he said, in a hoarse whisper. "Get away. I've seen what his type are capable of – what they'll do to an innocent like you."

I wondered why the guy thought I was an innocent. Cause I ain't pretty? I decided to give it up then. I obviously wasn't going to sell the poor guy on my safety.

"Don't feel the need to defend my good reputation," Naji said as we made our way up the stairs to the room, out of earshot of the innkeep. "I don't have one."

"Oh, I'm sorry," I said. "Did you want me to act like your prisoner or something? Slip him a note to send for help?"

"Please don't do that."

"What'd he think you were going to do to me anyway?"

Naji opened up the door to the room. It was smaller than the room I'd had on the edge of the city, and not nearly as clean. I thought of all the Confederation scummies that had passed through here and shuddered.

Besides which, there was only one bed.

"Blood magic, probably," Naji said, and I shut my trap at that, because I'd just seen how that part of the assassin stories was true and blood magic ain't nothing to mess with. Even Mama had warned me off it, before it became apparent my talents lie elsewhere.

"You can sleep on the bed," Naji said. "And you should sleep." He gave me a look like he expected me to sass him. When I didn't, he said, "And no, it's not because of the, ah, the oath. It's because I need you alert tomorrow night."

"What for?"

"I have some things I'll need you to fetch for me, so I can determine what we should do next."

He didn't expand on that, and I figured tomorrow I could make a case for our next step to involve convincing the Haariris not to kill me. I was awful tired, to be sure. I'd hardly realized it until we got to the room. Likely still running on the energy from the fight, the way you do during those sea-battles that go on for days and days. I collapsed down on top of the bed, not even giving any thought to the last time the sheets might have been washed. And, like any good pirate, I fell asleep immediately.

CHAPTER FIVE

I slept straight on through till nightfall, and when I woke up my entire body ached so bad I could hardly push myself off the bed. Naji was sitting over in the corner, his eyes glowing. I waved my hands in front of him a couple of times and when he didn't so much as twitch I went ahead and peeled off my dress, stiff with sweat and blood and sand, and put on a fresh one. I transferred the bag of coins into my new dress. Just cause he was protecting me didn't mean he wouldn't steal from me.

Then I sat down on the edge of the bed and waited for a few minutes. He didn't come out of his trance.

"Hey," I shouted. "Sure would be easy for me to sneak out on you right now."

That did it. The glow went out of his eyes and he stood up, unfolding himself gracefully like the fight hadn't affected him at all.

"Not as easy as you would think." He had taken off his armor and his cloak while I slept, and his arms were covered in strange, snaky tattoos the same ice-glacier blue his eyes got whenever he settled into a trance. He didn't say nothing, though I know he saw me looking at them.

He walked across the narrow width of the room, to the rickety old table where he'd draped his cloak, and began to rummage through it.

"I'm hungry."

"I'm sure you can get something downstairs."

"I don't have no money," I said, trying my hand.

"Nonsense." He peered over his shoulder at me. His hair fell in dark ribbons over his forehead, and I felt silly for noticing. "You have a pouch of pressed metal in your pocket."

Immediately, I forgot his hair. "How do you know that?"

He smiled, touched one hand to his chest in the manner of the desertlands, that gesture that's supposed to stand in for an answer you don't want to give. Then he said, "I would like you to go to the night market for me. I'll give you money for that, but I expect you to return with everything I request. And I will bind you to me if I feel it's necessary."

I scowled at him. "You can't go to the night market yourself?"

"No vendor would sell to me." He didn't look at me when he spoke. I got a weird feeling in my stomach, thinking about the innkeep from the night before, and blood magic I'd seen Naji perform out on the street. The threat of Naji tying me to him.

"What exactly are you going to do?" I said. "With the, ah, the things from the—"

"Nothing that'll hurt you." He pulled out a stack of pressed metal, gold and silver both and worth much more than what I had in my pouch. I took a more or less involuntary step forward, trying to see where he'd yanked them from. One glare stopped me.

"And what about the Mists lady?" I asked. "Don't you think she might come back after me?"

"No." But there was a gap in his voice, some information he was leaving out.

"You don't think she's going to try again?"

"Not her, no."

"But someone."

Naji rubbed his head. "They won't come after you," he said.

"They came after me before."

"No, you happened to stumble across them. It's not the same thing."

I watched him, trying to decide if I wanted to tell him that I didn't get the sense that I'd stumbled across anything. I'd almost made the decision to say something when he turned away from me and said, "Run downstairs and ask the innkeeper to borrow some paper and ink."

"You don't need to write it down. I'll remember." I tapped the side of my head. My stomach rumbled.

When I didn't move he glared at me again, and I did as he asked. It was a different innkeep from the one who tried to convince me I was about to die. Too bad. I kind of wanted to reassure the poor bastard, or at least see the expression on his face when he saw I wasn't dead.

The new innkeep gave me the paper and the ink without too much fuss, though he said he'd charge me if I didn't bring the ink down after I finished with it. I waved him off and then bounded back upstairs. The smell of food rolling in from the kitchen, spicy and warm and rich, made my mouth water. That didn't incline me toward screwing around with Naji just cause it would annoy him. The sooner he got me his list, the sooner I got to eat.

Unfortunately, he took his time writing it out. He had this special quill that he produced from out of his robes, long and thin and the kind of black that sucks the color out of everything. I sat down on the bed while he puzzled over his list, scratching things out, shaking his head, muttering to himself.

"I'm hungry," I said.

"So am I," he said. "But this is far more important than either of our appetites at the moment." He held the list at arm's length, squinting a little in the lamplight. Then he pressed it up against the wall and wrote one more thing.

"There," he said. "That should be it."

I jumped off the bed and snatched it out of his hand and scanned over his sharp, spiny handwriting. It was all in Empire, and most of the items were plants. Rose petals, rue, dried wisteria vines. Soil-magic stuff.

"Midnight's claws," he said. "You can read."

"Of course I can read." I folded the paper down as

small as it would go and slipped it into my pocket. "And why would you give me a list if you thought I couldn't read?"

"I assumed you'd hand it over to the vendors."

"Oh, that's wise," I said. "Let them give me some fountain grass when I paid for swamp yirrus. Whatever that is." I shook my head. "How'd you get your supplies before you met me, anyway?"

"Not from a night market."

I let him have the last word, cause I was so hungry I could hardly think straight. I stuck my hand on the doorknob and was halfway to turning it when he roared, "Stop!" like a troop of Empire navymen were about to come bursting through the door. I froze, all my aching muscles preparing for yet another knife fight. But Naji just slouched toward me, the heel of his hand pressed against his forehead. "Curses and darkness," he said.

"What the hell's wrong with you?"

He reached into his robe and pulled out the charm from the battle and tossed it at me. The minute it was in my hands he straightened up.

"I hope that'll stave it off," he muttered, more to the air in the room than to me.

"What are you talking about?"

"Wear that charm." He pointed at my chest. "Keep it on you at all times."

"Why?"

"It's for protection."

"I know what it's for. I'm more curious what it's protection against."

He glowered. "Probably nothing. But I... I don't like sending you out alone."

"You sent me downstairs."

"That was different. You were still in the building."

"So? You can look through walls or something? What if someone snatched me when the innkeep wasn't looking?"

"No one was going to snatch you."

"But someone's gonna snatch me at the night market?"

"Probably not."

"But you still need to give me protection?"

"Stop asking questions!" he roared. "I thought you were hungry!"

"I am hungry! I just want to know I ain't walking into a trap is all."

Naji rubbed at his forehead, his eyes closed. "You aren't walking into a trap. As long as you swear to me that you won't take off the charm, you'll be safe."

I stared at him.

He opened his eyes. "I need you to swear it."

"I don't swear," I finally said. "But I'll promise." I looped the charm around my neck. That feeling of safety drizzled over me. I thought the whole thing was off, like I'd just been handed a key to something I shoulda understood, but I was so hungry I didn't much care. I was out the door and into the kitchen before Naji could say another word.

The night market in the pleasure district was a lot bigger than the one where Naji had almost killed me. It stretched from the row of brothels all the way down to the docks, and I could make out the outline of ship sails in the distance, blocking out the sky's bright stars. Vendors crowded onto the street like weeds, shouting at me to come buy their charms and enchantments as I walked past. Mostly love potions and the like. I ignored them.

It took me less time than I expected to gather up all the things on Naji's list. Those plants I recognized – the powdered Echinacea, the rose petals, the hyacinth root – I picked up first, going from vendor to vendor so none of them would ask after what spells I planned on casting.

That left the weird stuff. Like an uman flower. Never heard of that before, and as it turned out, it was extremely rare and extremely expensive, and only grew in a particular swamp in the southern part of Qilar. I had to ask five separate vendors after it, and I eventually got sent to an old man tucked away behind a stand selling vials of snake blood. He was all shriveled up like a walnut, and he peered up at me through the folds of wrinkled-up skin around his eyes. "What you needing a weed like this for?" he asked.

"Magic."

"Don't sass me, girl." But he rummaged underneath his table for a few seconds and produced a plant that reminded me of a body wrapped in burial shrouds. It wasn't like any flower I ever saw, what with its twisted wooden stem, all deformed and grotesque, and its long, fluttering white petals.

"Be careful with her," the old man said. "You can call down the spirits, if you don't know what you're doing."

I thanked him, so as to seem polite, and then tucked the uman flower away in my bag so I wouldn't have to look at it again.

There was one rarity on the list that I did recognize: le'ki, which Mama had used sometimes in the tracking spells that helped us sift out the best merchant ships. I figured I could find that at the stands set up on the docks, and I was right. At the first one I went to, the vendor had a half-inch left, dried out and powdered like Naji had requested. Naji only wanted a quarter-inch, but I bought all the vendor had, cause it reminded me of home, that briny sea scent and opalescent pink sheen, like the inside of a shell.

I'd been half-avoiding coming down to the docks, but once I was there, I didn't want to leave. I had everything on the list but the swamp yirrus, and it wasn't even midnight yet. So I followed a dock away from the lights of the city, all the way out to its edge. Boats thumped against the water, that hollow wooden sound I always found so reassuring. Nobody was out but a single dock-guard, and he didn't pay me no mind. Not like one person can steal a boat anyway.

I sat down on the pier, the bag filled with Naji's supplies in my lap, my feet dangling out over the ocean. Mama used to tell me the sea had an intelligence all her own, though I'd never been able to feel it like Mama could. I loved the ocean, don't get me wrong, but for me and Papa it was just water, huge and beautiful and strong and bigger than everything in the whole world, sure – but never something I could sit down and chat over my problems with.

When I was younger I'd get up early sometimes and climb to the top of the rigging so I could watch Mama work her magic with the sea. Sometimes she stripped naked and swam in it, and the waves would buoy her around like a jellyfish. Other times she sang and threw offerings from our merchant runs – small things, like a few coins of pressed metal, or a necklace, or a bangled scarf. And the offerings wouldn't float away like jetsam, neither. The sea sucked them down to the depths, leaving a wisp of foam in their wake. Once Mama lowered a jar into the water and scooped that foam up and then drank it down. Three days later, we defeated the Lae clan in a battle everyone, even Papa, thought we'd lose.

Thinking back to my childhood, and to Mama and her magic, and even that horrible battle, I started getting real sad. And I didn't want to be on the docks no more, sea spray kicking up along the hem of my dress. So I gathered up my bag and made my way back to the twinkling lights of the night market. My melancholy left me feeling distracted and confused, and I didn't know I'd taken a wrong turn until I realized I was back in the city proper – not the night market.

I cursed and turned around, intending to follow my steps back to the docks. But the buildings all looked the same in the dim light of the magic-lanterns, and when I started going one direction I was sure it was the wrong way, so I turned and went another – and after doing that a couple times I realized it was hopeless. I was lost, and in a city, unlike the open ocean, it's best to just ask somebody for directions.

Course, all the buildings were locked up tight for the night. I wandered for a while, kicking at stones in the street, fiddling with Naji's charm at my throat. Nothing.

Then I caught the scent of incense.

Incense means a temple, and the temples are always open for prayers and sanctuary. Figured the priestess wouldn't mind giving me directions, neither.

I followed the incense for a few minutes, losing it on the wind and then finding it again, until I came across a little temple wedged up between a key-maker's shop and the office of a court magician. The lamps over the door burned golden with magic, and when I stepped inside, the light had a gilded quality that reminded me of the evening sun. There wasn't nobody praying at any of the portraits, but a priestess stepped out of the archway, her sacred jewelry chiming as she moved.

"You look like you belong to the sea," she said, slipping languidly into the light. Priestesses always talk like that, like everything they say has got to be poetry.

"That's right," I told her. "And I need to get back to it. Can you tell me the way to the docks?"

She gave me a disapproving smile. "You mean the night market?"

"No, I mean the docks. I gotta meet someone there."

"Why don't you ask the gods for help?"

Hell and sea salt. Figured I'd get a priestess who took her duties seriously.

"The gods like to take their time answering, and I need to get back straightaway."

She looked almost amused, but she handed me an incense stick and swept her arm out over the temple. I sighed and followed the line of portraits till I came to one of Kaol, the goddess of tides and typhoons, and the one who's said to watch over pirates. I lit the incense with the little white candle burning beneath her portrait, knelt down, breathed in the smoky sweetness, muttered something about having lost my way, and then stood up and looked expectantly at the priestess.

"Kaol doesn't usually answer requests," the priestess said. "You'd have done better to pray to E'mko." She pointed at the portrait hanging beside Kaol's, and where Kaol's ocean was darkness and chaos, a gray spitting storm and jagged scars of lightning, E'mko's was calm, flat, and dull, his benevolent eyes gazing down on his petitioners.

"Ain't a sailor," I said. "E'mko's for sailors."

The priestess tilted her head at me. "Are you a pirate?"

I shrugged. "I told you, I just need to be down at the docks."

"So you did. Kaol will help pirates." She smiled. "When the prayer finishes, we'll see if she answers."

I sighed again and knelt down beside Kaol's portrait to wait for the incense to burn away – for the prayer to finish, as the priestess had said. I wasn't sure about the gods, since they didn't do much to make themselves known, but Papa used to swear that Kaol always looked out for her children, and that was why a pirate ship could sail through a typhoon unharmed when a navy boat couldn't.

When the last of the incense burned up, I found myself holding my breath, half-expecting to hear a voice like thunder telling me the way back to the docks. Instead the priest took me by the hand and pulled me to my feet and said, "Follow the street until it dead-ends, then turn right. You'll be able to hear the sea."

I scowled at her. "You couldn't have just told me that?"

"I didn't," she said. "Kaol did."

I didn't believe that for a second, but I thanked her anyway and then rushed out onto the street. I'd one more thing to buy – swamp yirrus – and no idea where to find it. Maybe I shoulda prayed to Kaol to help me find that, as well.

The priestess's directions were good, at any rate, and soon as I heard the sea at the dead-end I followed the sound of it to the docks, and then I made way back to the night market. At the first vendor I came across, I asked after the swamp yirrus, but she shook her head.

"Don't got anything like that, I'm afraid," she said. I must've looked disappointed, cause she leaned in close to me and whispered, "There's a new stall down near Lady Sea Salt's brothel. He might have it." She straightened up and tilted her head back toward the city. "He's set up next to a lemon tree, and he usually has a gray horse tied up with his things."

I thanked her and set off. The crowds thinned out some, and a wind blew in from the desert, cold and dry as dust. Everybody seemed to huddle up inside of themselves, even the vendors. But then I spotted the lemon tree, twisted and bent with the direction of the wind. And the gray horse, just like the lady had said. It snorted at me as I walked up.

The vendor had his back turned. The wind toyed with the fabric of his cloak, and even after I cleared my throat a few time, he didn't look up. Eventually, I said, "Excuse me!" I felt like I had to shout to be heard over the wind.

"Yes, my dear?" He glanced at me over his shoulder. "You look a long way from home."

He said it kindly, but it still left me unnerved. How could some street vendor at a Lisirran night market know my home from anyone else on the street?

"Uh, I'm looking for swamp yirrus," I said. "Lady on the docks said you'd have it."

The vendor turned around, and my whole body froze up immediately. He had the same gray-stone eyes the woman at the dress shop had had. I might've chalked it up to a coincidence except looking at his eyes got me dizzy, like all I could see was that gray.

"Got one left," he said. He gave me a big dazzling smile. "I'll knock the price down some, too. Looks like you've amassed quite a collection of supplies there." He nodded at my sacks filled with Naji's stuff.

I didn't say anything. I couldn't stop shaking. There was nothing sinister about him, none of the warning signs Papa always told me to look out for. Except for those damn eyes.

"This is awfully advanced for someone like you, though," he added. "Someone so young."

"I'm an apprentice," I spat out.

He nodded and turned back to his jars and tins. "Give me just one moment…"

I didn't. I turned and hauled off down the windy street fast as I could, my dress flying out behind me, my hair whipping into my face. The bags of plants banged up against my hip.

I ran till I felt safe, and that meant getting out of the night market completely. I collapsed on a curb outside a drinkhouse, the scent of smoke and strong coffee drifting out into the night. Men laughed over some jangly music. A woman sang an old song I half-recognized. I figured Naji would let me have it for not getting everything on his list, but at least I hadn't spent all his money, and I had good reason.

Those gray eyes. I couldn't stop thinking about them, looming clear and steady in front of me, drawing me in. To the Otherworld. The Mists. I couldn't picture it, a world layered on top of ours, but something about the woman at the dress shop and the man at the stall wasn't human. Naji was a bit spooky, but I could see how he was a man. Those two – it wasn't just the eyes. It was the way looking at 'em made me feel like a mouse surrounded by snakes.

CHAPTER SIX

It took some time for my nerves to smooth over, but I dragged myself up to standing and worked my way back to the inn. The innkeep from the night before was at the counter, and his eyes widened when he saw me, and he ducked into the room behind the counter. I was too shaken up to take any joy from it.

Naji was sitting on the bed when I walked in, scrawling out something on a piece of thin-pressed paper. He had his thumb and forefinger pinched against his nose, but once I closed the door he dropped his hand to the table and let out this weird, contented sigh, like he was finally sitting down after a long day's journey. I didn't much know what to make of it.

His tattoos glowed, almost enough to cast light of their own. He went back to writing.

"Did you find everything? You were gone longer than I expected."

"Everything but the swamp yirrus." My throat felt strange when I said it, dry and scratchy.

He didn't stop writing. "Why not? The waterfront night market here is supposed to be indefatigable in its supply of nefarious properties."

It took me a second to realize he was making a joke, but I wasn't in much of a joking mood.

"Well?" He lifted his head and squinted at me. "Why didn't you get the swamp yirrus?"

"I brought you your money." I reached into my pocket and pulled out the last of the pressed gold pieces and tossed them on the bed. Naji stared at them. They glimmered in the light of the lamp flickering on the bedside table. Then he looked back up at me, and I could feel him studying my face, trying to get an answer out of me that way.

I realized there wasn't no reason to lie to him. Not about this.

"The one vendor selling it had gray eyes," I said. Naji didn't react at all, just listened to me. "The same as the woman from before. The one who–"

"So you didn't want to buy from him."

I shook my head. "Gave me the creeping shivers. I'm real sorry. But if a girl don't have her intuition, she don't got anything. That's what my Papa taught me."

"Sounds like a wise man, even if he was a pirate." Naji sighed. "Did the vendor… react to you in anyway? Mutter anything? Hum?"

"Act like he was casting a spell, you mean? No." I shrugged. "He did say I seemed a long way from home, which worried me a bit. That was before I saw his eyes. In every other way he seemed normal, like I was just some customer."

Naji nodded. "You did the right thing. They certainly sent him to try to find us." He paused. "I'm glad to see you didn't take off my charm just to spite me. He would have recognized you otherwise."

My hand went up to my neck, to the strip of worn leather. I'd forgotten I was even wearing it.

"I'll take that back now, by the way," Naji said. "I'm going to make you one of your own, so you can stop borrowing mine."

I slipped the charm off my neck and the air in the room felt different, darker, like the lamp magic had started to run out. Naji slipped the charm back into his robe and went back to writing. I hated to see it disappear.

"What did you need the swamp yirrus for?" I asked. "Was it important?"

"Everything on that list was important," Naji said. His pitch quill scratched across the paper. "But I can make do."

I wanted to sit down, but it seemed weird to sit on the bed next to Naji. So I made a place for myself on the floor and watched him write. When he finished he tucked the quill back into his robes and read over the sheet one last time. Then he started rifling through the bags, pulling out the wisteria vines and the rose petals.

"You don't have to watch me do this," he said, laying everything out on the bed.

Ain't no way I was ditching the inn after the run-in with Gray Eyes at the market, and downstairs there wasn't nothing but drunks and whores, and I wasn't of a mind to deal with either.

"I'd rather stay, if it's no trouble to you," I said.

He glanced at me. The scars made his face unreal, like a mask, but I didn't mind looking at him.

"You might find this unsettling."

I shrugged. Naji picked up the wisteria vine and started braiding the pieces together, threading in the rose petals and strips of acacia leaves. He chanted in that language of his while he worked. The room got darker and darker and his tattoos glowed brighter and brighter. I recognized some of what he was doing as dirt magic – the chanting over dead leaves and the like – but those tattoos and the darkness weren't like nothing Mama ever taught me.

Naji set the charm down on the bed. He reached into his cloak and pulled out that mean-looking knife from earlier, and then, so quick I hardly had time to realize what he was doing, he drew the knife over the palm of his hand. Blood pooled up in a line across his skin. He tilted his hand over the charm and dropped the blood a bit at a time into the twist of wisteria vines.

His tattoos glowed so bright the whole room was blue.

He stopped speaking and squeezed his palm shut. His tattoos went back to normal. Then the whole room went back to normal, though I could still smell blood, steely and sharp, hanging on the air.

He dabbed at his palm with a handkerchief, not looking at me.

The sight of blood ain't anything to get me worked up, but the idea of using blood in magic – Mama had told me it was a dark thing to do, and dangerous, though she'd made it sound like blood-magic always used someone else's blood, not the magician's. She always said it was the magic of violence.

"I want to apologize," Naji said. He slid off the bed, the charm resting in the palm of his hand. "I didn't want to bring ack'mora into this–"

"What's ack'mora?"

He looked down at the charm. "What you would call blood magic. I didn't want to use it, but without the swamp yirrus..." His voice trailed off. He shoved the charm at me. "This is for you. Please wear it at all times."

He sounded more formal than usual, like he was nervous. Weird that he should be more nervous than me. But I took the charm from him anyway and ripped a strip of fabric off one of my scarves so I could tie it around my neck. The sense of protection that wrapped around me was warm and thick, like blood.

"I've never seen anyone mix 'em up like that," I said. Naji had walked back over to the bed and was cleaning off the space. He looked over at me when I spoke. His face was pale, drawn, in a way it hadn't been a few minutes ago.

"Mix them up?" he said.

"Yeah, dirt magic and blood magic. Uh, ack'mora."

"Yes," he said. "I do combine them sometimes. I learned some – what did you call it? Dirt magic? – from my mother."

"You have a mother!" I didn't mean to blurt it out like that, but the idea of him coming from somewhere was too bizarre.

"Of course I had a mother." He scowled and yanked the uman flower out of the bag.

It took me a minute to realize he'd switched into the past tense. "I'm sorry," I said, and I really did feel bad about it. "It's just – you're an assassin, and I didn't think–"

"I had a mother before I went to the Order," he said stiffly. He obviously didn't want to talk about it. "I thought you'd prefer a charm born of the earth and not me, but, well, I had to make do."

I thought that a weird way for him to say it, a charm born of me, like he'd hacked off part of himself and handed it over.

"Thank you," I said.

"You're welcome," he said, and he actually bowed at me a little. Not a full bow, just a tilt of the head, but I got real warm and looked down at my hands. I was very much aware of that charm pressing against my skin, soft as a lover's touch.

"This next spell is a bit more involved, I'm afraid." He was laying out the rest of the stuff I'd bought for him, the powders and the uman flower. "I'll be stepping out of myself for some time. I have questions that need answering." A long pause, like he expected me to say something. "You really don't have to stay. It's… Well, I'm doing something very rare, full ack'mora – I wouldn't expect…" He straightened up, ran one hand through his tangled-up hair. "Though I ask that you stay in the hotel. My… oath. I'm not sure what would happen to me if you got caught up in danger while I'm away."

All that talking, and the only thing I could say in response was, "Away?"

He nodded.

"The Mists?"

"Curses, no." He shook his head. "We call it Kajjil – there's no translation."

"But it's a place?"

He stopped messing with the powder vials on the bed and looked me hard in the eye. "I'm not allowed to discuss it with outsiders," he said, and I understood that well enough, being a daughter of the Pirates' Confederation and all.

I used the language of pirates to tell him I understood, which was a joke, because I knew there wasn't no way for him to know what it meant. But he kind of half-smiled at me, not with his mouth but with the skin around his eyes, and got to work.

This one was a lot weirder to watch, cause it wasn't nothing like the bits of magic I'd dabbled in before. Most of it centered on the uman flower. He spent awhile mixing up pinches and shakes of the powders I'd brought him, in some big clay bowl that looked like it'd come from the inn's kitchen. Then he set the uman flower on the floor and cast a big circle around it with the powders. The knife came out again, only this time he cut along one of the tattoos on his arm, and he splashed the blood onto the circle, right on the floor like we weren't in an inn.

He said some words and then he sung some words and then he stepped inside the circle, and everything got real screwy.

The room fell dark, first off, even though the lamp was still flickering over in the corner. It just didn't cast no light. Neither did Naji's tattoos, which had taken to glowing as well. It was like the darkness was so thick it swallowed up any kind of brightness.

So all I could see of Naji were the swirls of blue on his arms, and the two blue dots of his eyes. And his singing got louder, and I smelled blood again, so strong it was like I had it running down my face, and I actually wiped at my cheeks, trying to get it off. But there wasn't nothing there, and after that I only got the medicine scent of Naji's magic, the one like a physician about to do you wrong.

Then the uman flower lit up, too, and it started writhing around, and another voice added itself to Naji's, one that was not human. Raspy and animalistic, more like. And the uman flower kept swaying and twisting, dancing like Princess Luni in that old story, the one where she dances herself to death.

Things stayed like that for a while. The singing and the uman flower and Naji's bright eyes. But despite all of it, I wasn't too fearful, even though I knew that made me a damn-right fool. I figured the charm was working, and that's where my complacency came from.

I couldn't say how long Naji was away. It couldn't have been too long because I hardly moved one bit and neither of my legs cramped up. When Naji did come back, it happened all at once. The singing stopped and the uman flower stopped dancing and the light came back into the room. Naji slumped forward onto the floor, knocking the uman flower aside, out of the circle. It skittered up to me and I jumped away from it, not so much out of fear but revulsion. Naji still hadn't moved.

I crawled over to him, stopping just outside the circle, and poked him in the shoulder. He groaned. I poked harder, and then I shook him. The part of my arm in the circle tingled. The smell of his magic was so overpowering, I could taste it in the back of my throat. But at least nothing in the room seemed to be shifting and changing from the magic-sickness.

Naji jerked up, so fast it startled me. He blinked a few times. His eyes were dark again. When he spotted me crouching by the circle he rubbed his head and said, "Don't cross the line."

"I know, I ain't an idiot." I frowned at him. "You alright?"

He nodded, his head hanging low. I scooted across the floor and leaned against the bed. "What'd you find out?"

"Find out?"

"You said you had some questions that need answering."

"Oh." His face darkened for a moment. "It seems we'll need to go across the desert." He stood up, using one hand to steady himself against the bed.

"What! The desert?" I was hoping that he'd seen the Hariri clan wherever he went – not them exactly, but the shadows of them, the way fortune-tellers do. I was hoping that he'd tell me that other assassin wasn't coming after me no more. "I don't want to go to the desert."

"You're in the desert now."

I shook my head. "No, I'm in Lisirra, and it ain't the same thing." I crossed my arms and glared at him. "Why do we have to cross the desert?"

"I need to see someone."

"That's it?" I said. "That's all you're going to tell me?"

Naji glared at me. He looked about a million years old.

"Yes," he said. "It's all that concerns you."

"Bullshit!" I stalked across the room, taking care to avoid the circle. I balled up my clothes and wrapped the scarves around them for a strap. I took the protection charm off and threw it on the bed.

"What do you think you're doing?"

"Leaving."

"You can't leave."

I went right up to him, close enough that I could smell the residue of his magic. "Sure can. I got money and my wits and there ain't nothing you can do to stop me."

"There's plenty I can do and you know it."

I didn't have an answer to that, so I stomped away from him, right out the door and into the hallway. I didn't think about what I was doing; it was a lot like when I left Tarrin, honestly. Get the hell out and come up with a plan later.

Naji screamed.

It stopped me dead in my tracks, cause it didn't sound like anger or magic, but like he was in pain, like someone had stuck him in the belly. The hallway was silent – nobody stuck his head out to see what was going on.

Then there was a thump and the door banged open. Naji spilled out into the hallway. He cradled his head in one hand, and his skin was covered in sweat. His tattoos looked sickly and faded.

"Ananna," he said, choking it out. "You can't–"

"What the hell is wrong with you?" Part of me wanted to bolt and part of me wanted to get him a cold washrag and a cup of mint tea.

He staggered forward, pressing his shoulder up against the wall. I kept expecting some angry sailor to come out and lay into us for interrupting his good time.

"You can't..." Naji closed his eyes, pressed his head against the wall. He took a deep, shuddery breath. "You can't go out there alone, without protection. The Hariri clan–"

"To hell with the Hariri clan. Let 'em send their worst."

Naji looked like he wanted both to roll his eyes and puke. "That's the problem," he said. "They will."

He pushed himself away from the wall and swayed in place. He didn't stop rubbing his head.

"Please," he said. "Come back to the room. You can't leave. I have to protect you."

That was when I figured it out. It sure took me long enough.

"Are you cursed?" I asked.

His expression got real dark. He jerked his head toward the doorway.

"Are you?"

"Get in the room."

I did what he asked. I tossed my dresses on the floor and sat down on the bed. The color had come back to Naji's cheeks, and his eyes weren't glassy and blank no more. He locked the door behind us and started sweeping at the used-up magic circle with his foot.

"Well?" I said. "You are, ain't you? That's why you have to protect me."

He didn't say anything. The circle was gone, replaced with smears of powders and streaks of drying blood, but he kept kicking at it. The dust made me sneeze.

Naji finally looked at me.

"Yes," he said. Then he turned his attention back to the powders.

I folded my hands in my lap all prim and proper like a lady. Naji wasn't protecting me cause of some stupid oath. He was protecting me cause it hurt him if he didn't.

"When did it happen?" I asked. "During the fight, I'm assuming?" I thought back to that night in the desert, crawling through the sand, flinging my knife at his chest, killing the snake–

"The snake," I said.

Naji stared at me for a few moment. Then he nodded.

"Was it a special snake?"

Naji looked weary, but he shook his head, his hair falling across his eyes. "It was just an asp, in the wrong place at the wrong time. But I suppose it would have bit me had you not killed it."

"Oh."

He stopped kicking at the circle and leaned up against the wall, arms crossed over his chest. "You saved my life. Now I have to protect yours."

"From the snake?"

"Apparently."

"So what you told me was true," I said. "About having to protect me and all? It just wasn't an oath." I frowned. "What happens if you don't protect me?"

"I imagine I would die." Naji turned away from me and fussed with the robes he had lying across the table. "That's generally how these sorts of curses go."

I didn't have nothing to say to that. I'd accidentally activated some curse when I killed that snake and now we were stuck with each other.

This was why untouched folks hate magic.

"So why are we crossing the desert? Is there a cure?"

That darkness crossed his face again. "I said I don't want to talk about it."

"What about the Hariris? You keen on killing me so bad you're gonna march through the desert just to get to do it? You're out of your mind if you think I'm going with you–"

"I told you we are not discussing this matter further."

There was an edge to his voice, anger and shame all mixed up the way they get sometimes, where you can't tell one from the other, and that shut me up at first. But the more I got to thinking about it, the angrier I became. This was worse than an oath, cause oaths can be broken. And I didn't want Naji's curse hanging over my head.

"Well, I think we should discuss the matter further." I stood up. "This don't just affect you, you know. I had plans. And they didn't involve tiptoeing around so some assassin wouldn't get a headache."

Naji glared at me. "There's nothing to discuss. If you try to stay behind with the other sea rats, I'll bind you to me."

"No, you won't."

He stepped up close to me, his scars glowing a little from the faint coating of magic in the room. "All I need is a drop of your blood. And I know I can fetch that easily enough."

I lunged at him, but he'd already whirled away from me and all I did was slam up against the wall for my trouble. He had pulled his pitch feather out and was scratching something across the top of his chest armor, trying his best, it felt like, to ignore me. I leaned up against the wall and watched him. I did still have the Hariri clan to worry about, and if I took sail with even a southern ship they'd probably catch up to me eventually.

"I'll go," I said, as if he'd put the decision to me in the first place. "At least until you take care of the Hariris."

Naji glanced at me. Then he tossed his quill aside, sat down on the floor next to the uman flower, picked it up, and started pulling off its petals in long, thin strips. We didn't say nothing, not either of us. The only sound in the room was a crackle as the petals came off the stem, one at a time, white as ghosts.

CHAPTER SEVEN

Two days later, we left for the desert. It was probably stupid of me, going to help cure a man who had been paid pressed gold to see me dead, but every time I thought about giving him the slip I heard that scream of his from when I tried to leave the inn and felt sick to my stomach. And so it seemed the matter was decided for me. Bloody magic. You'd think they could come up with a curse that didn't have to drag innocent bystanders into it.

Naji got me to buy all the supplies. He gave me a list of a few powders from the night market, but the rest of it was run-of-the-mill stuff, and he wasn't too picky about it. Most of that I stole, creeping into a closed-down day market one night for the food, making off with a couple of water skeins and some desert-masks one crowded, distractible morning. I did pay for the water itself, though, down at the well. Felt wrong not to.

With the leftover money I bought a camel. A real strong, fancy-looking one, with soft brown eyes and an elegant, spidery gait. I marched that camel up to the inn the morning we left. Naji was waiting for me in the shadows, his face covered like always. When he saw the camel he looked at it and then he looked at me and then he said, "You bought supplies, correct?"

"I got supplies."

His eyes crinkled up above his mask. I wondered if he was smiling.

We took off, me and the camel marching through the streets like we were important, Naji creeping though the dark places like a ghoul in a story. He didn't materialize again until we got to the edge of the city and the sun was peeking up over the horizon, turning the light gray.

"We need to head southeast," he said. "You know which way that is? I don't want you wandering off–"

"Don't insult me."

Naji looked at me.

"I'm serious," I said. "It was the first thing I ever learned, how to tell north from south." That wasn't exactly true – I learned east from west first off cause it's obvious – but I wanted to get my point across. I jabbed my finger out at the horizon. "There. Southeast. You look at the shadows during the day and the stars at night, assuming you don't got no compass." Which we didn't.

"Or you can cast a spell," said Naji. "That's what I did."

"My way's better." I patted the camel's neck, and he huffed at me like he agreed. "Anybody can do it."

Naji didn't answer. It wasn't too hot yet, but already I had the scarf on over my head to protect me from the sun, and Naji made me put on a desert-mask even though it itched my nose. Plus I'd stolen one of those light-as-air dresses before we left, the fabric soft and cool against my skin, almost like sea spray, and thin enough that my tattoo peeked through the fabric. I'd heard how bad it gets once you're away from the ocean. Some of the crew on Papa's boat had told stories.

Still, all the stories in the world weren't enough to prepare me for that trip. The first few hours were alright, but the sun got higher and higher, arcing its way across the sky, and I kept wanting all that sand to turn into the ocean, blue-green and cold and frothed with white. Instead it stung my eyes. My skin poured sweat, and the fabric of my dress only stuck to me and didn't do nothing to cool me off. And my feet ached from walking alongside the camel – we'd saddled him up with our food and water, and Naji said we could take turns riding if we needed.

"And why aren't we walking at night?" I asked him, tottering along in the sand.

"It'll be too dark," Naji said. "I can't risk casting lanterns. Besides, we'll be fine. I usually travel during the day."

"Cause you're magic. I ain't."

Naji sighed. "You'll get used to the heat." And that apparently was enough to settle the matter.

We stopped to eat and rest a little during the middle of the day. Naji pitched a tent real quick and neat and told me to sit in the shade, which I did without protesting. Then he brought some water – he rationed it out to me, said we had just enough for the trip – and a handful of dried figs. The sight of 'em made my stomach turn.

"Don't drink too quickly," he said. He crawled into the tent beside me and tossed back one of the figs.

I didn't listen to him with regards to the water-drinking and immediately my stomach roiled around, and I moaned and slumped up against the fabric of the tent. Naji pulled me up straight. "You'll knock the whole thing over," he muttered.

"I didn't know this kind of heat existed in the world."

"Have a fig."

I shook my head. Naji sighed. "There's energy in them," he said. "They'll help make the evening walk easier."

"What! This ain't us stopping for the night?"

"Does it look like night to you?"

I didn't bother to respond. The tent's shadow seemed to be shrinking, burning up in the sun. Sand blew across my feet, stuck to my legs.

When we set off again I did feel a bit better. I guess the air was cooler, but as the sun melted into the dunes, the heat still shimmered on the horizon like water, which set me to daydreaming about Papa's boat, first during calm weather and then during a typhoon, wind and rain splattering across the desk, drenching me to the bone. I would have given my sword hand to be stuck in a typhoon instead of creeping across the desert.

Naji finally let us stop for the night after it got too

dark to see. He set up the tent again, making it wide enough that we could both lie down. I stripped off my scarf and bunched it up like a pillow.

Naji brought me some water.

"Two weeks from now, we'll be at the canyon," he said.

"Two weeks!" My mouth dropped open. "Two more weeks of almost dying?"

"You didn't almost die." He looked at me. "And surely you've gone on longer journeys? I understand that Qilar alone is almost a month's trip–"

"That's on a boat!" I wished I had something to throw at him. "You ain't walking the whole time and you got the shade from the masts and the spray from the sea – Kaol, have you ever even been at sea?"

He didn't answer.

"I can't believe this," I muttered, cradling the skein of water up close to my chest. "Two weeks in the desert all on account of some assassin who doesn't know how to look out for snakes."

"If you hadn't killed that snake," Naji said calmly, "I would have killed you."

"Oh, shut up." I took a long drink of water. "Are you going to tell me where we're going?"

"I told you, to a canyon."

"Anything else?"

"No." He looked over at me. "Stay here."

"I ain't moving. Gotta rest up for the next two damn weeks."

He disappeared out of the opening of the tent. I drank

the skein dry and set it aside and lay back and listened to the wind howling around me and to the camel snuffling just outside the tent. At first I was thinking about how awful the next few weeks were gonna be, and how I was probably gonna dry out like a skeleton in the sun. Then Naji came back from wherever he went, his footsteps crunching over the sand, and then I smelled smoke, and I got kind of drifty and floaty, like I was in the sea. Best part of my whole day.

And then Naji was saying my name, over and over, and shaking me awake. It was completely dark save for a reddish-golden glow just outside the tent, and after a few bleary seconds I realized that Naji was sitting outside, tending to the fire and not touching me at all. My body was just shaking from the cold.

I sat up and pulled my scarf around me, trying to get warm.

"Ananna?" Naji stuck his head into the tent. "Oh good, you're awake. Come eat."

"Why in hell's it so cold?"

"It's night time," said Naji, like that answered it.

Now, I knew it got cooler in the desert at night. Lisirra certainly does. But I felt like I'd spent the night on the ice-islands. So I scrambled out of the tent and pressed my hands out to the fire, keeping my scarf drawn tight around my shoulders. Naji handed me a tin filled with salted fish and spinach cooked down to a sludge. The minute I smelled it my stomach grumbled and I scooped it up with one hand, slurping it off my fingers.

"Be careful," Naji said. "Don't eat too fast."

I thought about what happened with the water and slowed down.

It didn't take me long to warm up, what with the fire and the food. When we'd finished I walked over to the camel, who had folded himself up all elegant in the sand. I scratched him behind the ears and rubbed his neck, and he blinked his big damp eyes at me, and for a moment I felt weirdly content, even if I was surrounded by nothing but sand and sky and scrubby little desert trees, even if I was traveling with an assassin who wouldn't tell me nothing.

But the next day, during the absolute blazingest part of the late afternoon, I started tottering around on the sand, and I couldn't see straight. My head was pounding like I'd been in a fight. The sky kept dipping down into the sand and the sand kept swooping up into the sky, which was so hot it was white, and I couldn't even remember what clouds looked like.

The next thing I knew Naji had his arms around me. I blinked and looked up at him, at his dark eyes and the part of the scar I could see above his mask.

"You're going to ride the camel for the time being," he said.

"What happened?"

"Sun sickness."

He scooped me up, one hand beneath my knees and the other under my shoulder, and I got real dizzy, though if it were from the heat or from him carrying me I don't know. His chest was sticky with sweat, even through the fabric of his robes – he wasn't wearing his armor – and I kept thinking about it later, the way his chest felt against my cheek.

He set me on the camel and pressed one hand against my waist while I steadied myself. He took hold of the camel's rope and tugged on it and the camel pushed forward.

"I'm sorry," he said, not looking at me. "I should have listened to your complaints about the heat."

I squinted down at him, feeling a little smug and also a little touched that he'd bothered to apologize. He didn't say nothing more about it, though.

The next morning Naji let me sleep longer, and he made me drink twice the usual amount of water before we set off.

"Did it hurt you?" I asked. He was packing up the tent, folding it over on itself.

"Did what hurt me?"

"When I got the sun sickness."

He finished folding up the tent and shoved it into the carrying sacks. Then he stroked the camel's side, not looking at me, just petting the camel like it was a cat.

"Why does it matter?" he finally said.

I frowned. "I want to know."

I was sure he wasn't going to answer, but after a few seconds, he dropped his hand to his side. "It did, a little, but I caught you before you injured yourself, so it was nothing especially painful. And we had the camel, so…" He turned toward me. His face wasn't covered, and it was like looking at him naked. I wondered what it would be like to touch his scar. "That isn't something you need to worry about."

"I don't worry about it," I said. "I was just curious." Although that wasn't entirely true.

That morning's walk came much easier, because of the rest on the camel's back and the couple of extra hours of sleep I got in. Naji had me ride the camel in the evenings, and we carried on like that for the rest of the trip. He didn't seem to need the rest. I figured it was some trick from blood magic. He didn't offer an explanation, and I didn't ask for one.

The days bled together out there, the way they do at sea, turning into one long day, one long night. Eventually the landscape starting changing. The desert trees disappeared and the sand turned coarser. Our path was littered with little round stones and tufts of bristly brown-green plants.

"We're close," Naji said.

"Close to what?" I was hoping he'd trip up and give me some kind of hint as to where we were headed.

"The canyon."

"And what's in the canyon?"

"A river."

I didn't even care that he was weaseling out of telling me anything important. "A river?" I said. "Water?"

"Water generally comprises a river, yes."

"Oh, thank Kaol and E'mko both!" I closed my eyes and all the dusty dryness fell away, and I imagined diving into clean hard river water, sloughing off all the grime and filth of travel, a proper bath and not a useless sandscrub–

"We're not there yet."

I opened my eyes. Naji was looking at me with little lines creasing the strip of his face, his own eyes bright and sparkling.

"Are you laughing at me?"

"Never."

I lunged at him with an imaginary sword, and this time he really did laugh, all throaty and raspy, and I wondered what I could do to get him to laugh more.

The travel was easier, now that I knew our destination included a river. I didn't even need to hop on the camel that evening. Naji didn't push it, neither, which I appreciated. As we walked, I started telling him jokes, trying to get him to laugh again. Which he didn't do.

The next day started same as all the others, except I launched into my joke-telling straight away. I was building up to my best one, about a whore and a court magician, and I knew it'd get a laugh out of Naji for sure.

I never got to tell it, though, because the sky began to change.

Naji spotted it first, but he didn't say nothing about it, just stopped the camel and pulled his armor out of the pack. I went on walking a little ways before I noticed – I was trying to work out the best way to tell my joke – but then I realized I didn't hear the whisper-soft footsteps, and I turned around and saw Naji suiting up like he was about to go into battle.

"What are you doing?" I asked.

"Nothing you need to concern yourself with."

"Bullshit!" I stalked up to him, spraying sand and stones, building up a bank of all the best cusses I'd heard in my lifetime, when I saw it. This weird cloud on the horizon, snaky and dark, like ink dropped into water.

"What's that?" I stopped a few feet away from Naji, staring past him, out at the desert. The thing crawled across the sky, long thin strands like a ghoul's fingers. "Don't you dare tell me I don't need to concern myself with it!"

"It's a sandstorm."

"No, it ain't."

"And how would you know?" His eyes gazed at me from the top of his mask. "Do you see a lot of sand-storms out on the ocean?"

"I ain't never seen a sandstorm, but you wouldn't be suiting up if it were."

His eyes dropped away from me.

"Give me your sword."

He slapped the camel's thigh to get it moving again. "Absolutely not."

Naji walked beside the camel, and I followed behind Naji.

"Then give me that knife of yours. I want to be able to fight, it comes to that."

"You have a knife." He paused. "You stabbed me in the thigh with it, if I recall correctly."

"That knife ain't worth a damn. I want yours."

He sighed. "You realize things are easier for me if you don't fight. If you don't…" He tilted his head, like he was searching for the right words. "If you don't put yourself in danger. Besides, it might not be anything troublesome. A fellow Jadorr'a passing through."

"The hell is that?"

"An assassin, Ananna." The word kind of soured when he spoke it. "Someone from the Order. Someone like me."

"Oh yeah?" I shot back, though I did feel kind of bad about not knowing what a Jadorr'a was. "You usually leave a trail big enough to see from Qilar when you're passing through?"

He didn't say nothing. I patted the dress sash I had tied around my waist, where my knife was tucked away, to reassure myself.

Naji was walking quicker than he had earlier – not running exactly, but fast enough it was making me pant. The camel trotted alongside him. I kept glancing over my shoulder to look at the cloud, which was filling up the sky faster than I could track.

"We gotta stop," I said.

"Ananna–"

"What? We do."

He looked over at me, all eyes and mask. I hated that mask.

"Look," I said. "Something nasty's obviously about to catch up to us, and you damn near running like that's not gonna help. All it means is we'll be worn out when we've got to fight."

Naji blinked but didn't say nothing.

"We should rest," I said. "Rest up and face them head

on. They probably won't even expect it, if you usually run from a fight like this."

"I prefer to stay on the offensive," Naji said.

"Yeah, and that's why you're an assassin, ain't it, a bloody murderer-for-hire. Cause ain't no one ever gonna expect you and so you can fight like a coward or not fight at all."

He flinched when I said coward. Not a whole lot. Just a little squint of the eye. But I still saw it.

Then he did something I didn't expect. He told the camel to stay put, and he reached into his cloak and pulled out his knife. The blade glinted in the sun, throwing off sparks of light.

"If I give this to you, will it make you feel better?"

"A little. I still want to rest, though."

He shook his head. "You can't fight them. Not without magic."

"You got plenty of that."

"No." He stood close, bending down so our eyes were nearly level. "Any magic I do, it comes from me, do you understand? It takes a little piece of me with it. I can't simply cast any spell I want, any time I want – I have to give my body time to recover."

I set my mouth into a hard little line so he couldn't see what I was thinking. I felt stupid for not realizing that sooner, what the magic did to him.

"I cast a block over us before we left, but it was weak after the work I did creating your protection charm. You are wearing it, right?"

I lifted the mask away from my neck, showing him.

I was sure he knew I never took it off, but I wasn't gonna say it out loud.

"The black streaks are from the block. It's a warning, not an invitation to engage in battle. The canyon's close, we should be able to get there qui–"

The wind changed.

The whole time we'd stood there arguing the air had been hot and still and dry. Stifling. But then a breeze picked up and rustled the hem of my dress, and it was cold as ice. It sent a chill down my spine like a ghost had reached out and grabbed hold of me.

"Oh no," said Naji, like it was every curse in the whole world.

I was stuck in place, the breeze turning into a wind turning into a gale. All the sweat evaporated off my skin. My scarf unwrapped itself from my head and skittered across the sand, a thin twist of white disappearing into the encroaching darkness.

Naji started chanting in his language, his eyes glowing. I stumbled forward, my legs stinging like they'd been stuck with a million little pins. At least I could move again. Naji shoved his knife at me and then grabbed me by the arm as soon as I'd taken it. He pulled me up to him.

"Please don't fight unless you have to," he said, right close to my ear.

The camel made this horrible noise, a shriek-snort of fear, and galloped off, away from the darkness, all our food and water disappearing into the line of sunlight. I cried out for him to stay, but Naji put his hand on my arm.

"Let it," he said. "I might be able to call him after… after it's done."

"I thought you said it was impossible to win."

"It is," Naji said. "I didn't want to… to frighten you."

I was already frightened, but I wasn't going to tell him. Still, I pressed myself up against him as the darkness moved closer to us. Something was stirring up the sand. Figures appeared on the horizon. I kept imagining them all to look like Naji, a whole army of Najis, but they didn't.

They looked like ships crossed with enormous insects. And as they lurched across the sand, they let out this creaking noise, metallic and resounding. It made my ears ring. It shuddered deep down into my bones.

"What are they?" I shrieked, close to panic.

"I have no idea," Naji said.

"What!" I twisted myself to look up at him. His eyes were still glowing. "I thought you said–"

"A Jadorr'a is among them," he said. "But the Order does not deal in metallurgy."

Metallurgy. The word kind of lodged in my brain, like I should know what it meant but I couldn't quite grasp it.

The creatures shuddered to a stop. The sand settled. Thick black smoke belched out into the sky, mingling with the inky swirls of darkness from Naji's block. Their skins shone in the few beams of sunlight that made it through, like the side of a knife, like–

Like metal.

"They're machines," I said numbly.

Naji dug his fingers into my arm. "Killing a snake isn't going to save you this time."

Under any other circumstance that would've pissed me off, but I was so busy trying to overcome my panic that I didn't care.

The creatures stood there for a long time, creaking and heaving and letting off smoke. Naji murmured to himself, casting magic.

"Why aren't they doing nothing?" I whispered.

He chanted a little louder. The machines stared us down.

Then, like that, he stopped.

I didn't like not hearing his voice. As long as he was chanting, I felt like nothing could hurt us.

"Can you use a sword?" he said.

"Of course I can use a sword."

He slid his sword out of its scabbard and jabbed the hilt at me. His sword was even more mean-looking than his knife, thick-bladed and curving a little at the end.

"When they attack you, fight," he said.

"Planning on it."

"Try, please, not to get yourself hurt. Don't do anything foolish." Then he took a deep, bracing breath and walked off.

Just like that. He left my side and walked straight into the smoke, disappearing into the haze. I tried to call out to him, to remind him that he didn't have his knife neither, but the smoke got in my lungs and made me cough.

Then one of the machines opened up, its top peeling away like a lemon. More smoke poured into the air. I promptly forgot about Naji.

I used his sword to cut my dress away above the knee so I wouldn't trip on the skirt. Then I held the sword up the way Papa'd taught me a long time ago.

A figure dropped down to the sand.

A man.

Tarrin of the Hariri.

I gasped and faltered, stepping back without meaning to, but I didn't lower my sword. My thoughts felt like poison, turning me to stone out there in the light and smoke of those horrible machines. The Hariris. How long had they been tracking us across the desert? How long had they had this kind of magic at their disposal?

Tarrin was all decked out like a Qilari noble, the long coat and the knee-high boots and everything. He slipped off his hat as he walked up to me, clutching it next to his heart. His handsome face didn't fit the backdrop, all that dark smoke.

"We don't have to fight," he said.

"You sent an assassin to kill me!"

Tarrin's expression darkened. "No, I didn't. My parents did. I warned you."

My heart pounded hard and fast inside my chest. Sweat rolled down my back. I hardly noticed the heat, though. I didn't allow myself to. Part of me wanted to attack Tarrin then and there, just lay into him, even though it wasn't the nicest thing in the world to attack a man not holding out a weapon, but then I remembered Naji told me not to do nothing foolish. Laying into Tarrin, what with those machines backing him up? I wouldn't call it foolish, but I knew Naji would.

"Besides, he hasn't killed you yet," Tarrin said.

"Trust me, I noticed."

Tarrin frowned. "Mistress Tanarau, my parents are willing to give you one more chance. I talked them into it. Father lent me his landships and everything."

"That's what those are?" I squinted up at them, gleaming bright in the sun. Landships? Of all the abominable things.

"Please, just come back with me to Lisirra. We can get married on my ship – the wedding sails are still up – and if you come back as my betrothed, Father will let me fly his colors." He smiled at me, as dazzling as the machines behind him.

I thought about it. I really did. Marriage was still the furthest thing from what I wanted, and I didn't even know what I wanted. But it would have made things easier, to climb aboard one of those creaking monsters and let Tarrin whisk me back to sea, away from the sand and the dry desert heat. There was an appeal to it, is what I'm saying.

I lowered the sword, and let it hang at my side. My arms ached from holding it up over my head, and besides, I wanted to seem as unthreatening as possible when I asked what I had to ask.

"Could Naji come with us?"

Tarrin scrunched up his face. It made him look prissy. "Who's Naji?"

"My traveling companion."

Tarrin got this look liked I'd suggested we share a bowl of scorpions. "What? The assassin? Why would he come with us?"

"Look, I ain't too happy about it neither, but I can't just leave him."

"Of course you can."

I frowned. I thought about Naji screaming in pain when I tried to walk out of the Snake Shade Inn. What would've happened if I kept going? That scream was the scream of a dying man.

"It won't be forever," I said. "Just until we can get him cured."

"Cured? What are you talking about?"

"He got this curse on account of me, and until he finds the cure I pretty much have to stay around him. It won't be that big a deal. Just lock him in the brig."

"Are you insane? Do you have any idea what he does?"

"Kill people for money? Come on, you'd do it too if the price was high enough."

Tarrin scowled. "That's not what I was talking about." He lowered his voice. "You haven't dealt with the assassins the way my family has. They're dark. The magic they use – it isn't right. Isn't natural."

"Haven't dealt with them? What do you call walking across the desert for two weeks with one? He wouldn't use magic on your boat, I'm sure of it. Just as long we helped him cure his curse–"

Tarrin crossed his arms over his chest and puffed

himself up, like I was some recalcitrant crewman he needed to order down. "I can't have something like that on my ship. The brig wouldn't contain him, not with his magic. We spill one drop of blood up on deck and he'd be commandeering the boat–"

"Yeah, to get a cure for his curse."

"Please, mistress!" He threw his hands up in the air. "Just leave the assassin in the desert."

"Why don't you just let him onboard? He ain't as dangerous as you're saying. If anything he'll keep the boat safe."

"You don't really believe that, do you?"

"Course I believe it. Why won't you believe me?"

Tarrin sighed. "It's not that I don't believe you, it's that you're wrong, because you simply don't know what the assassins are like."

"Oh, just stop!" I snapped. "Why would I want to marry someone who won't even listen to me?"

Tarrin's face went pale. "Are you telling me no?"

"I guess I am. Maybe you could take this as a lesson, and treat your next lady with more respect."

"No, no, you don't understand." Tarrin shook his head wildly. "I have to come back with you as my betrothed, or as a corpse. It's the only way I'll get the colors…"

I stared at him, ice curling around my spine.

"I have my crew waiting," he said, jerking his head back toward the machines. "Our crew, if you'd just come back with me."

"And if I don't?"

Tarrin's face twisted up. "I want those colors, Mistress Tanarau."

"Well, I want a ship of my own, not yours. So I guess we're at an impasse here." I lifted the sword again.

Tarrin glared at me and reached for his own sword. I never did fight him, though, because light exploded out of the black smoke, a great blinding sphere of it, strong enough that it knocked me back into the sand and momentarily blinded me. Knocked over Tarrin, too, and he stretched out beside me, blood seeping out from a cut on his head – he'd hit a rock when he went down.

"Shit!" I scrabbled over to him, dragging my sword. He turned his head toward me, blinked his eyes a few times.

"As my betrothed," he choked out, and I saw the movement in his arms that meant he wasn't as hurt as he seemed, that he'd figured me soft enough to come coo over him while he went for a knife. "Or as a corpse."

It happened fast. He jumped to his feet and yanked the knife out from under his coat. But I knew it was coming – it was one of the oldest tricks in the Confederation, and one Papa had warned me against when I was a kid. I plunged the sword into Tarrin's belly. Blood poured out over the sand, and he gave me this expression of shock and dismay and for a moment I just stared at him, shaking. I'd been in sea-battles before, but this felt different somehow. It was too close, and Tarrin was someone that I knew.

"I had to," I told him, but it was too late.

I gathered up my courage and whirled around to face

the machine, cause I knew that, by killing Tarrin, I'd changed everything. And I was right.

First thing I saw was the crew clambering down a sleek metal folding ladder, brandishing their swords and their pistols – cause of course a fancy clan like the Hariris would have gotten their greedy hands on some hand cannons. Shit.

Second thing I saw was Naji, screaming words I didn't understand, his eyes like two stars.

Third thing was Naji's twin, a man in a cloak and carved armor, galloping through the smoke on a horse as black as night.

Those three things, they were all I needed to see. I lifted up my sword and screamed words of my own, all my rage and fear and shame at having killed Tarrin.

Then I ran into the fight.

CHAPTER EIGHT

The Hariri crew were terrible shots with the pistols – it helped that the black smoke crowded in around us, blurring the fight and making everything hard to see. I angled myself toward one of the shooting men, running fast as I could, dodging sword swipes. One man came barreling up to me and I stuck out my foot and tripped him. They never expect that.

A bullet whizzed past my head, close enough I could feel its heat, and I spun to face my attacker. Spotted her just as she was shoving in powder for another shot, and I dove forward, slicing across her leg. She screamed, dropped the pistol. I grabbed it and crouched down in the sand to finish packing off the shot. Stupid things ain't worth the trouble in this sort of fight, honestly.

There was another boom across the desert, another flash of light: a pillar this time, shooting up toward the sky. Everyone hit the ground but me since I was already there, giving me enough of an advantage that

I was able to jump to my feet a few seconds faster. I tucked the pistol into the sash of my dress and ran toward Naji cause I didn't know what else to do, now that I was matched in my weapons.

A couple of shots fired out but none of 'em hit me. Naji was crouched on the ground next to that black horse. Its rider was gone, and the horse chuffed at the sand. When I got up next to Naji he looked like he wanted to tell me to get away, but I spoke up first.

"We need a plan," I said.

"What?"

The other assassin appeared out of the cloud of smoke, limping a little, and the Hariri crew had recovered from the blast and were all aiming right for me, so I pushed myself away and fired the gun into the crowd. Somebody screamed. I threw the gun as far away from the fight as I could, since I didn't have no bullets and I didn't want one of the Hariri crew to reload it and shoot me with it. I lunged forward, whirling the sword, knocking at people rather than cutting if I could, and tripping 'em too, and praying to every god and goddess of the sea that not one of those bullets would make contact.

Another blast of light, and we all got flung to the ground again, even me. It knocked my wits out for a few seconds, and when I managed to get back up, some burly scoundrel was on me with a big two-handed sword, and I had to fight him off, plus another lady with a pair of knives. Got myself cut a couple of times, on the arm and in the side, nothing major. But I did wonder about Naji, if that hurt him, if it was hurting him worse than it hurt me.

I managed to get another pistol, same way as the last – by sneaking up and slicing and stealing. But I was getting real tired, every muscle in my body aching, and the crewmen kept coming, mean and devoted, and I kept thinking about Tarrin bleeding out on the sand.

Naji screamed my name.

The sound of it chilled me to the bone, despite the heat from the sun and the battle. I froze in the middle of the melee, sword halfway to some guy's gut, and it took the pop of a pistol a few feet away to get me moving.

He sounded like he was dying.

I pushed off through the crowd, ducking low into the smoke. Naji was sprawled out on the ground, white as death, face all wrenched up in agony. I crouched next to him, pistol drawn. The smoke swirled around us, cloaking us, which was a relief even if it set me to coughing.

"I can't..." He gasped, pulling in a long breath. "Help..." Blood bubbled up out of his lips.

"Ain't enough time for you to say what you've got to say," I told him and immediately set to looking for the wound. "Where's the other guy? Keep it short."

"Dead."

"That's something." He was bleeding from his chest, from underneath his otherwise untouched armor. A magic-wound. Shit.

A figure pushed through the smoke, sword glinting.

I fired off the pistol before he could get close to us. The figure dropped to the sand.

I knew we couldn't stay here, Naji and me. All the magic he'd been using had drained him dry, and me trying to stave off an entire ship's worth of crew just sent him spiraling into more pain.

Think like a pirate, I told myself. Think like Papa.

Ain't no shame in running from a losing battle, he told me once. Better that than dead.

"You have to get up," I said to Naji, tugging on him as I did. "You have to get up and get on that horse."

He nodded and pushed himself up about halfway.

The smoke had begun to clear, webbing out, revealing patches of white sky. Revealing more Hariri crew.

"Hurry!" I said. "I got to fight 'em off and if that hurts you–"

He wasn't standing. He'd dipped his fingers into the blood in his chest and was drawing a symbol in the sand.

"Get on the horse, Naji!"

"Protection," he croaked, and then he started muttering, and his eyes glowed sickly and pale, and the crew was descending on us, and I knew I had to fight. So I jumped to my feet and dove in, ignoring the pain in my body and the ache in the back of my throat that meant I needed water. And most of all I ignored the groans from Naji, cause I knew I was hurting him, but what choice did I have?

And then he said my name again. And he was on the horse.

I knew it was stupid, me right in the middle of battle like that, but I could've wept, seeing Naji slumped over that horse's back. I raced over and scrambled up to join him, wedging myself in front of Naji so I could take the horse's reins. Naji snaked his arms around my waist, pressed his head into my shoulder, and I dug my feet in the horse's side.

The horse galloped over the sand. Every part of my body hurt. Naji's breath was hot and moist against the back of my neck, even through the fabric of his mask, and it reassured me, it let me know he was still alive.

I rode the horse out of the smoke and craned my neck back up at the sky. The sun was nestled over in the western corner. Naji moaned something. I twisted the reins, sent the horse running off to the southeast.

Naji moaned into my neck for about five or ten minutes, and when he stopped I realized no one was following us. I halted the horse and turned him around. The desert was empty save for us. The cloud of black smoke stretched out over the horizon, a long ways a way.

"Can't... hold this... Get to the river." Naji's voice was right in my ear.

I didn't know if he meant he couldn't hold the protection spell or if he couldn't hold on to his life, but I wasn't taking no chances. I set the horse to running again.

"How far are we?" I asked, shouting into the wind and the sand.

Naji groaned and buried his face into my shoulder.

Even through his armor I could tell that his body was hotter than normal.

I rode the horse as hard as I could without having it collapse beneath us. Every time I slowed it down my hands shook and I made myself aware of Naji's breath, waiting for it to stop. But it never did.

The sun set. The protection spell held on. And so did Naji.

And then the landscape started to change. I didn't notice at first, in the gray twilight, but the shrubbery got more and more plentiful – it didn't look so much like a desert no more. The moon came out, full and heavy and fat in the sky, casting enough light to see. Naji's breath was thin, weak. The horse panted and trembled.

I smelled water.

Fresh, clean, sweet water. Then I heard it, babbling like voices, and I couldn't help it, I started to cry. I thought maybe I were imagining it, just cause I wanted it so bad.

"Canyon," Naji said. His voice made me jump. "Stop."

I slowed the horse down. The land dropped off not far from us, and I figured the river was down in the canyon, carving its way through the desert to the sea.

"How are we gonna get down?" I asked.

Naji didn't say anything, only gasped and choked and pressed up against me.

"Stay here," I said, and I climbed off the horse. Naji slumped forward, his head lolling. I crept through the shrubbery till I came to the edge of the canyon. Then I crouched down on my knees and leaned over.

The river was a line of starlight flowing through the darkness. The drop wasn't too far, but I couldn't risk jumping, not knowing the water's depth. And I had to concern myself with Naji and the horse, both of whom needed water. Fortunately the sides of the canyons sloped down pretty gently, and I figured the horse could probably climb down, assuming we did it slow.

I knew I couldn't wait till morning.

Naji was still slumped over the horse's back. His hands were dark with blood, and his blood soaked the back of my dress. I nudged him, and every second he didn't move, my chest got tighter. Then he rolled his head toward me.

"We're climbing down to the river," I said. "You have to hold on. I'm going to lead the horse."

He nodded and weakly threaded his hands through the horse's mane. I grabbed hold of the reins and tugged and the horse lurched forward. Its whole body was covered in white frothy sweat. I hoped it could make it down to the river.

The climbing was slow but not as difficult as I had thought. Showers of stone and sand fell beneath our feet, shimmering on their way down. Every noise we made echoed through the darkness, and the desert night's chill laid over the sweat and heat of my exertion.

At one point Naji nearly slid off the horse. I caught him and, with a burst of strength I shouldn't have had, shoved him back into place. I grabbed his wrist and checked for his pulse – still there, thank Kaol and her sacred starfish, even though it was faint, the whisper of a heartbeat.

I let myself get in one round of curses and then moved us on our way. Eventually the sand and stone gave way to soft pale grasses, and as soon as we stepped onto flat ground, onto the riverbank, I let out a holler of victory that rang up and down the canyon walls. The horse trotted up to the water and took to drinking, Naji still slouched on his back. When the horse bent down, Naji swung back his head and twisted sideways and I ran up to catch him and let him down easy on the riverbed. I pulled the mask away, my hand brushing against his scarred skin. He stirred and moved toward my touch, but he already looked like a dead thing. Ashen skin, sunken eyes.

While the horse slurped at the river, I scooped some water in my hand and dripped it across Naji's face, hoping to hell that he'd drink some of it. His lips, cracked and bleeding, parted a little, and I went back and forth, dribbling water a little at a time. Then I cracked open his armor, careful as I could. The inside was coated with blood, and the fabric of his robes was stiff to the touch.

I pressed my hand against the side of his face. His eyelids fluttered. "Naji," I said. "Naji, I need you to wake up. I don't know how to treat you."

He moaned something in his language, words like rose thorns.

"Damn it, Naji, I don't know what that means!" I

slammed my fist into the riverbed. Mud ran up between my fingers.

He moaned again, lifted one hand, and then dropped it against his chest, dropped it down to his side. His blood glimmered in the moonlight.

I sat back on my heels and stared at him and thought of wounds I'd treated back on Papa's ship, knife cuts and bullet shots, bruised faces and broken fingers. Ain't never anything done by magic. The rare occasion something like that came in, Mama took care of it.

Mama. I wished she were here now, her and her magic, the magic of the sea, of water–

The river.

I crawled down to the river's edge. Everything was silver and light, cold and beautiful. The horse had wandered off, blending into the shadows. I'd never been able to talk to the water. But Mama had told me you got to want it, and maybe before I never wanted it enough, maybe before I never needed it.

I crawled into the water. The cold cut right through me, made all my bones rattle. Silt drifted up around my bare legs. I closed my eyes, concentrated hard as I could.

"River," I said. My voice ran up and down the walls of the canyon. It became a million voices at once. "River, I ask to speak with you."

Those were the words Mama had told me a long time ago. And I waited, but the water just kept pushing past my waist, tugging on my dress.

Then I remembered. Mama casting gifts into the ocean. I had to give a gift.

The camel had run off with my money, so all I had left that belonged to me was the protection charm Naji made me and the knife I used to save his life. I threw the knife into the water. Mama always said the water knows the true value of things. And this was a trade, one way of saving his life for another.

I said my request again, louder this time, filling my voice with meaning and purpose, with pain and sorrow. If I let Naji die, my voice said, not in words but in tone, I as good as killed him.

The way I killed Tarrin of the Hariri.

This time, the babble of the river fell quiet. The river kept moving, swirling past me, but I couldn't hear nothing. And I knew I had permission to ask my request.

"Naji's dying," I said. "I need to know how I can fix him." I thought about it for a few seconds and then I added, "If there's anything in the river that can help him, please. I would appreciate it." Mama always told me to be polite when you're dealing with the spirits.

A heaviness descended over the canyon, a stillness that made me feel like the last human in the whole world. Then the river began to rise, inching up above my waist to my chest, flooding over the bed, washing over Naji, then under him, buoying him up. From somewhere in the darkness, the horse whinnied.

Then, quick as it flooded, the river retreated to normal.

River nettle. The name came to me like I'd known it all along, even though there ain't no way I'd ever heard it before. I splashed toward the shore, slipping over the stones to get to the riverbed. Naji gasped and wheezed, droplets of water sparkling on his skin. I walked past him, stumbling out into the grasses, feeling around in the dark for something that grew low to the ground, in places where the river flooded during that time of heavy run-off from the mountains. It would be covered in stiff, spiny leaves, like a thistle–

My hand closed around a thick stem, and my palm burned like it had been bitten by ants. This was it.

I yanked the nettle out of the ground, flinging clods of damp dirt across the front of my dress. Then I stumbled back over to Naji, who was panting there in the mud. The sound wrapped guilt around my heart and squeezed so hard it hurt.

"Hold on," I whispered to Naji, smoothing his hair back away from his face, wiping off the water that dripped into his eyes. "I got something to help you."

He gasped and shuddered and I knew he was dying and I knew I had to do this fast.

I used Naji's knife to cut his robes away from the wound. It wasn't like any wound I ever saw – it wasn't a cut or a burn, but a hole about the size of a fist in the center of his chest, like a well, a place of darkness and sorrow going all the way down to the center of the earth. I stared at it for a few seconds, and it seemed to get bigger and bigger, big enough to swallow me whole.

And that part of me that knew what to do, that knowledge that came from the river, told me the wound was hypnotizing me, that it wasn't no hole at all, and I had to concentrate.

I closed my eyes and shook my head and that dizzy

feeling went away. When I opened my eyes again I made sure not to look directly at Naji's chest.

I stripped the leaves off the stem, going partially by moonlight and mostly by feel. I didn't fumble or hesitate – it was like I'd known how to do this all along. Then I stuck the leaves in my mouth and chewed on 'em till they got soft and mushy. They tasted like river water, steely and clean, and I spat 'em out in the palm of my hand and pressed the mush to Naji's chest. For a few seconds I was sure that my hand would plunge into the darkness, that I'd fall through that hole and wake up surrounded by evil.

Naji's chest felt all wrong, spongy and decayed and hotter even than if he had a fever, but it was there, it wasn't no doorway to someplace else. I spread the river nettle over the wound. As I worked, I sang in a language I didn't know; the words sounded like the babble of water over stones, like rainfall pattering across the surface of a pond, like rapids rushing through a canyon.

When I finished, all that knowledge evaporated out of my head. I fell backward on the mud and looked up at the stars. They blurred in and out of focus. I wanted to stay up, to watch over Naji to make sure the magic held fast, but I couldn't. I was so exhausted I slipped over into sleep, where I dreamed of water.

CHAPTER NINE

The sun woke me up the next day. It was as hot out there by the water as it had been in the desert, and when I sat up my skin hurt. Face, neck, legs: anything that hadn't been covered up was burned. At least the air felt clean. No threat of magic-sickness.

Naji was gone.

That got me to my feet fast, sunburn or not. There were a few faint footprints headed in the direction of the river. The water threw off flashes of white sunlight, nearly blinding me. But Naji was there, floating out in the middle of the river without no clothes.

Now, I ain't normally a prude about things like that – most pirates are men so it wasn't nothing I hadn't seen before. And I'd had an encounter behind a saloon on a pirates' island in the west, with this boy Taj who sailed aboard the Uloi. But because this was Naji, my whole face flushed hot beneath the sunburn and I looked down at my feet. I wanted to go hide in the grasses until he came out and got dressed, but I was worried about him too, so I called out, "You alright?" without looking up.

"You're awake," he called back, which didn't answer my question. I heard him splashing around in the water, and I kept my eyes trained down until he padded up to me barefoot, at which point I had no choice but to look at him.

He'd tied his robes around his waist. His whole chest was covered in the same snaky tattoos as his arms. And though the wound had healed up as an angry red circle over his heart, he was still pale and weak-looking. I didn't think he should have been out there swimming, but I didn't say nothing.

"Are you going to have a scar?" I asked. He didn't answer right away and I realized I'd forgotten about his face. "Um, I mean–"

"Yes, it'll scar." Naji looked down at his chest, ran his fingers over the red, crumpled-up flesh. "I thought you couldn't do magic."

He said it like he was accusing me of something, and I flailed around a bit, trying to find the words. "I asked the river. My mama taught me, or tried to teach me. With the sea. And it worked. It ain't never worked before, but it worked this time."

"Oh, of course. I should have known. A pirate – you'd have an affinity with water." He stopped and squinted up at the lip of the canyon, like maybe he was expecting to see somebody. The Hariri clan maybe.

"You saved my life again," he said, still looking up.

"Yeah, hopefully I didn't just double the curse." The

irony of me saving his life a second time hadn't been lost on me. I had killed Tarrin only to make a deal with the water to save Naji. The thought made my stomach twist around.

"I doubt it works that way."

"Well, if it does, then I'm sorry."

He dropped his gaze and looked at me real hard, which made me shiver. "No," he said. "Don't apologize. I didn't mean–" He took a deep breath. "Thank you."

I got a dizzy spell then, and I thought it was because he'd thanked me, even though I knew how silly that was. But Naji caught me by the arm and said, "The magic exhausted you. We'll rest here a day before we go on. You should eat."

"What about you?" I said. "You were halfway to death last night, and you ain't looking too great this morning neither." My vision swam, the river turning into a swarm of light. The insects chittered out in the grasses, so loud it hurt.

"You're right," Naji said. He guided me down to the riverbed. It was nice to sit down. My head cleared. Naji sat down beside me. "We both need to rest." He paused. "I only suggested that because I'm used to this kind of healing. I do it constantly. You, on the other hand..." His eyes kind of lit up like he was going to smile, but he didn't. "That was some very powerful magic you performed last night."

"It was the river, not me."

"No, it wasn't."

I didn't say anything, cause I didn't know what he was getting at and I didn't want to ask.

We spent the rest of the day lying out by the river. I caught some fish by stabbing at them with Naji's knife – it was a lot easier than it shoulda been, I guess cause I was still in the river's favor. Naji got a fire going and cooked the fish on a couple of smooth, flat stones, and that fish tasted better than anything I'd eaten for the past two weeks. I got to feeling a lot better after that, but it seemed to wear Naji out, and he curled up in the grasses and slept.

I took that as an opportunity to strip down and bathe, scrubbing at my unburned skin with a small handful of pebbles. I rinsed out my dress – hardly more than rags now – and laid it out in the sun to dry. And cause Naji was still sleeping, I laid myself out in the sun to dry, too.

Kaol, that felt good, like all my muscles needed was the strength of the sun. I stretched my hands out over my head and listened to the bugs and the river and Naji snoring over in the grasses.

Every now and then, I thought about Tarrin of the Hariri, bleeding to death on the sand, and it gave me a tightness in my chest that hurt like a flesh wound. I know guilt won't get you nowhere if you're living a pirate's life, but it snuck up on me anyway, no matter how much I reminded myself that he would've killed me first. At least with the Hariri crewmen I didn't know for sure if they died or not – that's usually how it is in battle, all that chaos swirling around you. But

Tarrin stuck with me, and it wasn't just cause I knew the Hariri clan would have to take their revenge.

We set off the next morning. The horse was gone – it had wandered away in the night, off to join the camel in the desert. I didn't mind walking, but Naji was still too pale, and he moved slower than normal, shuffling along over the riverbed like an old man.

"It's only a few days' walk from here," he said.

"What is?" I looked at him sideways. "Don't you dare say a canyon."

He didn't answer at first, and I thought about laying in to him for never telling me anything, but then he said, "Leila."

"Who the hell is that?"

"Someone who can cure me."

"Oh. Right." I stopped and put my hands on my hips. Kaol, why couldn't we have met up with this Leila lady before the Hariri clan tracked us down? I didn't know how much it would've changed things. Tarrin still wouldn't have listened to me. But maybe I wouldn't have killed him, neither. Maybe I could have agreed to go with him and then found some other way out of marriage.

"What's wrong?" Naji turned toward me. He had his robes on normal again, but they gaped open at the chest from where I'd cut them, and he kept tugging them over the wound. "I thought you'd be happy to know we've almost arrived at our destination."

"Happy enough," I muttered.

Naji frowned. "Tell me. It could prove important–"

"Why should I tell you anything? Not like you haven't kept me in the dark since that night I saved your life – biggest mistake I ever made." I started walking more quickly, and I could hear Naji's footsteps catching up with me.

"Ananna–" he began.

"You really want to know?" Anger pulsed through my body, heating up my skin. Anger at Naji, at myself, and Tarrin for not standing up to his father. "I killed him. I killed Tarrin. He was a captain's son. I know that don't mean nothing to you–"

Naji didn't move.

"But a captain's son is special, cause he carries on the ship name. Ain't nothing to hire an assassin to kill a captain's daughter, but a son…" I hadn't let myself think about any of this yesterday, and now it was flooding over me like a tsunami. The Hariris would want revenge on me for sure. If they were willing to send an assassin just cause I spurned their son I didn't even want to think about what they'd do now that I'd killed him.

I wished my brain would just shut down the way it had yesterday afternoon.

"I do know what it means," Naji said quietly. "To kill a captain's son. I've worked with the Confederation before."

And then he put a hand on my shoulder, which surprised me into silence. I stared at the ridges of his knuckles, at the spiderweb of knife scars etching across his skin. His touch was warm.

"Leila is a river witch," he said. "I believe she can help lift my curse."

"Yeah, figured that out ages ago." I scowled down at the riverbed.

"Even when the curse is lifted," he went on. "I'll arrange for your protection."

His hand dropped away. The place where he'd touched me felt empty.

"Thank you," I muttered, looking down at my feet, my cheeks hot.

"Come," Naji said. "Once we get to Leila's everything will be fine. You'll see."

Yeah, I thought. For you.

But I walked along the riverbank same as before.

We followed the river for three days, and it was a lot easier than trekking through the desert, even without the camel. There was plenty of water and fresh fish to eat, and a lot more to look at. Little blue flowers grew along the riverbed, all mixed up with the grasses and the river nettle that I'd used to save Naji's life a second time, and the walls of the canyon grew taller and steeper the more we walked, until it seemed like the desert was another world away. And those walls were something themselves, stripes of golden-sun yellow and rust-red and off-white. Like the wood on the inside of a fancy sailing ship.

We had to stop quite a bit, though, so Naji could rest. His health didn't seem to improve. He stayed pale despite all the sun, and he'd stumble over the rocks sometimes, and I'd have to steady him. He slept longer than me and hardly ate much of anything. It was worrisome, cause I'd no way of helping him out if he got any sicker. There was no way the river would give me another cure, not without an offering – which I didn't have.

On the third day, we came across a house.

It was built into the stone of the canyon wall, with carved steps leading down to the river. There were three little boats tethered next to the steps, plus a flat raft that looked made out of driftwood from the sea. Bits of broken glass and small smooth stones hung from the house's overhang, chiming in the wind.

"Finally," Naji said. "We're here."

"This is it?" We were on the other side of the river from the house. I walked up to the water's edge. The house looked empty, still and silent save for that broken glass.

"Yes. Leila's house." Naji closed his eyes and swayed in place. Everything about him was washed out except for the wound on his chest. "She can help me."

But I got the feeling that he wasn't talking to me, so I didn't say nothing.

"Guess we got to swim across," I said. The water ran slow, smooth as the top of a mirror. Looked deep, though.

Naji opened his eyes. He nodded, and then he sat down and pulled off his boots and lashed 'em together with his sword and his knife and his quill, which I was surprised to learn hadn't been packed away on the camel. "My desert mask," he said.

"What about it?"

"Where is it?"

"I dunno."

Naji stood up, his boots and sword and all bundled up at his feet. "You don't know? You took it from me! I would never have lost it."

"Well, you didn't seem all too worried about it before." I honestly didn't know what had happened to the mask. It probably got left behind on the riverbed or knocked into the river proper.

"I didn't need it before."

"Why do you need it now? We still ain't in the desert."

Naji face got real dark, his eyes narrowing into two angry slits. "It doesn't matter," he said, turning away from me. He grabbed his boots and waded out into the water. I followed behind him, sure he was gonna pass out and I'd have to save his life again. The water was colder here, and I didn't know if that was cause of the depth or this Leila woman. Probably both.

At the other side of the river, Naji put on his boots, and drew his robes tight over the wound on his chest. Then he knocked on the door.

We had to wait awhile. Whoever Leila was, she sure took her sweet time. Naji knocked again. The glass tinkled overhead and cast rainbow lights all over the place.

"She ain't here," I said.

"Of course she is." Naji leaned up against the side of the house, tugging distractedly on the hair hanging at the left side of his head, pulling it over his scar. "She has to be."

At that moment, like she'd been standing inside listening to us, the door swung open. The woman who stepped out into the sunlight was beautiful. Curvy where she was supposed to be, with thick hair that curled down to her narrow waist. Big eyes and lashes long enough that she didn't need to wear no kohl to fake it. This perfect bow-shaped mouth. I knew immediately why Naji'd pitched such a fit about his desert mask.

Course, I didn't trust her one bit.

"Naji!" she cried, throwing up her hands. "My favorite disfigured assassin! What brings you all the way out here to my river?"

"Don't do this, Leila. You know why I'm here." But he didn't say it like he was mad. In fact, he kept looking at her with this dopey expression I'd seen a thousand times before, on the faces of the crew whenever a pretty lady came aboard. Ain't nobody ever looked at me like that.

Leila smiled and her whole face lit up like the river beneath sunlight. "Of course I do! One impossible curse, one round of spellshot to the heart. Which you seem to be mending up rather nicely on your own."

Impossible curse? My blood started rushing in my ears. Mama had told me about impossible curses once, back when I was still trying to learn magic. They were a northern thing, cold and tricky like the ice. And impossible to cure, of course. Naji had dragged me across the desert for a cure that didn't exist.

I was never going to get rid of him. And standing there by that dazzling river, I saw the life I'd imagined ever since I was a little girl sitting down in the cargo bay unfurl and then turn to dust. I'd killed a captain's son and now I had a lifetime bound to a damn blood magician.

Curse the north and its crooked, barbaric magic.

"The Order said you could help me," Naji said.

Leila dipped one shoulder and fluttered her eyelashes. I wanted to hit her. I wanted to hit both of them. But then she tilted her head toward the mysterious darkness of her house. "Come in," she said. "Her, too. I don't imagine you'll want her to wait outside. Gives you quite the headache, doesn't it?"

Well. I was starting to think she hadn't even seen me.

"Come on," Naji said, wrenching himself away from the house's stone wall. Leila waited in the doorway, gazing kind of haughty-like at Naji. I didn't want to go in. Course, maybe she really could help us.

I went in.

The house was small and dark and cool. It smelled like the river. Naji sat down at the stone table in the center of the room, and Leila disappeared through the back, calling out as she went, "I've something for that fatigue, Naji dearest, if you just give me a second."

I sat down beside him. Water dripped off my dress and pooled on the floor. I hoped she'd have to clean it up.

Leila came back with a chipped tea saucer and a kettle. She poured hot water into the saucer, and grass-scented steam floated up into the air. I watched

Naji drink, waiting for something bad to happen. But he just leaned back in the chair and closed his eyes and let out this long satisfied breath.

"Spellshot's nothing to mess with," Leila said to me, like I'd have any idea what she was talking about.

I glared at her.

She laughed. "Naji, where'd you come up with her? She's so sullen."

I clenched my hands into fists. Naji pushed himself up to sitting and leaned over the table and looked at Leila. "Thank you, I do feel much stronger."

"I heard my river gave you a handout a few days ago." She smiled again, and the whole room seemed to fill with light. Kaol, it pissed me off.

Naji's eyes flicked over to me a second. Back to Leila. "Can you help me or not?"

"Well, it's called an impossible curse for a reason." She leaned against the wall. "But I'll see what I can do. Stand up so I can get a good look at you."

For a few seconds Naji didn't move. Then he ducked his head a little and pushed away from the table. Leila sashayed up to him and walked around a few times as though she was sizing up a calf for slaughter. She moved like water, graceful and soft and lovely. Every part of me wanted to stick out my foot and trip her, just to see her stumble.

"Well?" said Naji, who hadn't looked up once.

Leila stopped. She was only a few inches from him, close enough he could have turned his head and kissed her if he wanted.

She pressed two fingers underneath his chin and forced his head up. She stared at his face for a long time, and Naji didn't say anything, didn't move at all.

"It's really a shame," she said. "You were such a beautiful man."

Naji jerked away from her, slamming his hip into the edge of the table.

"Leave him alone," I said, jumping to my feet, going for the knife that wasn't there no more. Wasn't enough that he had an impossible curse on him, she had to make fun of his face?

Leila glanced over at me and laughed, which made me feel smaller than a fleck of dust. Naji had sunk into his chair, his head tilted down, his hair covering up his whole face.

"Are you sure she's not the one cursed to protect you?" Leila slunk over to Naji and wrapped her arms around his shoulders and pressed her nose into the part of his hair. "Oh, don't be like that," she purred. "You know I was only joking."

"No, you weren't," I said. I wanted that knife so bad. It weren't so much cause of Naji but cause I can't stand a bully, and that's all she was. A bully who got away with it cause she was so beautiful.

"Ananna," Naji said. "Stop. She's going to help me."

"If I can," Leila said, her arms still wrapped around Naji's shoulders, her mouth right on the verge of smiling.

That was too much. I stalked out of the house, back out into the sunlight, all the way down the steps leading into the river. Naji's headache be damned. I sat down at the top step and stuck my feet in the water. Fish swam up to me and nibbled on my toes but nobody came out of the house. I didn't expect 'em to.

I stayed out there for a while, until the sun set and my stomach grumbled. I thought about swimming over to the other side of the river and setting up camp. But by now it was too dark to see, and I doubted I'd be able to catch any fish to eat. The air had gotten cold again, and the river was cold, and I kept on shivering out there in my ragged, cut-up dress.

My pride kept me from walking back in the house until it was late enough I figured both of 'em had fallen asleep. I crept back in slowly, pulling up on the door handle so the hinges wouldn't creak. The floors were stone, so my bare feet didn't make too much noise.

"I'm glad to see you came back inside."

I yelped.

Naji was stretched out on a cot in the corner of the room. He pushed up on his arm when he saw me.

"Where's Leila?"

"Asleep, I imagine."

I sat down on the floor beside the cot, drawing my feet up close against me.

"I don't like her," I said, pitching my voice low.

"I'd prefer not to talk about this." A rustle as he rolled over onto his back and pulled the thin woven blanket over his chest.

"She's beautiful," I said.

"I know."

I wanted to slap him for that, but I didn't, cause I

knew I didn't have no good reason. "It means she ain't trustworthy."

"What? Because she's beautiful?"

"Yeah. Beautiful people, things are too easy for 'em. They don't know how to survive in this world. Somebody's ugly, or even plain, normal-looking, that means they got to work twice as hard for things. For anything. Just to get people to listen to 'em, or take 'em serious. So yeah. I don't trust beautiful people."

"I see." He dropped his head to the side. I didn't look at him, but down at the floor instead, at the fissures in the stones. "No wonder you were so quick to trust me."

I heard the hard edge in his voice, the crack of bitterness. And so I lifted my head. He was staring up at the ceiling.

"You ain't ugly," I said.

He didn't answer, and I knew my opinion didn't matter none anyway.

CHAPTER TEN

Leila didn't do much to sway me over to trusting her those next few days, mostly cause she toyed with Naji, not giving him a straight answer one way or another with regards to the curse.

"He needs to rest," she told me that first afternoon. "Before I can examine him to see if I can help." She had come out to the river to gather up a jar of silt and a few handfuls of river nettle. I spent as little time inside the house as I could, and it surprised me that she said anything to me. I hadn't asked after him, although I'd been wondering.

"He's a lot more injured than he lets on," she added, scooping the silt up with her hand. It streamed through her fingers and glittered in the sunlight. "I'm surprised he made it as far as he did."

"I took care of him," I snapped, even though I was trying to hold my tongue.

She looked up from the half-filled jar. "Of course you tried, sweetling," she said. "But you aren't used to that sort of magic." One of her vicious half-smiles. "Or any kind of magic at all."

The water glided around my ankles, and I thought about that night the river spoke to me in her babbling soft language, that night she guided me into action.

"By the way," Leila said. "I have some old clothes that might work for you. Men's clothes, of course. You're not going to fit into anything of mine, I'm afraid."

I knew I really wasn't going to hold my tongue against that, so I slipped off the edge of the steps and into the river, the cold shocking the anger right out of me. I kept my eyes open, the way I always do underwater, so I could see the sunlight streaming down from the surface, lighting up the murkiness.

Naji'd told me Leila was some kind of river witch, but the river didn't seem to play favorites, didn't seem to care about the differences between me and her. It wasn't like Naji. And so I stayed under long as I could, cause it was safe down there, everything blurred, the coldness turning me numb.

Naji did seem to get better. I guess I'll give Leila that. He got the color back in his cheeks, and he didn't shake when he shuffled around the house. The wound was slow to heal, though, despite the river nettle Leila pressed against it every evening. Sometimes I watched them, studying the way her long delicate fingers lingered on his chest. When she sang, her voice twinkled like starlight, clear and bright and perfect. That was when I figured out that she and Naji had been lovers before he got the scar. Cause she touched him like she knew how, and he stared at her like all he thought about was her touch.

It left me dizzy and kind of sick to my stomach. At least she never did say nothing about his face again. Not in front of me, anyway.

We'd been there close to a week when Leila announced over dinner that she was ready to talk to Naji about the curse.

"Finally," I said.

Naji kicked me under the table.

"You need to be there too," Leila said.

"Be where?"

"The garden, I imagine," Naji said. He poked at the fish on his plate. All we ate was fish and river reeds, steamed in the hearth in the main room.

"There's a garden?"

"Yes, out back," Leila said.

That didn't make no sense. The house was built into the wall of the canyon, and even if she had stairs leading up to the surface, the surface wasn't nothing but desert.

"Magic," Leila said, and tapped her chest. I scowled. She smiled at me like I'd said something stupid that she found amusing.

I slumped down in my chair and pushed the fish around on my plate, my appetite gone. And I kept doing that till Naji and Leila decided they were finished up, at which point both of 'em filed out of the kitchen, toward the back of the house. I took my time, dawdling till Naji strode back into the main room. I was sure he was going to command me to follow, but instead he looked at me real close and said, "Please, Ananna."

I shot him a mean look, and he watched me for a few minutes like he was trying to think of something to say. I can wait out a silence just fine, so I crossed my arms over my chest and stared right back.

He said, "I went into Kajjil last night and spoke with the Order."

"What does that have to do with anything?"

"The Hariri clan hasn't hired another Jadorr'a. If you're worried that curing me will leave you vulnerable – if this is some pirate's scheme for protection–"

"I told you," I snapped, "I can take care of myself."

"Of course. I just thought that might be a reason for your reticence."

"Well, that don't surprise me none. That you'd think that." I gave him my best glare. I didn't want to think about the Hariri clan. I didn't want to think about Tarrin. "I just don't understand what Leila needs me for."

"She says that she needs your help."

"What?"

"You're part of the curse."

"Yeah, an impossible one. I don't see how I'm gonna make much of a difference–"

The expression on Naji's face stopped me dead. I'd never seen a man look so desperate. It made me aware of my own desperation, that ache that had settled in the bottom of my stomach after the battle in the desert.

"I just don't see what good it can do," I muttered.

"The least you can do is give me five minutes," Naji said.

That was enough for me. I followed Naji to the back of the house, through the dark, dripping stone hallway, past rooms glowing with something too steady for candlelight. And then the hallway opened up, the way corridors do in caves, and there was the garden.

So it was underground. There wasn't no sunlight in the room, though the ceiling had that same weird glow to it as the rooms in the house. And the plants weren't like any plants I'd ever seen: All of 'em were real pale, so pale you could almost see straight through 'em. They wriggled around whenever we walked past, as though they were turning to look at us.

Leila sat in the center of the garden, on a stone bench in the middle of a circle carved into the wet rock of the cave. She had on this floaty white dress that made her look like one of the flowers, and when we walked up she patted the bench beside herself. I let Naji take it. She obviously meant for him to sit there anyway.

"Everyone's gathered, I see." Like we were some big crowd, not three people who'd been living in the same house for a week. "Naji, I'll need you to look at me." That damn smile again. "I know it's hard for you–"

I took a step toward her, my hands balled up tight into fists, and so help me, her voice kind of wavered, and for a minute she actually shut up. Then she cleared her throat and said, "Look at me, and don't move. It's important you don't move."

Then she glanced over at me and said, "I need you over here too. Come along, yes, put your hand on Naji's hand there. No, palm down. Good."

She pulled out a blue silk scarf and tied Naji's and my hand together.

"Now," she said, looking up at me. "You need to stand there and not move your hand from his–"

"I'm tied to him," I said.

"And don't interrupt."

Naji didn't look at either of us while she spoke. He just kept his head down, his hair pulled over his scar.

"Don't give me a reason to interrupt," I said. "And I won't."

That got a glare from her and nothing else. She turned her attention to Naji. Put her hands on his shoulders. Closed her eyes. Hummed. The flowers trembled and shook and danced. Naji kept his face blank, and I wondered what was going through his head. I wondered if he bought it.

Cause I'd seen a lot of magic those last few weeks, and Leila's humming and swaying didn't fool me one bit. There was magic down here, for sure – have to be, with those creepy flowers – and Leila certainly could work a charm when she needed. But she didn't need to do anything right now. She was faking.

She carried on like that just long enough to be annoying. I shifted my weight around and tapped my foot and looked at Naji's scar. My hand was starting to sweat from being tied up with his.

And then she stopped. The cave seemed to let out a sigh.

Naji stared at her, and his eyes were so hopeful it almost broke my heart.

"Sorry dearest," she said. "There's nothing I can do."

"What!" Naji jumped to his feet, his whole body springing tight like a coil. The scarf fluttered to the ground.

I felt like the earth had been pulled out from under me. Nothing she could do. I realized then that I'd been thinking she could help too. I hadn't even recognized the hope for what it was until it got dragged away from me and I felt its absence in my heart. I couldn't let go of that old vision of my future life and the thought of what it was going to be like now.

"What do you mean? Nothing? Not even a charm against–"

"It's an impossible curse," Leila said lightly. "What did you expect?"

"But you said… And the Order…" Naji threw up his hands and stalked away from her. The flowers shrank away from him, curling up into themselves. "I can't believe this."

I was numb. I figured Leila knew from the moment she opened her front door that she couldn't help Naji, but she strung him along, cause – hell, I don't know why. Cause she was beautiful and he was all in love with her and so she could. This was why I hated beautiful people. They build you up and then they destroy you. And we let 'em.

"Naji, darling," she said. "I still might be able to help you, of course."

Naji picked up his shoulders a little, although he didn't turn around.

"Liar," I said. It didn't give me the satisfaction I'd hoped for.

She glanced at me as though I were as insignificant as a piece of pressed copper. Then she stood up and glided over to Naji, her dress rippling out behind her. She set one hand on his shoulder and whispered something in his ear. He sighed.

"The impossible curses are all from the north," Leila said. "A northern curse needs a northern cure. Even if it's impossible." She smiled. "Especially if it's impossible."

"What are you saying?" Naji asked.

"I can give you a boat."

"What'd you whisper to him?" I asked.

"None of your business." Leila swatted at me. "Naji, I can give you and your ward a boat and a promise of protection on the river."

"We can take care of the Hariri clan ourselves."

"I'm not concerned about some gang of unwashed pirates."

"What?" I asked. "Who else is after us?"

She twisted around, her hair falling in thick silky ropes down her spine. "The Mists, of course."

The garden suddenly seemed too cold. "What's the Mists got to do with it?" I was trying to sound brave, but my voice shook anyway, at the memory of a pair of gray eyes swallowing me whole. "Why didn't you say anything? I thought it was just the Hariri clan we had to worry about. I mean, you kept going on about us being under protection–" I was babbling. The words spilled out of my throat the way they always do whenever I let my fear get to me.

Both of them ignored me.

"The river will take you down to Port Iskassaya, where you can book passage to the Isles of the Sky."

"Kaol!" I shouted. "The Isles of the Sky!"

Naji and Leila both looked at me.

"I ain't going there," I said. "I ran out on Tarrin cause that's where he wanted to take me."

Leila gave me this teasing little smile, but I turned to Naji and said, "You can't really think–"

"It's the only way," Leila said.

"I ain't asking you."

"I agree with her, Leila," Naji said. "You know I can't go there."

"Thank you," I said. Finally, he had learned how to talk some sense.

"Oh, Naji, the enchantment from that charm is so strong I could feel it when you were three days away. They'll never catch you."

"I still don't understand why you'd send me there, of all places–"

"You know as well as I that if you want any hope of breaking an impossible curse, you'll need the magic of the Isles. And besides," Leila gave a bright smile, "it's where the Wizard Eirnin lives."

"I've never heard of him," said Naji.

"He's from the north, from the ice-islands. I studied under him as a child. Long before I met you." She smiled and pressed herself close to Naji and he sank into her like her closeness was a relief. "I've seen him cast impossible curses before. And a cure is only one letter off from a curse."

I snorted and kicked at the powdery dirt of the floor.

Naji gave her long hard look. "It's too dangerous."

"So cast some more spells. Someone as powerful as you…" She made her eyes all big and bright. Naji gazed moonily at her. "You'll be fine."

"And what about me?" I said. "Will I be fine? I know what happens when the untouched go to the Isles of the Sky. They get turned into rainclouds and dirt or they get sucked down to the depths and drown over and over."

"You aren't untouched," Naji said. "You healed me by the river."

I glared at him. "Well, I ain't as strong as you, then."

"I have to protect you before I have to protect myself," he said. "Leila is right about the magic–"

"Of course I am," Leila said, reaching over to toy with the curl of his hair.

I couldn't say anything, thinking about the idea that he was putting my protection before his own.

"It may be my only option," Naji said to me.

"My only option, too," I said. "You're not the only one cursed here. And I still don't want to go." But already I knew it might be worth it, if the Isles really could break Naji's curse. They were the place where the impossible happened, after all. It was just that their impossible was supposed to be the sort of impossible that's also horrible.

Naji gave me a sad, confused sort of frown.

"Of course," he said, "no merchant ship is going to agree to sail to the Isles of the Sky."

"No pirate ship, neither," I added. "And that's what Port Iskassaya is anyway, a pirates' port-of-call."

"How convenient," Leila said, "that you travel with a pirate."

Naji pulled away from her and trudged away from the flowers, back over to the center circle. "We need to talk," he said to me.

"Can't argue with that."

He gave me one of his Naji-looks. For a few seconds I didn't think Leila was going to let us leave the garden, but she didn't say nothing when Naji grabbed my upper arm and dragged me back into the dripping dimness of the house.

"Told you she ain't trustworthy," I said. "She's been planning that little performance the whole time we were here. I'd put money on it."

Naji didn't say nothing for a long time. Then he said, and it damn near knocked me over, "You're probably right. I was... hoping... that she wouldn't play any of her games with me. Not now. Not... with everything." He slouched down on the cot and stuck his head in his hands. "I knew she trained in the north, that's why I came here, but I truly hoped–"

"And what did she mean about protecting us from the Mists?"

Naji dropped his hands down to his sides. "Oh, her word is good for that," he said. "She wouldn't do anything to actually kill me."

"That don't answer my question."

"Because the answer doesn't concern you."

"Really?" I said. "'Well, in that case, this curse of yours don't concern me neither. So if you don't mind, I'll be on my way." And I slipped off my charm and headed toward the front door.

"Ananna!" Naji jumped up from the cot and grabbed me again. I wasn't really going to go. I ain't so heartless I'm gonna let someone be struck down with pain on account of me. Even if that someone is a murderer and a liar. Hell, murderers and liars used to sing me to sleep.

I yanked my arm away from him. "Look, you want me to go with you to the Isles of the Sky – and I can kinda see how maybe it's not the stupidest idea in the world, all things considered, even if it's definitely up there – but if you really want me to go, you have to be straight with me. You gotta tell me things."

"Tell you things," he said.

"Yeah. You know how you didn't tell me who Leila was, or what we'd find here in the canyon? Or what that black smoke was when the Hariri clan attacked?" I glared at him and after a few seconds he nodded. "Well, no more of that."

"I know what 'tell you things' means."

"Sounded like you were asking. Keep in mind that if you want to barter passage on a pirate ship, you will need me. You don't got the cash to buy your way onto one, and ain't no pirate in the Confederation's gonna let a blood-magician on board without some kind of leverage." I jutted my thumb into my chest. "Which is me. So if you want to go on with your secrets, that's fine, but you can expect to wait out the rest of your days in Port Iskassaya."

Naji got that flash of a smile around his eyes. I was too worked up to care.

"I think that sounds like a deal," Naji said.

"Now why the hell should I be worried about the Mists attacking us?" Kaol, even saying Mists sent the creeping shivers up my spine.

"Someone in the Otherworld wants me dead," Naji said. "They'll have no fight with you, but they want me. It's a long–"

Leila appeared in the doorway, that white dress swirling around her ankles. She had her cruel smile on, teeth shining in the lamplight. Naji stared at her the way he did, his face all full of longing. Then he turned back to me.

"Let me tell you on the river," he said.

"Fine." So he didn't want to talk in front of Leila. "But if I don't know the whole story by Port Iskassaya, I'm gone."

Naji's eyes crinkled up again. Then he stuck out his hand. I shook it.

CHAPTER ELEVEN

Leila lent us the largest of the boats that had been tied up out front. It had a newly patched sail and a rope-net for fishing. I didn't want to trust that boat, but as much as it pained me to admit it, I knew Naji was right when he said Leila didn't want us – or him, anyway – dead.

She gave us a basket filled with salted fish and some of the river reeds we'd been eating. I never wanted to look at another river reed again, but I accepted the basket anyway. She also produced a bundle of black cloth for Naji, which he unfurled into an assassin's robe. Leila had cut up his old robe when we first got here, for patching sails and blankets, and he'd been wearing the same cast-off men's clothes I had the past week.

"Where did you get this?" he asked.

"Surely you remember, dearest." Leila winked at him, and Naji looked down at his feet.

"I'm afraid I don't have anything for you," she said, hardly turning her head to look at me. I resisted the urge to make some rude gesture at her. "Oh, and Naji dearest, I put your armor down below."

"Thank you," Naji said, lifting his head. They regarded one another for a few seconds longer, and I turned away and set to fiddling with the ropes so I wouldn't have to look at them.

And then we took off. Port Iskassaya was a three-day trip down river, according to Naji. (Leila'd told him, of course, though he don't know nothing about sailing.) When we arrived we were to release the boat the way you would a camel – I thought of our own camel and wondered if he was still trotting through the desert weighed down with our clothes and money and food – and it'd make its way back up the river to Leila's house. Magic again.

Naji moped that first day, leaning against the railing and looking out over the river. He hadn't bothered to change into his robes yet, and his hair fluttered around his face so that he looked like a prince in a story. I tried to busy myself with the work of sailing, but the ship took care of herself, and after a while I was so bored I leaned up beside him.

He glanced over at me but didn't say nothing.

"You miss her, don't you?"

He kept staring out over the water and didn't answer. The sun was sinking into the canyon, throwing off rays of orange and red, turning the water silver. I don't know why I asked him that. It was like I wanted him to say something to hurt me.

"You don't miss someone like Leila," Naji said, after

enough time had passed that I figured he'd no intention of answering. "You merely feel her absence."

"That don't make sense."

"It's hard to explain. She's always played games, but it got worse after–" He stopped. "It doesn't matter. I only came here because I was desperate. I hardly see her anymore."

He leaned away from the railing. "Thank you," he said. "For coming with me to do this."

I was a little sore from hearing him talk about Leila, so I just dipped my head and said, "I told you. I don't want you hanging around me none, either."

"I'll find a way to repay you," he said. "When it's done. You'll be compensated."

I didn't like the way he said that, like I was some hired hand.

"I promise," he said.

I didn't respond, just left him there, muttering something about needing to check on the rigging. And he didn't say anything when I walked away.

I wished there was more for me to do on the ship, so I could throw myself into working and not spend all my time brooding. Mama would have called it the doldrums, but those always came when you'd been at sea for months and months and you were missing civilization so bad you're almost willing to fling yourself overboard and try to swim to land. And it wasn't the river that was causing my trouble anyway.

The second afternoon, Naji came out on deck and

called my name. I was up in the rigging – not working or nothing, just sitting up there watching the walls of the canyon slide by. I hung onto the rope and leaned over and watched him clomp around, swinging his head this way and that.

"Look up!" I called out.

He stopped and then tilted his head toward the sky, shielding his eyes from the sun. "How'd you get up there?"

I shrugged and then swung down on the rope, criss-crossing through the rigging, until I landed on deck, a few feet away from him.

"I owe you an explanation," he said.

"I thought you forgot. I was looking forward to ditching you once we made port."

He shook his head. His expression was soft, almost kind, and I wondered what he would look like if he smiled properly. Even with the scar, I bet it was nice.

"Alright," I said. "Let's hear it."

"You remember the woman from the desert? The one who gave you the spell to banish me to the Otherworld?"

"I thought she was dead."

"No. I sent her back where she came from."

"But she bled all over–"

"They don't die," Naji said. "It's not something I can explain – just know that they aren't human."

I crossed my arms over my chest. This was a lot to work through in my head. I'd seen sirens before, and the merfolk too, but you can kill 'em easy as you can kill a man. No wonder I got cold thinking about the Mists.

"So what'd you do to her?" I asked. "That got her so pissed?"

"I didn't do anything to her," he said. "She serves someone in the Otherworld, one of the thousands of lords constantly clamoring for power. I severed some of her master's ties to our world."

"What?"

"I killed some of the children he planted here. They weren't children when I killed them," he added, since I must have looked appalled. There are lines that shouldn't be crossed. "They were attempting to rub bare the walls between worlds, in a move to gain power in the Mists. It's complicated, but..." His voice trailed off. "He was willing to sacrifice our world to gain power in his."

The air was real still. The only movement came from the boat as it sliced through the river water.

"Oh," I said. "You saved everybody. The entire world." I gave him a little half-smile, even though it was weird to think of him as a hero. "I gotta admit, I'm impressed."

"Don't be." Naji frowned. "I was hired to do it. I didn't know who the targets were. In fact, I didn't understand the implications of what I did until much later, when she first attacked me."

I leaned up against the rigging and thought about everything that happened these last few weeks, everything that happened before Naji went from my would-be killer to my protector.

"You don't need to worry about it," Naji said, looking all earnest. "But that's why Leila offered us her protection against the Otherworld. Because–"

"Just as long as we're on the river."

"What?"

"She only offered her protection as long as we're on the river." I crossed my arms in front of my chest. "And don't lie to me. You said yourself you were putting my protection ahead of your own."

Naji sighed. "Fine. I'm worried the Otherworld will use you – the curse – to get to me."

"Put me in danger, you mean? So you'd have to come and save me?"

"More or less. Although really, you don't need to worry." Naji shrugged. "I've seen you fight. You could hold your own against any monster of the Mists."

I turned away from him, embarrassed. The water glittered around us like a million slant-cut diamonds. The sky pressed down, heavy and bleached white with heat.

"Thanks for telling me all that," I said. My words came out kinda slurred like I was drunk. "I appreciate you treating me like a partner."

"You're welcome."

I nodded out at the river, and that was that.

We sailed into Port Iskassaya at dawn, the air crisp from the night before. I was up at the bow of the ship, watching the city emerge out of the pink haze of the morning and thinking on how I didn't much want to leave the river for the sea, for the Isles of the Sky.

Naji came up from down below all decked out in his assassin robes and his carved armor, with a new desert mask pulled across the lower half of his face.

"That don't look dodgy at all," I said.

Naji sighed. "Ananna, these are my clothes. I feel comfortable in them–"

"I was talking more about your mask."

His eyes darkened. "I'm not taking it off."

"I know. I'm just saying."

I sweet-talked the bureaucrat at the river-docks into letting me and Naji set the boat for free. "We'll only be here half an hour," I said. "Won't be no trouble to you."

The bureaucrat gave me this long hard look. "I'm giving you twenty minutes. You ain't back by then, I'm letting her loose."

I smiled at him and gave a little salute and me and Naji went on our way. I figured he might cut the boat free or he might not, but whether or not Leila got her boat back wasn't something I was gonna concern myself with.

Naji got real quiet, quieter than normal, as we made our way through the port town, which wasn't nothing more than some drinkhouses and brothels and a few illegal armories tucked away in the back alleys. He stuck close to the buildings, weaving in and out of shadow. Soon enough we were getting stink-eyes from busted-up old crewmen who ain't got nothing better to do than sit out drinking that early in the morning.

I'd been to the Port Iskassaya sea-docks only once before, when I was a little girl. It ain't a major port, as it's surrounded by desert and the river don't go nowhere of interest, but somebody built it two hundred years back and since the merchants didn't want it, the pirates claimed it instead. Mostly folks use it as a place to stop off and refresh supplies before they head out to the open sea.

I made Naji go skulk off in the shadows – which he did without question, no surprise there – while I wandered up and down the docks, looking for the right sort of boat to take us out to the Isles of the Sky. Which ain't any kind of boat at all, when you get down to it.

I'd tried to make myself look as much like a boy as possible, though my breasts don't exactly bind easy. For one, the Hariri clan would be looking for a girl, but also it's usually easier to talk your way on a ship if you're at least trying to pass as a boy. Most people ain't that observant. I made my way through the docks as quick as I could, keeping my eyes on the ships' colors. I'd already decided against trying any Confederation ships since I didn't want word to get back to the Hariris, so my tattoo wasn't gonna do much good. As it turned out there weren't any Confederation ships at port anyway, but I did spot a couple of boats that obviously weren't entirely on the up-and-up.

The whole time I was looking I was thinking about whether or not I really wanted to go through with it – it couldn't be that hard to tell Naji no one was willing to take us aboard. Maybe we could just spend out our days in Port Iskassaya, swapping stories with the sailors down in the drinkhouses. Given our last trip in search of a cure, taking to port might prove more fruitful than sailing out to the Isles. At least that way there wasn't no chance of the curse turning out worse than before. I mean, we were heading for the source of magic. That's not something you can just trust.

But I patrolled the docks anyway, partly cause I promised Naji and partly cause I wanted my life to go back to normal. And after about twenty minutes I had two possibilities lined up: a busted-up old sloop that looked about a million years old, and a nice-looking brigantine with a crew that seemed to hail mainly from Jokja and Najare and the like in the south, all those strings of countries not bound by the Empire. I decided to try my luck with the Free Country ship, the Ayel's Revenge. Pirate's intuition, assuming it hadn't rusted out with disuse and bad decisions.

A few of the crew were sitting on the dock next to the ship, drinking rum and playing cards. I strolled up, acting casual, and one of 'em, a guy with a mean squint I could tell was mostly faked, jerked his chin up at me.

"You ain't a boy," he said.

"Leave her alone, Shan." It was the one woman at the table, and the one who looked like she had all the brains besides which. She lay down her cards and looked up at me. She had dark brown skin and wore her hair in locks that she tied back with a piece of silk ribbon. There was something calm and intelligent about her expression, and I liked her immediately. "Ignore him," she said to me. "I assume any girl dressed like a boy either needs all the help she can get, or none at all. Which is it for you?"

"I need passage," I said. "So probably the first."

"Passage? To where?"

"Wherever you're going."

She gazed at me appraisingly. The guys at the table shuffled their feet and exchanged glances with one another. I could tell they didn't want me around, but I knew their opinions weren't the ones that mattered.

"We're headed to Qilar," she said. "I suppose it's as good a place as any, for someone who doesn't know what they want."

One of 'em, not the squint-eyed one, muttered something about always playing captain. The woman ignored him.

"What can you do?" she said.

"My parents had a boat a bit like this." I nodded at the ship sloshing in the water. "Not quite as big, but I spent my whole life on her, and I know the rigging ain't that different." I squinted up at the ship's sails. "I know a bit of navigation, too, and I can hold my own in a fight, if the need arises."

"I hope the need won't arise." The woman smiled.

"One more thing," I said, trying to figure out the best way to say this. "It ain't just me. I got a…" I didn't know what to call Naji, exactly. I couldn't say assassin. "A ward, with me."

"A ward?" The woman raised an eyebrow. "Where is she?"

"He," I said. "He's back at the inn. He won't be no trouble, though. Keeps to himself."

"I take it he's not as knowledgeable as you?"

No point in lying. I shook my head.

The woman sat for a minute, nodding a little to herself. Then she stood up and held out her hand. "I'm

Marjani," she said. "Come back here in three hours. Bring your, ah, ward. I'll talk to the captain."

"Ananna," I said, touching my chest. "And thank you."

"Don't thank me yet." But she gave me a smile and I had a feeling it was going to work.

I left the docks and ducked into the alley where I'd left Naji. He materialized right away. Funny to think that trick once scared me witless.

"I think I found something," I said.

"Really?" His brow wrinkled up. "They agreed to go to the Isles of the Sky? That seems too simple..."

I kept my mouth shut.

"Midnight's claws, Ananna. We can't simply wander from ship to ship–"

"Sure we can," I said. "That's exactly how you do it."

"I don't think–"

"You don't know," I said. "Cause this ain't your world. It's mine. They're heading to Qilar, probably to Port Idai, and if there's anywhere in the high seas you'll find someone crazy enough to sail to the Isles of the Sky, it'll be in Port Idai." I glared at him. "I ain't just delaying the inevitable, you know."

Naji's eyes were black as coals and hard as diamonds, but he didn't protest further.

I decided to kill those remaining three hours down in the Port Iskassaya shopping district, where you'd find the few respectable types who lived out here. I ain't too fond of pickpocketing, but I figured some money was better than none.

Naji wasn't too happy about us splitting up again, but I yanked back the collar of my shirt and showed him the charm he'd made me.

"I'll be close by," he said.

I rolled my eyes at that. "You let me go to the docks without any fuss."

"And I could barely move from the headache it gave me."

I looked down at my hands. There were a million ways to respond to that, but I didn't want to say none of 'em.

The shopping district was crowded, which was good, though I really needed women's clothing to make this believable. I was a little too off as a boy. But I pulled some old tricks I learned from one of the crew of Papa's ship, this fellow who'd had a birthmark up the side of his face that made the usual sort of pickpocketing difficult, and after two hours I had a pocket full of coins and another full of jewelry. I scuttled out of the shopping district quick as a beetle and went down to the waterfront, where I found a dealer who didn't ask questions about how a young man-or-woman like myself wound up with a fistful of ladies' baubles.

When I walked away from the dealer, the shadows started squirming and wriggling. The sun was high up, right overhead, so Naji didn't have a lot to work with, just the dark line pressing up against the buildings and a few spindly tree shadows. I ducked into the first alley I could.

"I've never seen a more commendable bout of thievery," Naji said, rising up out of the darkness.

I smiled real big and handed him the pouch of coins from the dealer. He tucked it away in his robe.

"Keep that on you," I said. "Assuming they let us on the ship. But until we know the crew, it's best to not leave money lying around."

"As you wish."

"Also…" I took a deep breath, cause I knew he wasn't going to like this. "You have to take off your mask."

He got real quiet. "Why?"

"Because we need 'em to trust us enough to let us on their boat. You covering up your face like that, it's a sign of bad intentions."

"I usually have bad intentions."

"Well, you don't now, and even if you did, you'd still have to take off the mask."

Naji didn't say anything.

"Look, ain't nobody on that boat's gonna care about your face."

Naji's eyes narrowed.

"You never wear it in front of me. It ain't like Leila's around."

I knew I probably shouldn't have said that, but he didn't answer, didn't react at all. For a few minutes we stood there staring at each other, sand and heat drifting through the alley. Then he yanked the mask away and walked out into the sun.

When we arrived at the Free Country boat, the card-playing crewmen had all cleared out, and the ship rose up tall and grand against the cloudless sky. The sea, pale green in the bright afternoon sunlight, slapped against the docks.

"This is your ward?"

I turned around and there was Marjani with some big barrel of a man in the usual flamboyant captain's hat. He had his eyes plastered on Naji, who scowled and crossed his arms over his chest.

"Yeah," I said. "This is Naji."

"I was expecting a little boy," Marjani said.

"He acts like one sometimes."

Marjani laughed, and Naji turned his scowl to me.

"What business do you have in Port Idai?" the captain asked.

I spoke up before Naji could say anything to screw us. "Meeting with an old crew of mine. We got separated in Lisirra after a job soured. Got fed bad information. You know how it is."

"He part of your crew?" The captain jerked his head at Naji.

"No, sir. Picked him up after my own crew'd left me for dead."

"Bet you're not too happy 'bout that."

"Not one bit."

The captain kept his eyes on mine. "And so why exactly is he accompanying you?"

"He's got some history with my old first mate." Thank Kaol, Naji kept his face blank. "Needs to have words with him, you know what I mean."

The captain laughed. "What kinda history?" he asked, turning to Naji. "It about a woman?"

"It usually is," Naji said.

The captain laughed again, and I knew we had him.

Tell any grizzled old cutthroat a sob story about a double-cross and a broken heart and he'll eat right out of your hand.

"Well, if he don't mind sharing a cabin with the rest of the crew, I guess we can spare you."

Naji blanched a little but didn't say anything.

The captain nodded at me. "You can work the rigging, yeah? That's what Marjani told me."

"And anything else you need me to do. I grew up on a boat like this." And did I ever miss her, the sound of wood creaking in the wind, the spray of the sea across my face as I swung through the rigging – but I didn't say none of that.

The captain grinned, face lighting up like someone had just told him there was a merchant ship sitting dead in the open sea. "Exactly the kind of woman I like to have on board."

I ain't gonna lie, after weeks of following around Naji, not knowing what was going on, it felt good to hear that.

CHAPTER TWELVE

Marjani accompanied me and Naji on board the ship while the rest of the crew was setting up to make sail. She led us down below to the crew's quarters, all slung up with hammocks and jars of rum and some spare, tattered clothes. Naji wrinkled his nose and sat down on a hammock in the corner.

"I know what you are," Marjani said to him.

All the muscles in my body tensed. Naji just stared levelly at her.

"And what is that, exactly?" he asked.

In one quick movement, Marjani grabbed his wrist and pushed the sleeve of his robe up to his elbow. The tattoos curled around his arm.

"Blood magic," she said. "You're one of the Jadorr'a."

I pulled out my knife. Marjani glanced at me like she wasn't too concerned. "The crew doesn't know," she said. "They wouldn't recognize you. They're all Free Country, and we've got our own monsters to worry about. I only know because I studied Empire politics at university." She dropped Naji's arm.

"You went to university?" I asked. I'd talked to a scholar once, after we'd commandeered the ship he'd been on. He hadn't been nothing like Marjani.

"Are you going to tell them?" Naji asked.

Marjani set her mouth in this hard straight line. I was sure we were about to get kicked off the boat or killed or probably both.

"Why are you here?" she asked. She stuck her hand out at me. "Don't you answer. I want to see him say it."

Naji stared at her.

Don't screw this up, I thought.

"Revenge," he said. "As Ananna told you." His lips curled into this sort of twisted-up sneer. "Even the Jadorr'a fall in love sometimes."

A long pause while we all watched each other and the boat rocked against the sea. And then Marjani laughed.

"That's not what I heard," she said.

"Yes, I can imagine the sorts of things you heard, and I doubt very many of them have much bearing in reality."

Marjani laughed again, and shook her head. "Of all the things I thought I'd see. And no, I'm not going to tell the crew about you." She turned away from Naji, who immediately slumped back against the hammock, pressing his hand against his forehead. When she walked past me, she grabbed my arm and leaned into my ear.

"You should keep a close watch on him," she said in a lowered voice. "Once we get out to sea."

"I'm right here," Naji said. "I can hear everything you're saying."

"Good," Marjani told him. "You can get used to it. These sorts of whispers'll happen a lot more once we've been on the water a few weeks."

"Pirates gossip like old women," I said.

"When they get bored, they stir up trouble," Marjani said. "And you look like you'd be trouble if you got stirred up."

Naji didn't say nothing, but his face got real hard and stony.

"We'll be fine," I told her. "I'll keep 'em off him."

"I'm willing to help, but I can only do so much. I've got my business to attend to."

"You don't gotta do that." I paused. "But I'd – we'd both – appreciate it. Anything you can spare."

"I can take care of myself," Naji said.

"I'm sure you can." Marjani walked to the ladder and stopped there, turning to look at him. "But don't you dare cast blood magic on this ship. They may not recognize you, but they'll recognize that. Trust me. It'll get you and your friend killed. And probably me for bringing you on board."

Naji glared at her for a second or two, but then he nodded. "Thank you."

"Don't," Marjani said. "Just keep to yourself till we get to Port Idai. That's all the thanks I need."

She gave me a quick, businesslike nod and crawled up on deck.

• • • •

We set sail that evening, off into the sunset like a damned story. Naji came out on deck and leaned against the railing. I was up in the rigging, yanking at the rope to line up the sails properly when I spotted him down there, his black robes fluttering in the sea breeze. He didn't look happy.

We made it out to the open ocean not long after that, and the water was smooth and calm as glass, bright with the reflections of stars. The captain and the first mate brought out a few bottles of rum and everybody sat around drinking and telling stories and singing old songs. Some of 'em I knew, and some were Confederation standards that'd had the words changed, and some I'd never heard before. Like this story Marjani told, about an ancient tree spirit who fell in love with a princess. He turned her into a bird, so they could be together, but then the princess flew away, cause she didn't much love him back, and she flew all the way out across the sea, to an island where there wasn't nothing but birds, and she was happier there than she'd been as a princess. I liked it.

Then one of the crewmen started talking about the Isles of the Sky. He leaned in close to the fire so that his face didn't look human no more, and he told a story about an old captain of his who'd had a friend who got blown off course and winded up in the Isles. That friend had sailed between the different islands, his crew growing gaunter and gaunter until they were nothing but moonlight and old bones. The friend escaped cause he made a deal with the Isles themselves, but after he came back to Anjare all his thoughts were wrapped up in the Isles, cause the spirits were far trickier than he was.

Naji sat off in the sidelines all this time, shadows crowding dark around him. I got a couple of shots of rum in me after listening to that Isles story, to try and forget that was where we were headed to, and I slunk over to him and sat down. Everything was bright from the rum and the music, though Naji managed to swallow up some of the brightness just by sitting there. I thought of his pitch feather quill.

"You know any stories?" I asked him.

"No."

"Really? None at all?" I wanted to press up against him the way Leila did, but not even rum gave me that much courage. "Don't they tell stories back at the Order?"

Naji's hair blew across his forehead. "You aren't allowed to hear those stories." He pushed at his hair like it was some kind of spider crawling on him in his sleep.

"Why not?"

"Because they're sacred. Darkest night, do I really have to explain this to you?"

That stung me, and I slid away from him, and drew my knees up under my chin. Somebody brought out this old falling-apart violin and took to playing one of the old sea-dances, the one that asks for good fortune on a voyage.

We sat side by side for a few minutes while the crew spun out music and light in the center of the deck.

"Ananna," Naji said. "I have actually done this sort of thing before. With alarming regularity, in fact."

"I know." I said it real soft, and he leaned over to me like he cared what I was saying. "I just want to help you is all."

His eyes got soft and bright. I wanted him to smile.

"That's very kind," he said. "I don't have a lot of experience with kindness, but I… I do appreciate it."

I blushed. "And I wish you wouldn't be so sore with me all the time."

He blinked. The music vibrated around us, all shimmery and soft. Nobody was dancing.

"I'm not sore with you," he said.

I guess it shoulda made me feel better, but it didn't. The song ended and another started up. Another sea-dance, and still nobody was dancing. Maybe since they weren't part of the Confederation, they didn't know the steps. Or maybe they just didn't care. It took me a few seconds to recognize the melody without the dancing, and I realized it was the song asking for luck in love. On Papa's ship the crew had interpreted it as a prayer against brothel sickness.

"This ain't right," I said. "Nobody dancing."

Naji glanced at me out of the corner of his eye. His brow was furrowed up like he'd been thinking real hard about something, and I hoped it was me but knew it probably wasn't.

I jumped up and bounded back into the light. It took me a few seconds to remember the steps: a lot of kicks and jumps and twirls, but once I got it down the crew started hooting and hollering and clapping out the rhythm. Then this big burly fellow got up and started following along, and damn if he wasn't lighter on his feet than me. And the next sea-dance started up, asking for victory in battle, and I was laughing and spinning and any darkness Naji might've slipped into me disappeared – at least for a time.

Things fell into a routine quick enough; they always do, once you're out at sea and the novelty of departure wears off. I got all caught up in the routine, though, cause it'd been so long since I'd been on the open ocean – the movement of the boat beneath my feet, and the smell of rotted wood and old seawater and sweet rum. You don't realize how much you miss something till it comes back to you, and then you wonder how you went so long without it.

I tried not to think on Naji's curse too much. Didn't want to remind myself of the overwhelming possibility that it really was just impossible and my time on the Revenge would be my last time on a ship at all.

Captain put me on rigging duty cause I could scamper up the ropes easier than a lot of the men, even though by lady standards I ain't exactly small. By the end of the first week my palms had their calluses back, and I'd gotten to know some of the crew. I liked 'em well enough, even though they teased me and tried to embarrass me with crude stories and the like. Course, I had a few stories up my sleeve that made them blush.

One afternoon, when we'd been out on the water for

about a week and some days, a couple of the crew told
me about Marjani.

"Some big-shot noble's daughter down in Jokja," Chari
said. He was old and weathered and knew the ropes.
"Ran off when her father wanted her to marry some sec-
ond-rate Qilari courtier. Went to university, too."

It was noon and we were eating lunch up in the rigging, some hardboiled eggs and goat's milk cheese
and honey bread, all the fresh stuff that only lasts a
few weeks.

"She don't like people to know," Chari went on.
"Afraid they'll hold it against her, or somebody'll find
out and send her back."

I didn't say nothing, cause I figured it's none of my business what parts of their past people want to leave behind.

"Nah, she just don't want people thinking she's a
stuck-up bitch. Too bad it didn't work none," said Ataño,
who wasn't much younger than me and always out to
prove something. Chari threw a handful of crushed-up
eggshells at him and told him to shut up. That set me
to laughing, and Ataño gave me a look that might have
melted glass had I not gotten used to Naji's constant
scowling.

"What about you, sweetheart?" Chari asked. "You
got a story?"

I knew he really wanted to hear Naji's story. I wasn't
giving it to him, not the fake one and sure as hell not
the real one.

"Born under deck and grew up like you'd expect," I
said. "Don't need a story to know that."

Chari leaned back thoughtfully while Ataño glowered and picked eggshells out of his hair.

"Ananna!"

It was a woman's voice, and there was only one other woman on board that boat. Marjani.

"What we get for talking about her," Chari muttered.

I leaned over the rigging and waved, wondering what she wanted with me.

"I need to speak with you!" she called out.

Ataño made this kind of grunting noise under his breath. I ignored him and swung down, going through the possibilities in my head: Naji had screwed something up. Marjani was gonna blackmail us. The captain was gonna toss us in the open ocean.

"You said you'd done some navigation before?" she asked soon as my feet landed on the deck.

I stared at her. "A little." It was the truth: Mama'd showed me once or twice, but Papa liked to do most of the navigation himself. He kept saying he'd teach me once I was older, but then they tried to marry me off.

"Good enough. Come on."

I followed her down below, even though I still wondered why she needed my help.

We passed some crewmen sitting around telling fortunes with the coffee dregs. Marjani kept her head up high, the way Mama used to, and nobody said nothing to her. She had that same don't-mess-with-me expression Mama used to take on, the one I practiced in the mirror when I was younger and sure I'd get a ship of my own someday.

The captain's quarters on the Ayel's Revenge were nicer than what I was used to, brocades and silks hanging from the ceiling, with big glass windows that let in streams of sunlight. Flecks of dust drifted in the air, glinting gold. Marjani walked right through them.

"I'm having some trouble with a rough patch on the map," she said, stopping in front of a table. The map showed the whole world, the ocean parts criss-crossed with lines and measurements. Marjani pointed to a little brooch pin stuck in a patch of ocean right where we needed to go. The jewels glittered in the sunlight.

"Sirens," she said. "They move around, but I threw some divinations last night and it looks like they're staying put for the time being."

She looked up at me expectantly.

"Sirens?" I blinked. "You mean this really is just about the navigation?"

She stared at me for a moment before collapsing into laughter. "What, did you think I was dragging you down here to chase rats?" She laughed again.

"I thought you'd told on me and Naji."

Her face turned serious. She shook her head. "I told you I wouldn't. No, I just..." She looked down at the map. "Nobody on this ship knows anything. Well, the captain does, but he spends all his time on deck swapping rum with the crew." She rubbed at her forehead. "I feel like a wife."

"Well, I don't know much, just the bit Papa taught me..."

She waved her hand. "I know. All I wanted was

someone who'd understand when I tried to talk my way through it."

"Oh." I frowned. "I guess I can do that." In truth I was excited, though I tried not to show her. Knowing navigation gets you one step closer to being a captain.

She smiled at me, and I wondered how I ever thought she was gonna toss me and Naji overboard.

"So," I said. "Sirens."

"Have you ever dealt with them before?"

I shook my head. "Papa would always make a wide berth."

She gave me a weird look then, and I added, "Same with my last captain. Liable to lose your whole crew."

"That's what I was afraid of. But over here's Confederation territory, the Uloi and the Tanisia," she tapped a spot on the map, "and they've both got a major beef with the captain. And this direction," another tap on the map, "will take us too far out of our way." She looked up at me. "Suggestions?"

"I don't got any." I frowned at the map. "My last captain, he'd probably have gone through the Confederation territory." I didn't mention that's cause he was Confederation. "A risk of a fight versus the guarantee of delay or the sirens, you know? But he liked to fight, too."

"Not sure about fighting," Marjani said. "We have too much–" She stopped and glanced at me real quick out of the corner of her eye, and I knew she was talking about the cargo.

Marjani messed with the map some, tracing an arc around the sirens, up close to the northern lands.

Something shivered through me – but I doubted Marjani was taking us anywhere close to the Isles of the Sky. She ain't stupid. And as much as I wanted Naji to cure his curse, I wasn't sure I was ready to face the Isles just yet.

So I watched Marjani work, trying to memorize the movements, the way she used her whole arm as she worked, the little scribbles she took down in her logbook. Her handwriting was curved and soft and learned, and it reminded me of the calligraphy I saw in this book of spells Mama used to keep on her. Not plant-spells – something else. Alchemy. She never talked about it.

"It's the only way," Marjani muttered. "Up north. Curses! Captain's not going to be pleased." She looked up at me. "It'll take us over two weeks off course. Nearly three."

"We got the food for it?"

"We can make do."

I shrugged. "Well, if you don't wanna fight and you don't wanna lose half your crew to drowning, that's probably the only way." I shivered again, but Marjani didn't seem to notice.

"I might be able to shave it down." She wrote some figures in her logbook, crossing them out, scrawling in new ones. When she turned her attention back to the map, I asked if I could take a look.

"At my notes?"

I felt myself go hot, but I got over my pride enough to nod. "I always wanted…" My voice kinda trailed off. Marjani handed the logbook over to me.

"Wanted to learn navigation?"

I nodded.

"It's not terribly hard, once you know the mathematics behind it."

"Most mathematics I ever learned was how to count coins." I wanted to ask her about university, but she was frowning down at the map again. I ran my fingers over the dried ink of the logbook, reading through her scratched-out notes, all those calculations of speed and direction and days lost.

"I might have time to start teaching you," she said, interrupting our silence. Her divider scritch scritch scritched across the map. "Especially with this detour."

I looked hard at the logbook.

"I'd like that," I said. "I'd like that a whole lot."

That night, Naji emerged from the crew's quarters and slunk up on deck. The wind was calm and favorable, pushing us north toward the ice-islands, out of the path of the sirens. The captain had issued the orders to change directions that afternoon, and the crew had scrambled to work without so much as a grunt of complaint. I wondered what would've happened if Marjani had issued the order. Or me.

"Something's different," Naji said, sidling up beside me. I was standing next to the railing, looking out at the black ocean. "We aren't going in the same direction."

"You can tell that?"

"Yes." He frowned. "We were going east, now

we're going north. Did you manage to convince them to take us–"

I smacked him hard on the arm. "Are you crazy? Don't say that out loud!" Nobody was near us, though. The crew kept clear of Naji, though they sure saw fit to gossip about him whenever he was hidden away belowdeck.

"And no," I said. "We're still headed for Port Idai. But we're having to detour on account of some sirens."

"Sirens?" Naji stared out at the darkness. "I hate the ocean."

That made me sad. Sure, sirens are a pain in the ass, but how could he not see all the beauty that was out there – the starlight leaving stains of brightness in the water, the salt-kissed wind? I wanted to find a way to share it with him, show him there was more in the world than blood and shadow. The ocean was a part of me – couldn't he see that?

Of course he couldn't. He barely saw me half the time, plain and weatherworn and frizzy-haired.

"How far north is the detour taking us?" he asked.

I shrugged. "A couple weeks out of our way."

"That's not what I asked."

I looked over at him. His face was hard and expressionless. "I ain't sure," I said. "Not so far we have to worry about ice in the rigging."

Naji frowned. "Are you wearing that charm I made you?"

Course I was, though my wearing it didn't have nothing to do with protection. Still, I nodded.

"Good," Naji said. "Don't take it off."

I knew there was something he wasn't telling me, probably something about the Mists, and as much as Naji claimed to hate the ocean he sure seemed content to stare all gloomy at the waves.

"It ain't so bad," I said.

"What isn't?"

"Being out here." I glanced at him. "I know something's got you spooked, but I'm safer here. Ain't been in danger once. So there ain't been no hurt for you."

The wind pushed Naji's hair across his face, peeling it away from his scar.

"You haven't been attacked, that's true." He sighed. "But you spend all day scampering among the ropes like a monkey."

"That hurts?" I was almost offended. I've been messing about in ship's rigging since I was four years old. It's about as dangerous as walking.

"Not really," Naji said. "I get a headache sometimes." He looked at me. "But you could fall."

"In fair weather like this? Not a chance." I frowned.

The water slapped against the side of the boat, misting sea spray across my face and shoulders. The ocean trying to join in on your conversation, Mama always told me. It's her way of giving advice.

Naji let out a long sigh and wiped at his brow with his sleeve. "I'm going back to the crew's quarters."

"Wait."

He actually stopped.

"Listen," I said. "First off, it ain't healthy for you to stay down below so much. You're gonna get the doldrums faster'n a bout of crabs in a whorehouse. Second..." I groped around for the words a bit. "Marjani's gonna teach me navigation, but I don't know none of the math."

"Alright," he said. "What does that have to do with me?"

The words hit me like one of Mama's open-hand slaps. "Because," I said, faltering. "You... you're educated. I thought you could..."

He was staring at me, only his face wasn't stony and angry no more.

"I thought you could help me." I looked down at my feet, my face hot like we were out in the sun. "Marjani's so busy, you know, and I thought – and you spend so much time by yourself."

"Oh." He took a step or two closer to me. He was close enough that I got these little shivers up and down my spine.

"It'd give you something to do," I said.

"Yes." He paused, and I lifted up my head to look at him. He had his eyes on me. They were the same color as the ocean at night. "Mathematics were not my strong suit, I'm afraid."

"You still know more'n me."

"I suppose I do." He took a deep breath. "I would be happy to help you, Ananna."

"Really?"

He nodded.

I hugged him. Just threw my arms around his shoulders without thinking, like he was Chari or Papa or one of the Tanarau crew. I realized what I did quick enough, though, when he stuck his hand on my upper back all awkward, like he wasn't sure what to make of me touching him. I pushed away, dropped my arms to my side. "Sorry," I muttered.

"Your enthusiasm for learning gives me hope for the future," he said. "We can start now, if you'd like. You don't seem to be… working."

"I'm the daytime crew." I squinted. "I thought you wanted to go down below."

He took his time answering. "Well, the air up here is much more pleasant."

"Yeah, never was clear how you could stand the smell."

He looked like he wanted to laugh, but cause he's Naji he didn't.

"We'll need something to write on. And some ink."

"I'll ask Marjani." The whole night seemed brighter now. Naji wasn't glowering no more, and I was about to learn something neither Mama or Papa'd ever saw fit to teach me proper.

Naji nodded at me, and I ran off to the captain's quarters, to find some ink and scraps of sail.

CHAPTER THIRTEEN

Marjani taught me the basics of navigation in the evenings, mostly, after mealtime when the bulk of the crew was up on deck drinking rum and watching the sun disappear into the horizon line. It was a lot of measuring and taking notes, and at first she just had me work off the records she took so I could learn how to do the calculations. And Naji gave me practice equations during the day, when there wasn't no sailwork for me to do. He came up on deck and everything, and we sat near the bow of the ship while I worked through them.

The crew ignored us the first few days, just went about their business like we weren't there. Then Ataño picked up on us and took to swinging down when I was working, asking me what I was writing for but staring at Naji while he asked.

"Ain't none of your business," I told him, scribbling with Naji's quill. It didn't work no magic for me. Wouldn't even tell me the answers to the equations.

"I dunno, looks like you're charming something." He dropped to his feet and squinted at Naji. "You know magic, fire-face?"

"Ananna's learning mathematics," Naji said.

Ataño howled with laughter, too stupid or too intent on acting the bully to notice that Naji hadn't answered his question. My face turned hot like it had a sunburn but I kept scribbling cause I wanted to learn navigation more than I wanted Ataño to like me.

"The hell?" Ataño asked. "That's even better'n the idea of her writing spells." He laughed again.

"Don't you got deck duty?" I muttered. It was hard to concentrate on the equation with him standing there gaping at me.

"You can't tell me what to do," he said.

"She will once she learns navigation," Naji said, "and you're serving under her colors."

I stopped writing, embarrassed as hell but also a little bit pleased that Naji thought I could be a captain someday.

There was this long pause while Ataño stared at Naji. "She ain't never gonna be my captain."

"Yes, that's probably true," Naji said. "Since I doubt she would require the services of someone as incompetent as you."

I bit my bottom lip to keep from laughing, but then I noticed Ataño staring at Naji with daggers in his eyes. Naji didn't seem to care much, but it occurred to me that we probably shouldn't be stirring up trouble when we were riding on this boat as guests.

Fortunately, the quartermaster stomped up to us and cuffed Ataño on the head before he could say anything more. "Get your ass to work," he said to Ataño, before fixing his glare on me.

"Doing something for Marjani," I said real quick, which was what she'd told me to say if any of the other officers caught me practicing. The quartermaster wrinkled up his brow, but he nodded and sauntered off.

"You shouldn't have said that to Ataño," I told Naji. "You made yourself an enemy just now. You see his eyes?"

"I'm not afraid of children."

I frowned and started working real hard on the next equation so Naji wouldn't see my face. The ink blotted across the sail.

"You're pressing too hard," Naji said.

"I ain't a child," I muttered.

"What?"

"Ataño's the same age as me." I didn't mean to tell him but it came out anyway. "And I ain't a child."

Naji stared at me. I stared back as long as I could but Naji was always gonna win a staring contest. I dropped my gaze back down to the equations. They looked like scribbles, like nonsense.

"You're the same age as him?" he asked.

"Uh, yeah. Seventeen."

This long heavy pause.

"Hmm," Naji said. "I put him at thirteen."

"Oh, shut up. You did not."

"Well, I'd put him at thirteen by his actions. Thirteen

or seventeen, it doesn't matter. He can't hurt me." He hesitated. "I won't let him hurt you–"

"Oh please." I tossed the quill and sail scrap down to the deck. "You think I'm scared of Ataño? You really think–"

Then I saw that sparkle in Naji's eye and knew he was laughing at me.

"See?" he said. "Now you know how it feels."

I glared at him for a few seconds. He looked so pleased with himself, but he also looked kind of happy, and that was enough for me to turn my attention back to my equations. I was happy, too, about finally learning navigation, and the possibility that I could become an officer on a ship, which was the first step to having my own boat. And there hadn't been any whispers about the Hariri clan, either. I was starting to see my future again.

As long as I didn't think about the Isles of the Sky. As long as I didn't think on how Naji's curse was an impossible one. Cause I knew that just cause I could see my future again, that didn't mean it was going to happen.

After a while, Naji started coming with me to my lessons with Marjani. He didn't ask – of course he didn't ask – but he did show up at the captain's quarters one evening after dinner looking sheepish. Marjani had me perched over the maps with a divider, tracking a course from Lisirra to Arkuz, the capital city of Jokja, where she told me she had been born. She'd asked me my birthplace but I just said Lisirra, cause the stormy black-sand island where I'd been born wasn't even on the map. And then Naji was banging on the door, asking to come in.

"I hope you don't mind if I join you," he said. "But I find the crew…" He hesitated. Marjani looked like she wanted to laugh.

"A pain in the ass?" I offered.

"Tiresome," Naji said. He tugged at his hair, kind of pulling it over his scar, and I frowned, wondering what the crew had said to him.

"I have to go with Ananna on this one," Marjani said. "But you can sit in here if you want."

Naji settled down in this gilded chair in the corner and watched me and Marjani work without saying nothing. It took me awhile to chart the course from Lisirra to Arkuz – I was using some calculations Marjani had given me, from an old logbook. I felt like I'd taken way too long to get it done, but when I finished Marjani looked sorta impressed.

"Nice work," she said. "You're a quick learner." She smiled. "You would've done well at university."

That made me real happy, cause nobody had ever said nothing like that to me before.

"Yes," Naji said. "She would have."

Marjani glanced at him. "Where did you attend?"

"In Lisirra. The Temple School."

"Oh." She flipped through the logbook and handed it back to me. "Lisirra to Qilar," she told me. "Go."

I sighed like I was annoyed but really I thought the

drills were fun. Marjani turned to Naji. "The Lisirra Temple School," she said. "That's a school of sorcery, isn't it?"

Naji nodded and said, "I didn't study ack'mora there, if that's what you're asking."

"I'll admit I was curious." Marjani smiled. "I've no ability for sorcery, myself. I studied mathematics and history. At the university in Arkuz."

"I've been there. It's lovely."

"The city or the university?"

"Both."

It was like they were speaking a whole other language. Universities and history and sorcery. I wondered what I would've studied if I'd got to go to university. Piracy's probably not an option.

"I've been to Arkuz," I said. "We sailed up the river into the jungle to trade with some folks there."

"Really?" said Marjani. "I always hated the jungle. You never know when it's going to rain." She leaned over the map. "Oh, good work," she said.

"I've got it?" I'd been so wrapped in listening in on Marjani and Naji's conversation that my hands must've kept on working while my brain lagged behind.

"You've got it," Marjani said.

After that, Naji came to my lessons about every day, I guess cause he and Marjani had bonded over both going to university. He didn't have a lot to offer in the way of navigation, but he and Marjani would tell me about other stuff they'd learned, like all these weird stories about the different emperors over the years, or how to calculate the volume of an empty container without having to fill it with water first. It was fun.

Then Marjani got me to start helping her with the true navigation, the navigation that was taking us around the sirens and three weeks out of our way and, as far as me and Naji were concerned, delaying the trip to the Isles of the Sky. One morning she called me down from the rigging and handed me her logbook and a quill and the sextant.

"I need measurements," she said. "You know how it works. Get going."

The crew stared at me while I stood there fiddling with the sextant. Marjani trotted off to speak with the captain up at the helm, and I felt real conspicuous with everybody's eyes on me. But then I lifted up the sextant and peered through it up at the sky and the whole boat fell away.

I stopped doing as much work in the rigging after that, since Marjani had me taking measurements for her every day. Seems that charting a new course on the water's a bit risky, as you're creating a new path in addition to the usual work of checking where you are in the water. But we stayed on course, still moving up toward the north and to the east, and Marjani said it was partially cause I helped her. I didn't necessarily believe that, mind, though I suppose I had no reason not to.

One afternoon I crawled up on deck to make the usual round of measurements and noticed immediately that something was off. There were a lot of voices shouting and yelling, but it wasn't about rigging or wind or none of the usual complaints. At first I thought we must be under attack, that some tracker from the Mists – or worse, the Hariris – had followed me and Naji all the way to sea. Immediately my heart started pounding and I went for the knife at my hip. Which I still hadn't replaced. Stupid. I needed to ask Naji for his knife or nick it off him while he slept.

But then I realized I didn't hear the clank of sword against sword, or the pop of a pistol. And nobody'd sent out the call to arms, neither. It was just yelling. And jeering.

And my heart started pounding all over again.

I raced across the deck to where Ataño and a couple of his cronies were crowded around the railing. Naji was there, too, staring at them stone-faced. Ataño said something I couldn't make out, on account of the wind blowing in off the waves and beating through the sails, but he pushed up the skin of the left side of his face until it snarled the way Naji's face did sometimes and his cronies laughed like it was the funniest thing they'd seen in a year.

Me, I felt like someone had punched me in the stomach.

"Fuck off!" I screamed. All three of 'em turned toward me and I took off running. Half the crew was up in the rigging or clustered over on the other side of the ship, not participating but not doing nothing to stop it neither.

And then Ataño was flat on his back, Naji crouched on his chest with his sword at Ataño's throat.

I stopped dead in my tracks.

Naji made this hissing sound through his teeth and pressed his sword up under Ataño's chin. A trickle of blood dripped onto the deck, glistening in the sunlight. Ataño whimpered, his eyes clenched shut.

"Look at me," Naji said in a voice like an ice storm.

Ataño opened his eyes.

"This is the last time you will ever look at my face. If you see me coming, look the other way. Because if you look at me again, or speak to me again, I'll make sure your face comes out worse than mine."

Nobody on deck was moving. Even the wind had stopped. In the silence, all you could hear was Ataño's pitiful little moans.

"Do you understand?"

"Y... Yes," Ataño said.

Naji pulled his sword away. Ataño scrambled backward, his head twisted over to the side, looking everywhere but at Naji. His cronies stumbled after him.

Naji wiped the blade of his sword on his robe.

And like that, the spell broke. A couple of the bigger crewman bounded across the deck and grabbed Naji by the arms, pulling him into a lock, though I could see that Naji didn't have no intention of fighting back.

I could see that if Naji had wanted to fight back, both of those crewman would've been dead.

And anybody else he wanted, too.

When he'd attacked Ataño, he'd covered close to five feet so fast I hadn't seen him move. He hadn't even moved that fast during the fight in the Lisirran pleasure district – this time, I hadn't seen him go for his sword, or even noticed the twitch in the arm that meant he was thinking about it. One second he'd been standing there like a victim, the next he could've slit Ataño's throat before anybody knew what was happening.

The two crewmen dragged Naji down to the brig, and all I could think about was that night in the desert, and how he hadn't done what he just did to Ataño – to me.

The brig smelled like rotten fish and piss and the air was thick with mold. Saltwater dripped off the ceiling and down my back as I made my way over the dank floor. I had Naji's desert-mask tucked into the pocket of my coat.

He was curled up in the corner of his cell, sitting with his chin on his knees. His eyes flicked over to me when I came in but he didn't say nothing.

I stared at him for a minute, his hair all tangled up from the sea wind, the lanterns illuminating the lines of his scar. Looking at it I got this phantom pain in the left side of my face.

"They take your knife off you?" I asked him.

He shook his head.

"Can I see it? I'll give it back."

Naji stared at me.

"C'mon, I ain't gonna do nothing bad."

He reached into his cloak and then there was a thwap and the knife wedged into the wood of the ship a few inches from my head. I was real proud of myself cause I didn't even blink, though I did see him go for it this time – something told me it was cause he wanted it that way. I yanked the knife out of the wall and walked up to the lock on the bars. Shoved the knife into the keyhole and wiggled it around like Papa'd taught me. When the lock clicked I snapped it open and stepped into the cell with Naji.

"I brought your desert mask," I said, pulling it out of my pocket and dangling it in front of me. Naji didn't move. I started thinking this might've been a bad idea.

But then he took the mask away from me and straightened it out on his knees.

"You sure it won't look suspicious?" he asked, his voice full up with sarcasm, and I looked down at my feet, shamed.

"I'm sorry." My voice kinda cracked. "I didn't think – on Papa's ship they would never–"

"Forget it." Naji pulled the mask across his face, hiding his scar. "Of course you're correct, the young men on your father's ship never once jeered at a disfigurement. Upstanding citizens the whole of them, I'm sure."

I didn't know what to say. My face got real hot, and Naji kept glaring at me.

"You have no idea what it's like," he said. "To look like me. To be what I am on top of that – people think I'm a monster."

"I don't." But I said it so soft I'm not sure he heard me.

I wanted to get out of the brig. I wanted to run up on deck till I found Ataño so I could pummel the shit out of him. Instead, I sat down next to Naji, the floor's cold damp seeping up through the seat of my trousers. He didn't talk to me or look at me and the air was heavy with his anger and I tried to think of a way to fix it. I couldn't come up with nothing.

After a while, Naji said, "I'm sorry."

The sound of his voice made me jump.

"I'm sorry I was cold with you," he said. "I don't think it was your fault."

"Oh. That's good." I chewed on my lower lip and looked at the pool of scummy seawater that had collected over near the bars. "I tried to stop it–"

"I know you did."

We sat for a few moments longer.

"Can I ask you a question?" I said.

"Depends on the question."

"It's not about–"

"Just ask it, Ananna."

I took a deep breath.

"You could've killed Ataño and been down below before anybody saw you. I ain't never seen a man move as fast as you."

Naji didn't say nothing.

"I get why you didn't kill him, that's not my question. But..." I forced myself to look over at him. "Why didn't you do that to me? Before I started up the curse and everything? In the desert? You could've laid me out faster'n a jungle cat. I know there was a protection spell but it must've worn off by then, cause you did cut me and all..."

My voice kinda trailed off. Naji stared straight ahead.

"It's true," he said. "There wasn't a protection spell on you in the desert."

"Then why...?"

Naji took his time answering.

"Because," he said. "I didn't want to kill you."

I stared at him. My heart was pounding all fast and funny, and I felt like I'd forgotten how to speak.

"Ananna! Get the hell out of there before the captain comes down and sees you."

Marjani. I jerked up in surprise, banging my head against the back wall. Naji glanced at me but didn't ask me if I was alright or nothing. His voice kept echoing around in my head: I didn't want to kill you. I'd no idea what to make of that.

Marjani pushed the cell door open and stood there expectantly. She didn't say nothing about Naji's mask. I handed him back his knife, and once I'd stepped out she slammed the bars shut. The clang of metal against metal rang in my ears.

"Crew's saying you move like a ghost," she told him, leaning up against the bars.

Naji didn't reply.

"Fortunately, the captain doesn't believe in ghosts."

"He ought to," Naji said.

"Is he gonna toss Naji overboard?" I asked.

"The captain?" Marjani looked at me. "No."

Over in the corner, Naji didn't even stir.

"Ataño's a worthless little shit," Marjani said. "But

it seems he's done more work in the past three hours than he's done in the past three days, so – the quarter-master's happy." She smiled. "Captain's letting you out tomorrow morning."

"Wonderful," Naji said, though he didn't sound like he meant it. "Curses and darkness, I want off this ship."

"Well, it's four weeks till Qilar. You've got awhile. Whispers are gonna be worse. You need to remember that you're here on the captain's good graces. You're lucky he's not a superstitious man."

Naji lifted his head a little. "No, I'm lucky he has a navigator clever enough to dispel any residual belief in ghosts and ghouls."

Marjani didn't say nothing, but I could tell from the way she tightened her mouth that he was right.

CHAPTER FOURTEEN

Whatever magic Marjani worked on the captain held fast; he released Naji at sunup the next day. I filched a knife off the cook when he wasn't looking and made sure I was down in the brig when it happened, tucked away out of notice in a back corner. Ataño wasn't nowhere to be seen.

The captain had a couple of crewmen standing by with a pair of pistols each, all four barrels pointed at Naji's forehead.

"I see any hint of magic," the captain said as he unlocked the cell. "Any hint of weirdness, I'm tossing you out to sea."

He didn't say nothing about tossing me off the boat along with Naji, but then, I can't kill a man in less than a second.

"I understand," Naji said. He'd kept his mask on but his words came out clear and even.

The captain nodded like this was good enough and pulled the cell door open wider. The crewmen kept their pistols trained on Naji as he strolled up to the ladder. Naji glanced at me when he walked past but didn't say nothing. The captain stopped, though.

"What're you doing down here?" he asked.

"Checking up on my friend."

The captain chuckled. "Ain't gonna hurt him, little girl. Not unless he pulls a knife on me."

"He won't." I shifted my weight from foot to foot. "Sides, and with all due respect, sir, I was more worried about Ataño striking out revenge."

The captain roared at that. Even his cannon-men kind of looked at each other and laughed. I frowned at them.

"Ataño ain't gonna cause no more trouble," the captain said. "Can't believe I put a man in the brig for scaring some discipline into that boy." He laughed again and all three of them climbed up out of the brig.

Things got back to normal after that. I kept on working for Marjani, taking down measurements and tracking our course toward Qilar. Naji went back to spending all his time in the crew's quarters, scribbling over the sail scraps left over from my mathematics lessons. I went down there once or twice to keep him company, but he didn't much talk to me, just muttered over his work.

"What're you writing?" I frowned. "It ain't magic, is it?"

"Don't be ridiculous. When I said I wanted off this ship I didn't mean I wanted to be thrown into the open sea." Naji handed me one of the sail scraps. It was a story – an old desertlands story about a little boy who gets lost in the desert and has to strike a deal with the scorpions to make it back home.

"Why're you writing this?"

"I need something to do." Naji leaned back in his hammock.

"Nobody writes down stories."

"They do when they're trapped at sea and bored senseless." Naji hunched over his sail scrap and wrote a little swirl of something. "I hear from Marjani you're plotting part of our course each day."

"Getting us to Port Idai as fast as possible." Not that I liked the idea of leaving the Revenge. Any boat crazy enough to take us to the Isles wasn't one I'd want to work on.

Naji stopped writing and looked up at me, all dark hair and dark mask and the little golden strip between them. "I appreciate that." He looked down at his sail scrap. "Although I can't say I'm much looking forward to our second journey north."

"Me, neither."

Naji picked up his quill and began writing again.

"You think it'll work?" I asked him.

"Will what work?"

"Do you think we'll find a cure?"

Naji's hand twitched, but he kept writing, and he didn't look at me. "I don't know."

That was not the answer I wanted to hear. I left him to his stories and stomped back up to deck, where Marjani was waiting for me with the logbook and a quill, and things fell back into their routine, ocean and wind and salt and sails.

It felt like the beginning of the end.

A week later, the weather turned.

I was helping with the rigging, cause the wind had been strong all afternoon, blowing in from the south, hot and dry and tasting like dust and spice. It had everybody in a mood, especially the more superstitious fellows in the lot, and so there were a lot of charms getting tossed around, and certain words getting uttered. And everybody was drinking up the rum, superstitious or not. I'll admit that my hands kept going to my throat that day, rubbing at Naji's charm.

The wind picked up, and it howled through the sails, flattening 'em out and then billowing 'em up. Water sprayed out from the sea, huge glittering drops of it. Not a cloud in the sky, though, the sun hot and bright overhead.

Crewmen were crawling all over the rigging, and Marjani was up at the helm, throwing her whole body into keeping the ship steady. A big green wave splashed over the railing and slammed into me, and I fell across the deck, hitting up against old Chari's worn-out boot. He hardly offered me a glance as he pulled at the rigging, shouting curses and prayers alike. I scrambled to my feet and grabbed hold of the rope to help him out. The whole thing felt like a typhoon if not for the sun and the weird spice scent on the wind. Maybe it was that noble from the Mists, drawing the worlds together like Naji had said...

For a half-second, I caught a whiff of medicine, sharp and mean, like spider mint, and I shot back to Lisirra, to the entrance of the night market. The rope slipped out of my hands.

"The hell's your head, girl!" shouted Chari. "Hold on tight if you don't want to get knocked overboard."

The smell of Naji's magic disappeared. He can't, I thought, scrambling to pick up the rope. It has to be the Mists. He can't be doing this. It'd put me in danger–

And then another wave crashed over the side, and I managed to hold on tight, and all thoughts of Naji's magic washed away with it. I had a ship to keep afloat.

By then somebody was ringing the warning bell, the clang clang clang that meant an attack or a storm or just plain ol' trouble. Seawater showered over us like rain, the salt stinging my eyes and the sores in my hands. Chari turned around and grabbed my wrist and shoved me over to the foremast. "Get up there!" he shouted, jabbing his hand toward the rigging. Water streamed over my face, blurring my vision, but then I saw it: The storm sail had come loose.

"Shit!" I scrambled up the rope, slipping and crawling, my clothes plastered to my skin. The wind threatened to knock me off the rope but I dug my nails into the fibers, clinging with every bit of my strength. The sail flapped back and forth, snapping like a whip, though at least it was dry up here, away from the fury of the waves. I reached out and made a grab for it. Missed. Righted myself. Took a deep breath. Watched the sail and waited for it to snap back toward me. This time I caught the edge and yanked on it one-handed even though the wind had other ideas. My arms shook. My eyes watered. I screamed, trying to gather up the will to do this without dying.

And then I had it. That split-second between wind gusts and I had it. I tied the sail back into place, looping the rope with aching fingers.

The boat jerked, tilted, and I fell, grabbing at one of the riggings before I crashed down on deck. I cried out but the wind swallowed my voice right up and no one down below even noticed me.

I kicked out my feet, swinging up like a monkey. The wind kept on howling. I started crawling back down, my arms hating every second of it. Every part of my body ached.

And then I heard this low creaking groan, and I knew they were shifting the boat so we could run with the wind to safety. Under normal circumstances it ain't nothing I can't handle but with the wind and the hurt in my body it was too much. The movement knocked me loose. I managed to hang on with one hand, swinging out over the deck. What with the seawater and the sunlight, everything down there was covered in rainbows.

Then I lost my grip, and I fell.

I woke up and all I knew was the hurt. Pain vibrated through my body, all the way out to the tips of my fingers and toes. My head throbbed. But I was laid out on something soft, a pile of rope and old sails, and I guess that was why my brains hadn't spilt out all over the deck of the Ayel's Revenge.

She was moving, at least, soft and smooth, and there wasn't any wind or water splashing over the railing. No voices, neither, only the purring ocean, the occasional snap as the sails rippled overhead. I pushed myself up on my elbows, and when that wasn't the bone-breaking trauma I expected I forced myself to sit up halfway, my back aching, my head lolling.

The air was cold.

That bothered me. Ain't no reason for us to be anywhere near coldness, not at this time of year, and not where we were sailing. Don't care how bad that storm knocked us off course.

Not a storm, I thought, remembering the sunlight, the scent of spider mint, but I shoved the thought out of my head.

I took another few moments to pull myself up to standing, and then took even longer to recover from it, standing in place and swaying a little. Then I shuffled forward, limping from a twinging pain in my left thigh.

We were someplace else. I knew that soon as I came out from the under the shadow of the rigging. The sky was the color of a sword's blade, and the water lapping up at the sides of the boat was dark gray, nearly black, and everything smelled like metal and salt. We were north, up close to the ice-islands, maybe. I'd only been there a few times in my life but I remembered the smell of the air, that overwhelming scent of cold.

A handful of crewmen were bunched up at the port bow of the ship, all huddled together, not talking.

Chari was there, and Marjani, her arms wrapped tight around her chest. I limped toward them.

"Hey!" My voice came out strangled, raspy. Nobody turned around. "Hey, what's going–"

I stopped. We were in sight of land. Way far off in the distance was a line of green, that vivid dark-almost-black green you only get in the north.

And below the line of green was a line of black beach and below that, a strip of gray. The sky. A gap between the island and the sea.

And like that, all the pain in my body got replaced with the icy grip of dread, and I remembered how I'd smelled medicine back during the storm, before I–

Marjani glanced over at me, her eyes widening. "Ananna!" she said. "Oh, Aje, I thought you'd been thrown overboard! I–" She stopped, covered her mouth with her hand. "You look like hell."

I tried to choke out some kind of nicety, something about falling into the rope, something, anything to make her think I had nothing to do with us being within swimming distance of those horrible islands.

Instead, I turned away from her and hobbled over to the ladder that'd take me down below.

"Ananna? What're you... Stop, it's flooded–"

"Stay there," I said, cause what else could I do? She didn't listen, of course, and came chasing after me, grabbing hold of my arm. Pain shot up through my elbow.

"Let me go! I need to..." Do what? I didn't want to put it into words.

"Need to what?"

"Naji." It was all I could bring myself to choke out. I jerked away from her and half-slid, half-climbed down the ladder. Down below the floor was covered in a half-foot of dirty water, rum bottles floating by like they might hold some kind of message for me, and scraps of clothing and pieces of dried fish. I splashed through the water, the chill setting my whole body to shaking. Marjani had stopped at the ladder.

"Ananna, come back!" she said. "It's too cold. You'll get hypothermia…"

I didn't have the faintest idea what that was, and I didn't care, neither. I pushed my way into the crew's quarters.

The first thing that hit me was that horrible medicine smell, stronger than anything that ever soaked its way into the air of the crew's quarters before. My eyes watered and my throat burned and my skin prickled from all the leftover magic. The ship walls down here were all blood-red, transformed by magic.

And there was Naji, slumped across a hammock, blood trailing down his arms, his skin white as death. Bits of sail floated in the water around him like flower petals, leaving streaks of red in their wake.

He lifted his head when I came in, just enough that I knew he wasn't dead.

I splashed forward and picked up one of the scraps of cloth. His writing was all over it, the ink a brownish-red color, not black like Marjani's ink. It wasn't a story. I stared at it for a long time, not making any sense of those symbols, knowing full well it was a spell.

I balled the cloth up in my fist and dropped it at my side. Naji moaned, dropped his head back. My anger swelled up inside me like a wave.

"You son of a whore," I said. "You filthy, mutinous, lying sack of shit–"

Naji tried to say something, but his words came out all slurred, and for a second I wondered how bad it had hurt him when I fell out of the rigging, if his body shattered like it was made out of glass. I hoped so. And then my anger was this flash of white light, hot and searing, and I waded up to him, pulled my arm back, and punched him square in the face.

"Ananna! What are you doing?"

Marjani crashed into the room. I hit Naji again, open-handed this time, and he tried to squirm away from me, shoving his hands between us to block me. I grabbed his wrist, dried blood flaking off on my fingers, and yanked him up off the hammock and punched him again. He slammed up against the wall.

And then Marjani had her arms around my waist.

"Stop it," she said. "Stop." She pulled me away from him, dragging me through the water. I strained against her, arms flailing, but it wasn't no use.

"Calm down," she said, over and over. "Ananna, this isn't the time. Calm do–"

She froze in place, staring at the walls, and I wriggled out of her arms and turned to look at her. Over on his hammock, Naji moaned my name.

"Shut up," I told him. My heart pounded up against my ribs and it didn't have nothing to do with the fight.

"The air," Marjani said. "It's all wrong…" Then she picked up one of the sail scraps and stared at it good and hard. I stood there with my chest heaving, waiting for her to get angry, as angry as I was. But she only seemed sad.

She looked up at Naji. "You shouldn't have done this."

"You don't understand," Naji said. "The curse–"

"Shut up!" I screamed at him. "You're going to get us killed." I turned to Marjani. "We were always headed for Port Idai, like I said. I never thought he'd do something like this."

"Neither did I," Marjani said. She splashed over to me. "I know about the curse," she said, her voice soft. "He told me."

"What?" I said.

"I tried…" Naji gasped. "Tried to save–"

"Get him," she said, jerking her head at Naji. "And come up on deck. And for Aje's sake, play along."

"You knew?" I said. "How long?"

She didn't answer, just made her way out of the crew's quarters, the water splashing up around her knees. I turned to Naji. He'd sat up some, and there was a bruise forming around his eye from where I hit him.

"You heard the lady," I said.

"We are… The islands? We're… here?"

"Shut up."

I grabbed him by his arm and jerked him up to standing. He slouched against me. Fine. I threw his arm around my shoulder, and together we waded through the ship's belly. I wasn't screwing around with this. We'd been caught, flat-out. Having Marjani on our side helped, but it wasn't just Marjani who'd caught us, it was everyone. The crew. The captain. If we were lucky we'd be thrown in the brig for the rest of the trip. I didn't think we'd be lucky.

It took us a while to get up on deck, cause I pretty much had to push Naji up the ladder. He pulled himself up through the hatchway, Kaol knows how, and then he slumped against the deck, wheezing and grasping for breath. The captain and Marjani were waiting for us, standing side by side with the rest of the crew fanned out behind 'em.

"This true, Ananna?" the captain asked me. Marjani had this right mean look on her face. Play along.

Naji coughed and pushed himself up on his hands. His hair pressed in thick clumps against his face.

"I did it," he said. "Don't blame her."

The captain looked like he wanted to whip out his sword and take care of the problem the old-fashioned way, but instead he just spat at Naji and turned to me.

"Wasn't asking him," he said.

I closed my eyes. All I could feel was my heartbeat, the blood rushing through my body.

"Well?" he said.

"Yeah, it's true." I forced myself to meet his eye. Any of that kindness I'd seen before had disappeared. "I didn't know he was gonna do it, though, or I'd have stop–"

The captain held up one hand, and I shut my mouth. I was shaking from the cold and from fear, wondering what he was going to do to us.

"Blood magic," the captain said, spitting the words out. "Can't believe you'd bring something like that on board. I trusted you, little girl."

I flushed with shame, but I didn't hang my head. Kaol, was I proud of that.

"Believed that whole damn story you told..." The captain shook his head.

"I'm sorry," I said, looking at the captain, looking at Marjani. She frowned, little lines appearing around her eyes.

"Throw 'em overboard," the captain said.

Marjani whipped her head toward him. "Captain, I don't think... In this water, that will kill them."

"Good," he said cheerfully.

I about started to cry. I've cried out of desperation twice in my life and both of those times were nothing compared to the mess I was in right now, about to get cast out in the icy northern sea cause of a blood magic assassin with no manner of patience.

Marjani gave me this look of full-up desperation, quick as a flash, and I knew whatever plan she'd made just fell through. I'd never felt so small and vulnerable and doomed.

And then Chari spoke up.

"Sir," he said, stepping forward out of the crowd. "I agree we shouldn't keep this pair of hijacking mutineers on board, but I did see the girl during the, ah, storm and she about near died trying to save this ship."

The captain stared at him. Chari held his gaze. He was the kind of old that commands respect.

"So what do you suggest?" the captain said.

"Give 'em a boat," Chari said. The crew didn't like that, and they all hissed and booed behind him. "Or a piece of plank board, captain. Enough to get 'em to the island."

I wanted to kiss the old son of a bitch, I really did.

"They'll be good as dead there anyway," Chari said. "It's what you'd do if we were down in the south."

Something flickered though my head. Ain't got nothing to lose.

"Confederation rules," I said. "Mutineers are always stranded. Not killed."

Everybody stopped talking and turned to me.

"We ain't part of the Confederation," the captain said.

"I am," I said. I pushed out my chest and took a deep breath. "My full name is Ananna of the Tanarau. My father is the captain of that same ship." Then I lifted up the hem of my shirt to show him my Confederation tattoo.

The captain's face got real dark.

"You drew that on," he said. "You're faking me."

"You want to risk it?" I said. I nudged Naji with my foot. "You have any idea what he's capable of this close to death? That's blood magic's nexus, captain, death. This close to the other side, he could send a message to my father so quick you'd be dead in a week."

The crew fell silent, so I figured I must have convinced most of 'em at least half-way. The captain didn't look too doubtful himself, either.

"I don't want no business with the Confederation," he said. "I could kill you right now and not worry about a thing."

And then Naji started chanting.

It gave me pause, ain't gonna lie. I thought maybe he was working some kind of darkness over there, maybe calling down demons to swoop in and save us. But when I glanced at him his eyes were dark as night, not glowing at all. And I realized he was faking for me.

"You hear that!" I shouted, getting into it. "Speaking straight to my father, he is. You can't kill me now. Neither one of us."

The captain's eyes went wide with fear. Marjani's didn't. She glanced back and forth between me and Naji but didn't say nothing. But the chanting got the crew into a tizzy, and they all backed up against the railing.

"Make him stop," the captain said.

"Can't," I said. "He don't listen to me. If that were the case, we'd still be on our way to Port Idai."

The captain took a few steps back from Naji. "Fine," he said. "You want me to treat you like some Confederation mutineer – Marjani, get them a boat."

"And a pistol," I added. I didn't want to push my luck but those were the Isles of the Sky.

"And a damn pistol." He spat on the deck.

Marjani dipped her head and disappeared over to the starboard side.

Naji stopped chanting and slumped over. The captain took a deep breath and looked relieved.

Then he jerked his head back to the crew and called

up a couple of the rougher fellows to drag me and Naji over to the side of the ship, where Marjani was waiting with a rowboat and a pistol and a thinly-hewn rope net that she probably meant to serve as a blanket. The crewmen shoved Naji and me into the boat. One of 'em looked like he wanted to spit on me, but he glanced at Naji and nothing happened.

"Leave," Marjani said to 'em.

They didn't.

"Do what I tell you," she said, pulling out a thin little knife I didn't even realize she carried.

And what do you know, both of the crewmen took off.

She held the knife up to my throat and leaned in close. I could tell she didn't aim to use it, but still. Nobody likes having a knife at their throat.

"Listen," she said, talking real close to my ear, hissing like she was threatening me. "He said something the other day about somebody following him."

"What–"

"He tried to get me to change course. He wouldn't tell me details, but just – be careful." Her face got kind of soft and understanding. "Stay on that island," she said. "And for Aje's sake, stay alive. Keep warm and keep dry. There are ways off every island."

And before I could respond, she turned away from me and cut the ropes holding the rowboat aloft. We crashed down into the black sea. The Ayel's Revenge rose up in front of us like a leviathan, and I had no choice but to grab hold of the oars and row us away.

CHAPTER FIFTEEN

The island really did float. Once we'd cleared the Revenge, once my arms got so sore I could barely move 'em, I drew the oars back into the boat and drifted along the choppy water, shivering from the cold, from my injuries, from the distracting knot of fear coiling in my stomach. Up ahead the island hovered above the sea, chunks of smooth black stone tapering into points beneath the gray beaches and the trees. In the distance, you could just make out the other islands through the haze drifting off the water.

"Hey." I shook Naji's shoulder. He was curled up on the net and didn't move. "E'mko and his twelve dancing seahorses, you better not be dead."

He stirred, moaning a little. His breath blew out in a white cloud.

"That spell of yours have any way for us to get on land?"

That must have gotten his attention. He sat up, pushed his hair back away from his face. "We're here," he said.

"Of course we're here," I said. "We just got kicked off the Ayel's Revenge for it." I frowned at him.

His expression glazed over as he stared at the island. The sight of the damn thing made me dizzy, so I stared at Naji even though I wanted to throttle him.

"Vaguely. I vaguely remember..." He dug his hand into his good eye. "I can't seem to keep my thoughts straight."

"Oh fantastic." Figures I'd get stuck with a blood magician who'd driven himself insane.

Or maybe it was the island, working its magic like in the stories. Changing him, making him forget himself and who he was. I studied the angles of his face, looking for some sign that his bones were pushing out of his skin. He looked gaunter than usual, but maybe it was because of the spell. I hoped it was because of the spell.

"It's cold," he said, and his voice sounded small, like a kid's.

"Not a whole lot I can do about it." We drifted along, the water pushing us toward the island, like it was a normal island and there was a tide to pull us ashore. Part of me wanted to look back, catch a glimpse of the Revenge as she sailed away. But I didn't. Water slapped up along the side of the rowboat, spraying us with a cold fine mist. Naji moaned and rubbed his head, and I was still dizzy myself.

The rowboat jerked up, her bow clearing the water in an arc of gray water drops, and then slammed back down.

"What the hell was that?" I shouted. I yanked the oars in even though it didn't do much more than make me feel more vulnerable, the two of us sitting there in the open ocean like that. Naji slumped down, his eyes wide, and mumbled something about being weak.

"Shut up," I said. I didn't hear nothing unusual: just the howl of the wind, the rush of the waves.

The boat jolted again, knocking me forward into Naji's lap. I bit down on my tongue to keep from screaming.

"Ananna," he said.

"We need to get on land." At least on land any enemies couldn't lurk beneath the depths. "Is it safe to row?"

"Don't... I don't really know."

"Kaol!" I shoved the oars into the water and pushed us toward the island. We weren't far, almost to the line of shadow the island cast onto the water. I tried to lift the oars up but the left one wouldn't move. I shrieked and let go, and it slid into the ocean without a sound.

I yanked the other oar into my lap and sat very still, heart racing. We floated underneath the island. Dark as night down there, although the ocean water gleamed silver. The boat bumped up against a hunk of low-hanging stone. It was too smooth to be any use for climbing, and besides which, it would only take me to the underside of the island. I didn't have time to try to make some kind of rope throw.

The boat tilted again. Naji gripped the sides and his eyes gleamed like the water.

I had an idea.

"How weak are you? Can you do anything?"

"What?"

"Your shadow thing," I said. "Can you take me with you?"

He didn't answer.

"Naji?"

"Under normal circumstances, I could."

"Naji! There's something in the water!"

Naji didn't answer, and I glared at him in the dark.

"Maybe somebody shouldn't have used up all their energy blowing a brigantine off course. But you wouldn't know anything about that, would you?"

"It wasn't just the magic," he said darkly.

"Yeah, you put me in a spot of trouble with that wind. Damn near killed me."

"It nearly killed me as well."

"Well, I imagine we're both going to die if we don't get on land." My whole body was tense, waiting for the boat to rock again, but the water stayed as smooth and still as a mirror. "Do your thing."

"My thing?"

"Damn it, Naji! The shadow thing. We're in shadow now. There's shadows up there – have to be, all them trees. So do whatever it is you do to get both of us out of this boat and on that bloody island."

Silence. I sucked in a deep breath. I could barely make out his outline in the silvery shadow of the island.

"This might hurt me," he said.

"I don't care."

He didn't say nothing. I shoved the pistol into the waistband of my pants. Nothing happened.

"Well?" I said.

"You have to touch me," he said. "Well, not just... We need to... Come here."

And then he reached out his arm and drew me into him. His touch surprised me, and suddenly I wasn't cold anymore.

"We need to be close," he said. "As close as possible."

I slid across the boat, pressing up against his body. He didn't have his armor on and I could feel him, the muscles in his chest and his arms. He smelled like magic and sweat and the sea, but there was something else beneath all that, something sweet and warm, like honey, and just for a moment I didn't feel afraid anymore.

I was furious at him, and I was terrified, but I didn't want him to stop touching me.

Then the shadows started moving around us, slinking like cats. I stiffened, thinking that it was the island and her magic, but Naji tightened his arms against my back and said, "It's fine." I let out a slow, careful breath. Something prickled against my skin, cold and damp. It soaked through the fabric of my clothes. It pressed my hair against my scalp.

And then I couldn't see nothing at all, just blackness. And there was this roaring in my head that scared the shit out of me. But at least I could still feel Naji even though I couldn't see him. I could still smell him, that scent like honey.

And then I smelled soil and pine and rotting wood. We were on the island. It was like I'd opened my eyes and here we were, curled up together beneath a tree taller than any ship I'd ever seen, the sand of the beach not ten feet away.

Naji's arms loosened and he fell with a thump against the soil and the fallen pine needles.

This might hurt me. His words echoed around inside my head and I thought maybe he said hurt when he meant kill and I rolled him over onto his back and pressed my fingers against his neck until I felt his pulse fluttering beneath his skin. I lay my head on his chest and listened to his heart beating.

"You're alright," I said, just in case he might've heard me.

A breeze blew in off the sea, biting and cold. I remembered what Marjani told me: stay warm and stay dry. We weren't doing too good on neither count.

And I hoped those woods didn't hold the same kind of monsters as the water.

I pushed that thought out of my head so I could concentrate on not freezing to death. I left Naji lying beneath the tree and picked my way down to the beach. The sand was rough and dark, coarse like Orati salt, and littered with bone-gray twists of driftwood. I gathered some of the driftwood, trying not to think about how it got there, and stacked it in the sand. Then I sprinkled some powder from the pistol into the wood and fired off the one shot I'd been allowed, wincing as it rang out through the trees, echoing and echoing.

Streaks of white birds erupted from the trees and I slammed down on the sand, fumbling around for my knife – but they were only birds, and they flew off and disappeared into the gray clouds.

Thank Kaol, the shot took. The powder sparked and smoldered and burned. I watched the fire for a while, sitting close enough that the heat soaked into my skin. The light of it made me feel safe.

I walked back over to Naji. He was still passed out. I took off his boots and his cloak and lay them out by the fire to dry. Then I gathered up my strength and wrapped my arms around his chest and dragged him over the pine needles and the sand to the fire. He squirmed a little, twisting his head this way and that. I brought him as close to the heat as I could. He moaned and fluttered his eyes and kind of looked up at me and then at the fire.

He said something, but I couldn't understand it. I sat down beside him and took off my own boots so they'd dry out. I stuck my feet close to the flames. I warmed up pretty quickly, all things considered.

Just once in all that work, I let myself look out at the horizon, to see if I could spot the Revenge one last time before she left us. And I did. It wasn't nothing but a few specks of sails against the gray sky, but Kaol, did it ever fill me with despair.

I was dozing on the sand, drowsy from the heat of the fire, when Naji shook me awake hours later. I rolled over and looked at him.

"You're alive," he said.

"Course I'm alive," I snapped. "You're the one who keeps passing out."

"I feel better now."

He didn't look better. Still death-white and haggard. One bruise blossomed out on the unscarred part of his face and another ringed around his eye. Kaol, I got him good.

When he reached up to shove his filthy, clumped-up hair out of his face, his hands shook.

"We need to find fresh water," I said, really meaning I would have to do it, cause in his state he didn't need to be traipsing through the woods. "I hope it won't turn us into monsters." I squinted up at the soft gray sky. "Do you think it's gonna snow?"

I'd seen snow once when we sailed to the ice-islands, and I knew that it was cold as death and not anything we'd want to mess with in our present state.

"It shouldn't," he said, and I didn't know if he was talking about the snow or the water's magic, and I didn't ask.

I sat up best I could – my body was stiffer than it'd been before, like I'd just gone eight rounds with a kraken. "I don't know about you but I ain't too keen on dying." I grabbed my boots and patted the leather. All dry, but also stiff and shrunken. I kneaded at it while I talked. "One of the first things I learned. You get stranded, look for water. Then find a place to protect yourself." I jutted my head at the fire. "I made an exception on account of you getting us stranded in the forsaken north. Figured water wasn't no good if we both froze to death."

Naji closed his eyes and let his head loll between his knees.

"Though I'm also a bit concerned with whatever the hell's following us."

That jerked him back up to full alert.

"It's the Mists, ain't it?"

"The Hariri clan would not have followed us this far without attacking."

I sighed and started kneading at the other boot.

"Ananna, your detour took us through a part of the world where the barriers are thinnest. They'd picked up on my trail while we were out at sea. I was trying to save the ship." He leaned forward. "You must be careful. This place is part of the Otherworld that found its way to our own..."

His voice trailed off as though speaking had worn him out. I stared at him with my mouth hanging open.

"Are you kidding me!" I shouted. "You couldn't have told me that earlier?"

"We need to find the Wizard Eirnin."

"Don't ignore me."

"You have no idea... I'm utterly incapacitated by this curse... If the Otherworld finds me, if they find you–"

"I'll hand you right over! You don't think this curse is hurting me, too? Kaol! I should have let you die in the desert."

Naji's face turned dark as a typhoon sky, and I immediately regretted shooting off like that. I didn't really want him to die, curse or no. So I pulled on my other boot and stood up. I hated stepping away from the fire, but it'd gotten big enough that its warmth spread all up and down the beach. I did not want to go into those woods, though, all dark and misty and shivering.

"Stay here," I said. "I'm going to find a stream or a pond or... or some dew. Something for us to drink." I glared at him. "You probably need it more than me, and I've fallen out of sail rigging once today."

I stalked away from him before he could say anything, up to the treeline. When I figured I was far enough away I chanced a glance back at the fire, and there he was, yanking on his boots to follow me. Fantastic.

Still, I waited for him.

He leaned against a tree to steady himself.

"You ain't going to make it," I said.

"I'm fine." He wobbled a little in place. "And I'll be worse if you go off on your own. We shouldn't... We shouldn't stay too long–"

"Naji, we're stranded here!"

I took off deeper into the green shadows. The air was damp and cold and wrapped around me like an old wet shawl. Everywhere I stepped I made noise, branches snapping, pine needles crackling. But so did Naji, and he was usually as graceful as a Saelini dancer and twice as silent.

We walked for twenty minutes when I heard pattering up in the tops of the trees, distant and soft. I cursed. All rain would get us was wet – we didn't have nothing to collect it in.

"We gotta head back," I said. "I don't want to lose our fi–"

I stopped. Naji was leaning up against a pine tree, his skin waxy like he had a fever.

"Kaol's starfish," I said. "You look like you're dying."

He moaned a little and rubbed at his forehead. "I'm not sure I can go on. I was hoping the spell would lead me to Eirnin, but..." His voice trailed away.

I glared at him, not wanting to think about his spell, the whole reason we were gonna die on a magic floating slab of rock in the first place.

"I used the last of my magic to bring us on land," he said mournfully. "It's run out."

"Good," I snapped. "If only it'd run out when we were on board the Revenge." Then I turned and stalked away from him, blood pounding in my ears.

"Ananna! Wait!" I heard the snap of branches that meant he was following. "You don't understand."

"I understand plenty. You stranded us here without any kind of protection." I whirled around to face him. He looked shrunken and old. "That's what you're going to tell me, isn't it? You can't do your protection spells?"

He didn't have to say anything to answer.

"At least you were able to get us on land before the ocean sucked us down." I dug the heels of my palm into my eyes. I was exhausted and in truth all I wanted was to lay out by the fire and sleep. But I knew I couldn't.

"Give me your sword," I said, "and go back to the fire."

He tried to stare me down, but he was too weak. So he just handed me his sword, nodded, and turned away.

I picked my way through the woods. The rain misted across my hair and the tops of my shoulders and set me to shivering, and the forest pressed up against me, impossibly tall trees and thick green cover and ropy vines. I kept the sword out, although I wasn't sure if a sword could stop whatever creatures the island had hidden.

Every now and then I stopped and listened for the bubbling of a river. But there were just forest sounds, leaves rustling and water dropping off the tree branches and critters scurrying around in the underbrush, and beyond that, a distant chiming sound like some weird far-off music. I didn't trust it. Didn't trust the normalcy of it. That's when magic's the most dangerous: when it feels like the untouched world.

The woods grew darker from the rain, and mist started rising up from the forest floor, gray and cold and wet. I tightened my grip on the sword, trying my best to ignore the panic rioting around my chest. I got a flash of pirate's intuition: I wasn't safe in the forest.

I should go back to the beach.

My left hand peeled itself away from the sword and found Naji's charm still looped around my neck. I thought about him leaning up against the tree, rubbing his forehead, pale from exertion. He was probably in pain now, all on account of me. I wondered if it was keeping him from healing.

But if we didn't have water, we'd die of dehydration within a couple of days. And even magic-tainted water was better than that.

So I kept walking.

After a while, the forest brightened a little, not from the sun peeking out behind the rain clouds but because the trees were different, tall and skinny and pale, with white crystalline leaves that clinked against one another in the wind. This must have been the chiming I heard earlier – this bright, strange forest. I tensed and hoisted up the sword. Nothing about this forest was natural, and yet after a few moments that sense of danger had passed. The forest chimed and sparkled around me, and I was just too exhausted to stay alert.

That was when I heard the faintest murmur of water. It was hard to make out over the chiming, but I listened closely and wandered about, trying to find its source. I don't know how long it took me, but I finally stumbled over a spring bubbling up underneath a big normal-looking pine tree, the water clear and clean-looking. I plunged my hands in and scooped it up to drink without thinking. Water was splashing down my chest when I remembered that I was on the Isles of the Sky, that this water could destroy me.

I fell back and stared at the spring, waiting for something to happen, for something to change. Nothing did that I could feel. And although I still didn't trust this normalcy, I allowed myself a bit more of that sweet-tasting water, and I prayed to Kaol and E'mko to keep me safe from the spirits.

The rain stopped, and I sat beside the spring, listening to the chiming from the trees, half-waiting for the mist to form again, to come creeping along the forest floor. But nothing happened. And after a while I started thinking on Naji, thinking on his curse. He cast a spell so strong it wiped out his magic, and we didn't even know if we could cure his curse. Hell, we didn't know if the Wizard Eirnin was even on this rock.

Maybe he'd die out there on the beach and I'd be free of the curse just long enough to get swallowed by the Isles of the Sky.

Maybe I shouldn't have left him alone after all.

So I ripped some strips of fabric off my trousers – they were soaked through with rainwater anyway – and knotted them in the tree branches as I made my way back to the beach.

The fire had burned out, just like I said it would, and the driftwood lay blackened and ashy along the horizon line. Naji was crouched beside the remains, his head hanging in his hands, hair stringy from the rain. He stirred as I walked up to him, but he didn't say anything, didn't even look up.

"I found a spring," I said.

No answer. I sat down beside him and balanced the sword on my knees and stared at the remains of the fire, trying my best to ignore the dampness in the air.

"A spring," Naji said after a while, muttering down at his feet.

"Yeah. You know. For drinking. I had some and it didn't do nothing to me, so hopefully..." I couldn't finish that thought. We sat in silence for a few moments more.

"I'm sorry I said I was glad your magic ran out."

Naji lifted his head but he still didn't look at me. I could hear the waves crashing beneath us.

"It happens," he said, "when I exert myself."

"I know."

Another moment of silence.

"I hope to be recovered enough within the next few days to cast a tracking spell on the Wizard Eirnin, but I don't..." He dipped his head again. "I've never run out like this. And with the curse – I just don't know."

I toyed with the hem of my shirt and looked down at the sand. My head felt thick with what he had just told me. Maybe he didn't have to die for us to get sucked into the island's magic.

"Maybe we can find the wizard the untouched way." Not that I liked the idea of wandering the island.

"I doubt we'll be able to find him just by searching."

"Ain't that big of an island."

Naji glanced at me out of the corner of his eye, and even with just that tiny look I caught a glimpse of the weariness and the hurt I'd caused him as I had traipsed alone through the woods. "The size of the island isn't the issue," he said. "I doubt very seriously the Wizard Eirnin will be easily found. Most wizards aren't. Not unless you know where to look."

I didn't have no answer to that.

"I might be able to conjure up a fire tomorrow," he said. "A small one."

"Maybe you should focus on getting better first."

"Perhaps you should show me the spring. You are correct that we'll need water to survive." He sighed. "We can look for food and shelter tomorrow."

"I can look for it to–"

"No." The word sliced through the air, left me colder than any rain ever could. "No. Once was enough."

I didn't need to ask him what he meant.

"I'm sorry," I said softly.

Naji pushed himself to his feet, and I noticed that he was shaking. If it was because of the cold or because of the way he wore himself out or because he was as scared as me, I couldn't say. But I didn't say nothing about him not being able to make it. I didn't say nothing about the spell he cast onboard the Ayel's Revenge.

We walked side by side as I led him through the woods.

CHAPTER SIXTEEN

That night I made a little tent out of fern fronds and fallen sticks not far from the spring, and I fell asleep to the gurgle of water and the glow of Naji's tattoos as he started healing himself. It was weird sleeping so close to him, and at first I lay on my back and looked up at the pattern of shadows created by the ferns, my hands folded over my stomach so I wouldn't accidentally touch him.

I woke up the next morning covered in ferns and rainwater. The tent had collapsed in the night, probably cause of some storm, and Naji was curled up on his side, his tattoos dull and flat against his skin. I pushed the ferns away and peeled off my soaked-through coat and shivered in the cool, damp air. The spring bubbled and churned a few feet away. Naji didn't move.

I shook his shoulder. He moaned and fluttered his eyes.

"Naji?" I asked. "Are you alright?"

He rolled onto his back, shedding a cascade of fern fronds and rain drops.

"Ananna?" he asked. "Where are we?"

"Kaol! You really don't know?" Anger rose up in me and turned to panic. I pressed my hand to his forehead. His skin was hot. "I think you have a fever."

He closed his eyes. I lay my ear against his chest to listen for the rattle of the northern sickness, but his breathing was steady and even.

"Need to rest," he murmured.

"Naji!" I shook him again. He stirred but didn't respond. At least his chest was rising and falling, and his tattoos had taken to glowing again. I stood up and paced back and forth in front of the spring. If he was sick, he needed warmth and shelter. And I didn't much like the idea of us staying in the woods, neither.

So I stole his sword and took off for the beach. The chiming forest was rioting in the pale morning, the trees throwing off glints of light, everything sounding like temple bells after a wedding. I picked my way through those narrow trunks, leaves drifting through the air. They stuck to my skin, and when I tried to wipe them away they shattered and smeared like the spun-sugar figures in a fancy Lisirran bakery.

Still, I made it to the shoreline easy enough. The sand dropped off toward the sea, which churned below the island, frothy and roiling with the wind. I rubbed at my arms to try and take out some of the chill; it didn't work, and so I put my coat back on even though it was still wet. I didn't know which direction to go, which direction would lead me to shelter. All the damn trees looked the same, and the clouds covered up the sun.

I shouldn't have left him at the spring.

But if I'd stayed behind, what could I have done then? Watch him burn up with a fever? Watch him sink into the soil and become part of the Isles?

No. I had to do something.

I trekked along the sand, gathering up the largest pieces of driftwood I could find and stacking them together close to the treeline. The beach felt safer; it was out in the open, which meant it was easier to spot any creatures that might come our way. But I wasn't sure if the tides came in here, and I didn't much want to risk it.

Once I had the driftwood gathered I ventured into the fringe of the woods. I didn't want to bother with fern leaves again, but there really wasn't much I could use in the way of shelter-building. I pulled the sword out of its scabbard and crept deeper into the forest. Here, the light turned a syrupy golden color I didn't trust one bit. Ain't no way the northern sun could give out light like that. But there was a certain type of tree in this part of the woods, one that I hadn't seen before, with trunks covered in a chalky pale white bark that peeled off in long wide strips. I didn't trust it, but sometimes you gotta trust the thing you don't want to.

Course, following that particular bit of Papa's advice was what got me in my current predicament in the first place. I guess it came down to a matter of choices. And I didn't have much of any at the moment.

I stacked the driftwood up into a lean-to against one of the pine trees – those at least I recognized from the ice-islands. Then I wove the tree bark into a sort of roof, which I tied to the driftwood using some twists of old vine.

When I finished, I took a step back and admired my work. I almost forgot where I was. I almost convinced myself I was just on the ice-islands, having the sort of adventure I used to dream about.

But then a wind blew in from the forest, and it smelled like musty damp and magic. I had my sword out before my brain could even figure out if I was in danger or not.

The beach stayed as empty and desolate as always.

I crawled into the lean-to and peered out the opening and through the cracks in the branches I'd left in so we could keep look out. I figured there should be enough room for me and Naji to both stretch out and sleep, and it was high enough that when I was sitting down I could reach up and my fingers would just barely graze the underside of the tree bark ceiling.

Since I'd managed to take care of our shelter problem for the time being, I figured I should look into food. The truth was I didn't trust anything on this island enough to eat it. Even if the water had turned out fine.

But my stomach was grumbling and I figured Naji was gonna need food if there was any hope of him getting better. So as I picked my way through the forest, back to the spring, I watched for any edible plant that I might recognize from the ice-islands. I didn't find nothing.

When I came to the spring, the ferns were scattered across the ground, and Naji was gone.

All thoughts of food flew out of my head. I had my sword out, my body tense and alert, and I stalked around the spring, stepping as careful as I could.

"Ananna?"

I froze, and then turned around slow and careful. Naji was leaning up against a tree, holding his shirt up like a basket.

"You left," he said. "And you took my sword."

I let the sword drop. "I thought you were dying. And we needed shelter. Real shelter, not leaves." I kicked at the ferns.

"I'm not dying. But the healing is taking a long time." He stumbled forward and I noticed his hands were shaking.

"Should you be wandering around the woods, then?"

"Probably not. But I was hungry." He knelt down in the remains of our tent and flattened out his shirt. A handful of dark red berries and little brown nuts spilled across the ground.

"I know these are safe to eat," he said. "They grow in the ice-islands, too."

I scowled, irritated that he'd been able to find something when I couldn't.

"Have some," he said. "I can show you where to collect more."

I picked up one of the berries and sniffed: It smelled sweet as rainwater. I was too hungry to be cautious. I tossed it into my mouth.

Best berry I'd ever tasted. After that first one didn't kill me, I took to shoving the rest of the pile into my mouth. It wasn't enough to satisfy me, but it took the pang away. When I finished, Naji was staring at me.

"I'm glad I ate some on the way back."

"Sorry."

His eyes brightened a little, and seeing it made me feel weirdly happy even though I was surrounded by gloom and magic.

"I made a lean-to," I said.

"Ah, so that's where you disappeared off to."

"I guess it didn't hurt you too bad."

Naji shrugged. "It wasn't as bad as yesterday, no."

"Well, I figured we needed shelter. And fire, too, although I don't know if I'll be able to start one in all this damp." I stood up and rubbed at my arms, trying to work out the chill. "Do you want me to show you? I don't… I don't much like staying in the woods."

Naji tilted his head a little and looked at me like he wanted to say something. But he only nodded.

It was slow going back to the beach. Naji stumbled over the underbrush and kept getting caught up in the woody vines that draped off the trees. Although he let me carry the sword, I was on edge the whole time, waiting for something to come creeping out of the shadows. It didn't help that every now and then I'd hear these weird chiming animal calls off in the distance, and the wind had a quality to it that sounded like a woman's whisper. At one point, Naji slumped against a tree, his forehead beaded with sweat. I only just caught him before he collapsed.

"Not safe," he whispered. His face twisted up and he pressed his hand into his forehead. "Not safe. For you."

"What's not safe? The woods?"

He cried out in pain and groped around my shoulders. His fingers were clammy and cold. I peeled the collar of my shirt away. The charm he made me was still there.

"Thank the darkness," he whispered, and he slumped up against me, as if all the air had been let out of him. "I'm sorry I can't protect you better."

The forest was rustling around us, dropping down feathery green leaves, and my breath was coming out fast and short. I knew we couldn't stay here – knew I couldn't stay here. But I wasn't leaving Naji behind.

"Here," I said, shoving the sword at him. "To protect me with."

His fingers fluttered around the handle. He straightened up a little, and his face no longer seemed so drawn and haggard. Stupid curse. It ain't like I don't know how to use a sword.

"Let's run," I said. "To keep me safe."

He stared at me like he didn't understand. But then he said, "Yes, I think that might work."

So we ran.

I ran faster than him, flying over the ferns and fallen tree trunks, but he kept up better than I might have expected, and I guess the running really did count as a way of keeping me safe. We burst out of the forest and the sea wind didn't carry the same cold whispers as the forest wind. I collapsed on the sand, panting, my stomach cramping up from the berries I'd eaten.

Naji knelt down beside me and took a long, deep breath. "Thank you," he said. "I couldn't think straight."

"Yeah, you looked pretty rough." I sat up and twisted around so I was facing the forest. I didn't like having it out of my sight. "You want to see the lean-to?"

I stood up and helped him to his feet, cause he was shaking and trembling like an old man. The lean-to wasn't far; I could see it crouched next to the treeline like an ugly gray toad.

"Ain't much, I know," I said. "But hopefully it's sturdier in a rainstorm. I bet it can last us till we find the wizard." I tried to sound sure, cause I figured it wasn't too fair to burden Naji right now. But inside I was afraid we'd never find the wizard at all.

I helped Naji crawl into the lean-to. He stretched out on his back and closed his eyes. I hardly had a chance to ask him how he was doing before his chest started rising and falling in the rhythm of sleep.

I took the sword off him and crawled back out onto the beach. I didn't want go too far – I certainly didn't want to go into the woods. We did need a fire, though. Papa had shown me how to start fires back when I was a little girl, since Mama couldn't start 'em with magic on account of her being a water witch. I figured it was safe to burn the wood since nothing had happened with the first fire, plus I'd already built a lean-to out of it, and I'd drunk the island's water and ate its berries without any trouble. And I was shivering so hard, too. This time it wasn't just 'cause of the fear.

I wandered down the beach looking for driftwood I hadn't already gathered up for the lean-to. When I got my courage up, I'd dart into the woods and pluck some dead, fallen branches off the ground. Never went in more than a few feet, though. Never went into the dappled shadows.

Stones were easier to come across. They were scattered across the beach in big piles, like someone had come through and set them that way as a message to the gods or to the spirits of the Isles. Part of me hoped it was the Wizard Eirnin, that maybe I'd stumble across him and we wouldn't have to wait for Naji to heal himself. But I never saw anybody. No animals, no birds, no wizards.

The lean-to was glowing when I came back, intense pale blue, a color that made me feel colder just looking at it. I checked in on Naji and the light from his tattoos seemed to overpower his whole body.

Maybe he'd heal quicker than he thought.

I piled up the wood and sat in the sand and struck stone against stone until a spark caught. You're supposed to feed the fire dead dry grass, which is easier to find in the south, so I made do with twigs from the dead tree branches. Luck was on my side. I had the fire going just as the sun, what little of it I could see, was dropping down to the horizon. In what I was pretty sure was the east.

I tried not to dwell on it.

The fire grew and grew as the island fell dark. Naji kept on sleeping, the blue from his tattoos mingling with the orange firelight. I never crawled into the lean-to myself, 'cause I didn't want to leave the heat and light of the fire, and so I fell asleep out there in the open.

The next morning, I rolled over onto my back, sand crunching beneath my weight. It was still dark, although whether that was 'cause of the time or 'cause of the rainclouds I couldn't stay. At least the fire was still burning, casting light up and down the beach–

Except it wasn't.

I sat straight up and screamed. The fire was nothing but a pile of dark ashes. The light was coming from me.

I screamed again and pushed myself up to standing and stumbled down to the edge of the island. Streaks of light radiated out behind me, and I froze in place, terrified. The sea crashed and churned beneath my feet. I took a deep breath and held up one of my hands and squinted at it, and I could see bright lines moving beneath my skin, those veins and arteries where my blood should be.

"No," I whispered, because I knew that all those stories about the Isles were true, that I really was turning into moonlight. "No, no." I took stumbling, shambling steps, trying to work through my panic. We couldn't build a boat and live out on the water, and we couldn't stay on land, neither.

Tears squeezed out of the corners of my eyes, blurring my skin's light and turning it into golden dots that scattered across the beach. I stumbled over the sand. The wind picked up, smelling of brine and fish–

"Get away from the edge!"

Hands grabbed me by the arm and dragged me backward, away from the churn of the ocean. I flailed and screamed. It was only Naji, but he was glowing too. Not just his tattoos. All of him.

"We're turning into moonlight!" I screamed.

"No, we're not. You almost ran off the side of the island. Come."

His voice was stronger, the voice I remembered from that night in the desert. He led me back to the lean-to and sat me down next to the fire remains.

"What's going on?" I wailed.

Naji blinked at me. It was unnerving to see him with his bright skin and his dark eyes, the opposite of how his magic worked.

"We're fine," he said. "Do I look like I'm in pain to you? There's no danger. At least as long as you stay away from the edge of the island."

"But the stories–"

Naji reached over pulled the charm out from under my shirt. "It's keeping you safe," he said. "As far as you're concerned, this is just… an effect. A courtier's trick." His glow brightened for a few seconds.

"Are you sure?"

"Yes." Naji pushed a piece of my hair out of my eyes. The movement was distracted and careless, but the minute he did it he dropped his hand into his lap and looked away. I felt myself growing hot and I realized that my own glow had brightened and turned a rich syrupy color. "I imagine it was caused by drinking from the spring. In a few days' time I should have enough strength to cast a spell to keep it from happening entirely."

I sighed as my panic mostly disappeared.

"Think of it this way," Naji said. "We won't need to worry about lanterns when we walk down to the spring."

"What! The spring! You said that's what's doing this to us!"

"It's also giving us water. Which we need if we aren't to die. Which I need if I'm ever to be well enough to track Eirnin."

"You seem well enough now," I muttered.

"I'm not." He stood up and held out his hand.

We trudged through the woods, our glow throwing off weird, long shadows that seemed to wriggle and squirm between the trees. Naji had the sword, but I had to stop myself from reaching over and grabbing it from him. I always feel safer with a sword in hand.

The spring was waiting for us, looking as normal as ever. Naji knelt beside it and took to drinking, but I hung back. His glow shimmered across the surface of the water.

"Ananna," he said, "I swear to you that it's safe."

I was thirsty. And I knew I couldn't go without

water. What would be the use of coming all this way, just to die of thirst?

"Fine," I said, and I sat beside him and drank my fill.

Nothing happened on the walk back – no whispers on the wind, no flare-ups of Naji's curse. He led me off the path we'd flattened out on our trips to and from the spring to pick some nuts and berries, and I was so hungry I ate 'em without waiting till we were on the beach. This time, they seemed enough to fill my belly. The sun pushed out from behind the clouds and washed out enough of the glow that I almost got to thinking everything was normal.

"We shouldn't stay," Naji said.

"Are you hurting?"

"No. I just don't want to linger."

Stepping out on the beach eased my tension up some, the way it always did. Out in the open, my glow had almost entirely disappeared in the pale northern sunlight.

"The lean-to," Naji said.

"What about it?"

"It's gone."

I stopped in place and squinted down the beach. He was right. All I saw was trees and shadows and sand.

The fear slammed back into my heart.

"Someone knows we're here," I said. "The wizard? He's trying to scare us off?" My voice pitched higher and higher. "He ain't gonna help you after all? We got stranded here for no reason?"

"I don't think that's it." Naji pulled away from me

and marched to the place where our lean-to had been. And that's when I saw it: the smear of ashes from our fire. The lean-to had been replaced by an enormous bone-gray tree, twisting up toward the sky.

"Curse this island," Naji said.

I couldn't speak. The best I managed was little gasping noises in the back of my throat.

"It's the magic," Naji said.

"I know it's the magic!" I shouted. "This island ain't nothing but damn magic!" Desperation welled up inside of me. He wasn't never gonna get better and the wizard wasn't never gonna cure his curse and we were gonna die here just cause of some glimmer of hope Lelia had nestled inside him. "What if we'd been inside?"

Naji turned toward me. Even though the glow was mostly washed out by the sun, his eyes seemed much darker than normal. "We should be grateful that we were not."

I turned away from him and walked over to the fire ashes. Kicked at 'em with my boot. The tree that had been our lean-to rustled its branches at me and showered down a rain of gray, twisting leaves. Everything about the island was gray. The sky, the sand, the shadows, our home.

I was becoming more and more convinced that the rest of my life would be nothing but gray.

We spent the next few days sleeping in fern tents that I built out on the beach. A storm rolled in one afternoon and soaked through all the wood and our tent, but Naji had gotten enough of his magic back that he was able to build a little fire afterward. It must have exhausted him, though, cause he stretched out on the sand afterward and slept, the glow of his skin and the glow of his tattoos fighting it out in the dark.

We always moved our location, and we always used different ferns for the tents. We took different paths to the spring. Naji said that would keep the island from changing too much, though he didn't explain how. At least that was back to normal.

Things fell into a routine. I didn't get used to 'em, but they were at least a routine.

Then one morning I woke up and Naji was gone. The familiar sick panic set in. I was on my feet immediately, tearing the tent apart, screaming Naji's name. A million possibilities raced through my head. Maybe he'd turned into moonlight after all, and I was next. Maybe he'd turned into a fern and I was ripping him into shreds in my fear.

I dropped the fern and I stepped back, almost stepping into the fire. The beach was silent save for the wind and my racing, terrified heartbeat.

"Naji?" I said one last time. All my hope was lost. That wasn't much of a surprise, though, cause I really didn't have much of it left.

"Ananna? Are you alright?"

Naji popped up in the shadow of a tree.

"You!" I shouted. "What's wrong with you?"

He blinked at me.

"I thought you got turned into a fern."

"Oh. Oh, Ananna, I'm sorry, I didn't think–"

"You go on and on about how I can't be left alone and then you just leave me here?"

Naji walked up to me. He moved with his old grace, slinking across the beach instead of shuffling. I'd hardly noticed that particular quality was coming back along with the magic.

"I was restless," he said. "I'm sorry. You weren't in danger."

I suppose that was something, but my heart was still beating too fast.

"I have something to show you."

"What could you possibly have to show me? Did your sword turn into a courtier's dress?" I narrowed my eyes at him. "Or did you find the wizard? Did you–"

"No. I'm not that well yet. But I think you'll appreciate it nonetheless."

He turned and headed off down the sand. I followed him because I didn't much want to be left alone again. After fifteen minutes we came across an old falling-apart little shack, set back into the woods, still within sight of the beach.

I didn't trust it at all. "Does somebody live here?" Though I had to admit it looked long-abandoned, the stones in the walls cracked and warped, the thatched roof dotted with holes.

"Look at it, Ananna. But the answer's no, no one lives here. I cast a history spell. A small one, but enough to tell."

I stepped up to the shack's door and nudged it with my

foot. Inside, the stone floor was coated with sand and old ashes and the thin, glassy sheen of sea salt. There was a tiny hearth in the back, where Naji had started a fire, and a pile of stone jars and a rotted bed in the corner.

The warmth spread over me, welcoming as an embrace, but I just looked on it with suspicion

"It's some island trick," I said, turning toward Naji. "It'll be like the lean-to. We'll go fetch water and come back to find it turned into a big pile of stones." I thought about the stones on the beach and shivered.

"It's not. I cast a history spell, remember?" Naji leaned up against the doorway. "It's been here for almost seventy-five years. And the first spell cast on it was one of protection."

"And it's still working?"

"It was very strong magic. Very old magic."

I glowered at him. He stepped inside and the fire flickered against his rotting clothes. "Would I do anything to put you in danger?"

He'd done plenty to put me in danger. He'd dragged me across the desert in the white hot heat. He'd gotten me stranded on the Isles of the Sky. But I'd let him. I'd done it all cause I wanted to break the curse as much as he did.

I shrugged and didn't look him in the eye.

"You should sit by the fire. It's a work of magic in and of itself that you haven't gotten sick yet."

"I'm fine."

"Let's not risk it."

I had to admit, the firelight looked awfully inviting.

And Naji looked healthy, not in any pain at all. I took one step cautiously through the doorway, and then strode across the shack to the hearth. The heat soaked into my skin, and I sat down, drawing my knees up to my chin. Naji sat down beside me.

"Why'd you do this?" I asked.

"Do what?"

"Find a shack."

"Because we need it," he said. "I don't know how long it will be until I'm fully healed, and it isn't helping that we have to sleep out in the cold every night."

I didn't say nothing, just leaned closer to the fire. Naji got up and paced around the room liked a caged jungle cat.

"I hope the wizard can break your curse," I said, speaking into the fire.

Naji stopped pacing. I looked over at him, and he stared back at me from across the room, the firelight flickering across his scars. But he didn't say a word, not about the curse, and not about anything else, neither.

CHAPTER SEVENTEEN

The shack looked halfway destroyed, but I was grateful for it when a storm blew through later that week, cold driving rain and dark misting winds. There was a hole about the size of my fist up in the roof, and water sluiced across the far wall, opposite the hearth, but me and Naji huddled up next to the fire and stayed dry. Naji kept rubbing his head, though, and I think it might've had something to do with the whispering on the wind. This time I could make out what it was saying: a voice speaking a language I didn't understand.

The next morning, the sun broke through the clouds, sending down pale beams of light that dotted across the beach. It was hard to imagine the storm from the night before and harder still to remember the voice, which seemed more like a dream as the day wore on. I thatched the roof with fern fronds and pine needles, and Naji swept out the inside with a broom I made for him from more pine needles. When we finished, we sat down to eat berries and some pale creamy tuber Naji dug out of the ground. Neither were very satisfying.

"I might be able to catch some fish," Naji said after we'd finished. "I think that may be the reason I'm not healing as quickly as I expected. I don't have enough strength just eating berries."

"We'll need a line. I guess I could make one out of that net Marjani gave us–"

"That won't be necessary." He paused, and the wind blustered in off the beach and knocked the pine trees around. "The island casts enough of a shadow over the sea that I can move through the water that way. I've done it before, in the Qilari swamps."

"How long you been well enough to do that?" I didn't have my usual strength, neither, although I'd thought it was cause of the island, or that I was spending energy on glowing.

"A few days."

"What! Then why haven't you done it already?"

"I don't like leaving you alone."

"You've done it before."

He frowned out at the ocean line. "Things were different."

I thought about the whispers on the wind.

"I got my charm," I said.

"I know you do."

"If I don't get us some fish we'll probably both starve to death and then it won't matter if the Mists show up. That's what you're worried about, isn't it? The Mists?"

He didn't answer.

"Hell and sea salt! Naji, you promised me that you'd start telling me things."

"I'm telling you now." He unfolded himself and the wind pushed his hair away from his face. It was cloudy and a bit of his glow peeked through his skin, his scar shining a pale soft white. "While I'm gone, you must promise to stay in the shack."

"Fine. I just hope it won't turn into a tree."

"It won't." Naji frowned, and then glanced over his shoulder at the woods. "Come."

"Into the woods? Why?"

"I need to gather up something." He plodded over to the treeline and then ran his fingers over the greenery spilling onto the sand. He plucked three narrow, shiny fern leaves, twisted them together, and muttered in his language. His glow dimmed for a few seconds, and then he handed me the bundle of ferns.

"Hang this above the door," he said.

I turned the ferns over and over in my hand. They were much heavier than three twisted-up leaves should be.

"Go on," he said. "You have to do it."

"What's this to protect me from?" I asked as we made our way back over to the shack. "The Mists or the Isles?"

"They're practically the same thing," he said.

A chill went down my spine.

I jammed the ferns into a crack above the door, and Naji slipped off his sword and scabbard and handed it to me.

"Stay inside," he said.

"Go," I said. "I'm starving."

He nodded, stepped into the shack's shadow, and disappeared.

He was gone for longer than I expected, not that I knew how long it took to sneak up on fish and catch 'em that way. I got bored and started tossing leaves that had fallen through the hole in the roof into the fire to watch 'em smolder and curl in on themselves. When I ran out of leaves, I stood in the doorway, Naji's sword and scabbard looped around my hips, and stared out at the shadowline along the trees. Nothing. I drummed my fingers against the doorway. Glanced up at the bundle of fern leaves. Thought about Naji telling me to stay put.

Something flashed out of the corner of my eye.

I had the sword out even though my brain was telling me it was only Naji. Except it wasn't Naji. It wasn't nobody at all, just a gray mist that was slinking out of the woods, shrouding my view of the forest, of the beach, of everything–

"Darkest night! Get inside!"

Naji looped his arm around my chest and pulled me backward into the shack. I cried out and dropped the sword in a clatter on the floor. The door to the shack slammed shut with a force that rattled the stones in the walls. I could hear Naji breathing in my ear. He smelled like the sea and like the cold nights of the ice-islands.

"What the hell!" I shouted. "Where did you come from?"

"The water." Naji let me go, and I whirled around

to face him. He was as dry as when he left, but he had a big silver-striped fish in one hand, and he didn't look furious the way I expected him to, only tired. "I felt you about to do something stupid. I told you not to go outside."

I slumped down on the floor, my heart pounding. "I was just bored," I muttered.

"Fortunately, they didn't see you," he said, laying the fish out on a slab of stone that was next to the hearth. "They'll only get stronger, though. You need to be more careful." He leaned in close to me, and I stared up at him, dizzy with the rush of my fear, and with something else I couldn't identify. "Promise you won't go out alone."

"You're the one that left me be–"

"Promise."

"I promise. Kaol. I'm sorry I stood in the damn door."

He slid away from me and pulled out his knife. "Midnight's claws, I wish I could heal faster. If only I knew how long I had to keep them from you–"

"Me! You're the one they're after."

He slid the knife up under the fish's scales, his movements quick and assured. If I hadn't been annoyed with him, I might've been impressed. "I'm currently far more protected than you are," he said. "I have the strength of the Order behind me."

I scowled. "Don't cut that fish too thin. It'll burn up in the fire."

He stopped cutting and looked at me. "Would you rather do it?"

"I can do it better than you can."

He pulled out the knife and handed it over like it was a peace offering. Cleaning the fish calmed me down a little. It helped that Naji didn't nag me about the Mists no more, and by the time we had the fish cooking on the fire, I had forgotten about the mist curling through the woods outside the shack. I was inside, I was surrounded by warmth and the smells of real food, I was safe.

The two of us finished off the entire fish. Its flesh was flaky and almost sweet-tasting, and it snapped clean and bright inside my mouth. The best meal I'd had in ages.

When we finished eating, Naji pulled out his sword and started sharpening it against the side of a rock he had brought in from the beach with him. It didn't take him long; he was sure practiced at it.

He held the sword up to the fire. It glittered, throwing off little dots of silvery light.

"You had that sword long?" I asked him. Some people, soldiers especially, make a big deal about their swords, and you can get 'em to talk about the things forever. Never been one for that sort of thing myself. A weapon's a weapon.

"I received it when I took my vows." Naji lay the sword over his knees.

"What kinda vows?" Celibacy? I thought, though I didn't say it. Nobody keeps a celibacy vow anyway.

Naji lifted his head. "I'm not supposed to discuss it with outsiders."

"Oh, course not." I picked the sword up by the handle and swiped it through the air a few times. But without the threat of danger, it only reminded me of Tarrin of the Hariri and I dropped it on the floor. Naji gave me one of his looks and slipped it back into its scabbard.

"Can I ask you a question?" I said.

"I'm not divulging any secrets of the Order."

"Not even one?"

Naji narrowed his eyes, and I realized he'd probably been joking, in his way. I took a deep breath.

"Why didn't you want to kill me?"

Naji looked away, toward the fire-shadows flickering across the doorway.

"Well?" I prompted. "Or is that a secret of the Order, too?"

Naji sighed. He leaned back against the wall. He didn't look the least bit like an assassin, what with the firelight and his seaworn clothes. In truth, cause of the scar and his long hair, he looked like a pirate. Even the tattoos reminded me of ocean waves.

"Do you know who the Jadorr'a are?" he asked.

"Assassins."

My answer made him look worn out.

"No, do you know their involvement in the history of the Empire?"

I shrugged. Not much use for knowing history on board a pirate ship.

"They used to prevent wars," he said. "Before the Empire bound together the countries of the desertlands, they were a way to put a cease to the constant fighting between kings. Better to kill one man than allow soldiers to destroy the countryside, raping and burning their way across the desert."

War between countries was something the Confederation didn't much get involved in beyond its own internal squabbling. Though there hadn't been war for a long time, not since I was a little girl, and that was over on Qilar anyway. The Empire had formed long before I was born.

"I don't see what any of this has to do with me," I said.

"It doesn't," Naji said. "That's my point. The Order was always paid for its services, but once the Empire formed, gold lust opened them up for use by any merchant with enough wealth to provide payment."

"Like Captain Hariri?"

"Like Captain Hariri." Naji shook his head. "I joined the Order after my strength manifested itself – after I learned my magic came from darkness and death, not the earth, the way it did for my mother, my brother–"

"You have a brother?"

Naji fixed me with a steely gaze. "My mother sent me away. She said I could harness my darkness into something good, that I could stop the Empire from destroying all the people living under its banners..." He laughed, a short, harsh bark. "I suppose I've done that. Once or twice. But mostly it's errand-running for rich men. I despise wealth."

I didn't say nothing to that. Wealth is power, Papa always told me. Wealth is strength. But I could see where Naji was coming from, too.

"So that's why you didn't want to kill me?" I finally said. "Cause you didn't think it was worth your time?"

Naji looked up at me. "No," he said. "I didn't want to you kill you because I thought it was wrong."

I dunno why, but my face flushed hot at that. Hotter than the fire.

"I won't tell nobody," I said.

"It doesn't matter. No one's going to believe you escaped an assassin."

"A Jadorr'a," I said.

He looked at me again, and I still couldn't read his face none. Not even his eyes.

"Yes," he said. "A Jadorr'a."

And his voice was soft as a kiss.

I woke up to rainfall pattering across the roof. It was awful hard to tell the passing of days here, on account of the cloud cover and the way the sun didn't always rise and set in the same place. The rainfall was constant, though. It was a shame you couldn't keep track of the days through the rain. All I knew was that I'd heard that soft rustle of rain more often than not.

This morning something was different, though. The shack was lit not by the usual faint golden glow of our skin, but by bright blue light. Light the color of northern glaciers.

I sat up, mussing the pile of pine needles and leaves I used for bedding. Naji sat in the corner next to the fire, his eyes and tattoos glowing. My heart pounded. Was he tracking the wizard? Or maybe he was talking to the Order. Maybe they'd have a way to bring us home.

For the first time since we landed on the island, I felt a dizzying twist in my brain that I half-recognized as joy.

A pile of berries was lying next to the hearth, and I ate 'em and checked the water jar. It was empty. I cursed and sat back down on my pile of leaves. Figured he'd think to pick some berries but not go fetch some water. And I was thirsty from sleep.

I watched him in his trance for a while, my head leaned up against the stone walls. He didn't move. Not even his chest rose and fell with his breath. It was eerie, truth be told. I'd never watched him this closely during a trance before. I'd always had better things to do with my time.

"Naji!" I said, waving my hands in front of his face. "I'm thirsty."

Naji didn't move, and the light in the shack didn't change.

"If you don't come out of that trance I'm gonna go fetch water myself."

Nothing.

I sighed. His sword was lying across the bed. It wouldn't take long to walk down to the spring, I knew the different paths so well now, and I was in such good spirits I felt invincible. I hadn't even seen any mist in the last week. Hadn't heard no voices, neither.

And I was wearing my charm. It'd protected me from the Mists man in the night market in Lisirra. It'd made him look right through me. Maybe it could do the same with the island.

And Kaol only knew how long Naji would be under.

I scooped the sword off the bed and grabbed the water pot. Naji was wearing the scabbard, so I just carried the sword with me out into the rain. The drops were cold and stinging, the way the rain always was here. Made me miss the warm soft rains that fell across the pirates' islands. But once I got into the thick part of the forest the leaves caught most of the drops, and I trudged over pine needles and crushed ferns, shivering and miserable. My brain started churning up like the sea, thinking on the curse and getting kicked off the Revenge and fighting the Hariri clan. I thought about Tarrin, who I'd managed to shove down deep inside me when we left Port Iskassaya. The memory was back now: his breath tickling my ear, how easy the sword had slid into his belly, the heat of his blood spilling over my hands. And it was this sword that had done it, this sword that I'd used to kill Tarrin.

I suddenly couldn't stand the thought of the sword touching me no more, and I tossed it off into the greenery, my chest heaving, my heart racing. I watched it disappear in a spray of ferns, and for a split second I wondered what I'd done. But then my thoughts went elsewhere.

The woods had gone silent.

There's always noise in the world.

But not now.

I stopped and that's when I heard it, that emptiness of sound, like the forest was holding her breath. I got this creeping chill up my spine, and my palms turned cold and clammy, and here I was alone and with no manner of weapon cause I'd just thrown it away, and what sort of stupid girl does a thing like that?

A shimmer appeared up ahead, a curl of mist, pale silver and hazy. I took a step backward, trying to figure out the best way to run. I was in the chiming forest, all those skinny trees covered with bone-white bark, weird transparent leaves disintegrating in the rain–

"Ananna of the Tanarau."

A woman stepped out of the mist, her body long and thin, her eyes that same eerie silver as the woman in the dress shop. But this was a different woman. The woman in the dress shop had been human enough to fool me; this one had a narrow feral face, her chin too pointed and her cheekbones too sharp. And the silver in her eyes blocked out all the white.

"I don't know who that is," I told her.

The woman laughed. Her teeth were filed into points.

"You don't know who you are?" she asked me.

"I know I'm not Ananna of the Tanarau."

The woman laughed again, and I knew it was pointless to lie. I wished to the deep dark sea that I had waited for Naji to finish his magic.

"Who are you?" I asked.

She tilted her head and little lights danced in the shadows around her. Whenever I looked at them I felt dizzy.

The woman drifted up beside me. It took me a minute to realize that she didn't have feet, that her skirts ended in a cloud of creeping mist that got up under my clothes, all cold and damp. Those little lights swirled outside my line of vision, and I used all my willpower to keep my sight focused on the bridge of her nose. I knew better than to look her in the eye.

"Surely you know," she said. "You've met my kind before. Harbor. Although she did insist on a fully human body." The woman laughed. "Stupid of her. At least she bled all over your world and not mine."

"That ain't what I'm talking about. I know you ain't human." I took a deep breath and steadied myself. "You know my name. Only seems fair I know yours."

The woman gazed at me for a long time. I stood my ground, even though the mist crept and crept around me.

"You can call me Echo," she said.

"You expect me to believe that's your name?"

"I didn't say it was my name. I said it's what you can call me." She gave me this sly, slow smile that reminded me of a fox. It showed just enough of her teeth.

"So what do you want?"

"Now that," she said, "I'm certain you already know."

"You'd be wrong." A lie, of course. I knew damn well what she wanted.

She stared at me for a long time, like she couldn't decide if I was lying or just that stupid. I could tell she figured either one was a possibility.

"Your companion," she said finally. "The assassin."

"Oh, him." I frowned. "I don't know where he is."

She tilted her head. "Don't confuse me with Harbor," she said. "I've been doing this much, much longer than she. That charm she lent you was one of my own devising. It should have worked. But the assassin had taken precautions I didn't realize."

The woman ghosted her hand along the line of my throat, coming close but never quite touching. I could feel Naji's charm pressing against my heart. "You seem to have taken precautions yourself."

"Figure I can't be too careful, out in the wild."

She drifted closer. Her body gave off cold the way a normal person's gives off heat. She still didn't touch me, though, and I figured I could thank Naji's charm for that.

"You can still help me," the woman said. "It will be of your own accord, and that way is always better. And I would never expect you to work for free."

Her silvery eyes drifted over my face and came to rest on the charm.

"Oh yeah?" I asked. "What would you give me?"

She laughed. "Whatever you want."

"Money? Empire money, I mean, not some worthless Mist coins."

"We can acquire wealth, yes. Human wealth."

I looked past her, to the gray space where she'd first appeared. It shimmered in the trees, a thundercloud that lost its way out of the storm. From where I stood, the Mists were grayness. They were nothing.

"My lord would be pleased if you brought him the assassin," she said. "He would grant you a boon." She smiled. "A hundred boons."

Her hand traced over the line of my forehead. She couldn't touch me, but it was still like walking straight into a typhoon.

And I got these pictures in my head. Me with my own ship, sleek and tall, with sails the color of blood. And that ship of mine, she had a crew that listened to me even though I was a woman, and together we sacked the coasts of Qilar and all the lands of the Empire. The Confederation fell cause of me and that ship. All Confederation pirates became part of my armada, and I ruled the oceans, the richest woman in the world. I took lovers more handsome than Tarrin of the Hariri, more handsome than Naji. I wielded Otherworld magic that put the seas under my control and gave me power over typhoons and squalls and sunshine and steering winds.

I became the most perfect version of myself, fierce and terrifying and even beautiful.

I wanted to take her up on it. I wanted to wrench that charm off my neck and stomp it into the ground and race through the woods till I found Naji crumpled up in pain in the shack. I wanted to, cause on the surface it was the most common-sense thing to do. Always take the money, Papa said. You can always double-cross on the deal later if you don't like the terms.

But I also wanted to do it cause Naji didn't see me,

he would never see me, and for reasons I couldn't decipher, that bothered me.

I wanted to do it. I just couldn't do it.

I stepped away from her, my forehead damp from where she'd almost touched me.

"You liked that, didn't you?" she asked.

"It had appeal, ain't gonna lie." I took another step back, hoping my legs weren't shaking too bad. "But I think I'll leave you to it on your own. You don't need my help."

Echo's eyes turned flat as mirrors. Darkness roiled through the woods. The trees shook. The earth rumbled.

"You can't hurt me," I said, thumping the side of Naji's charm with my thumb. "I ain't afraid of you."

She bared her teeth, sharp and bright, and let out a low, snaky hiss. But I was right. She didn't move to attack. I was protected.

"Protected?" she sneered. "You think you're protected?"

"Course I do. You can't even touch me." I tried not to think about her reading my thoughts.

"Why do you think you threw your sword into the woods?" Her voice was nothing human. She glided up to me, and there was that cold dampness again, but I held my ground. "I can control you, I can force you to lead me to him–"

"Then why don't you do it?"

She snarled, her face twisted and wild. I was not going to flinch. I was not going to run away.

And then something darted out from the underbrush, something swift-moving and black as pitch. A sword flashed. It sliced through the woman and her dark mist, and this time there wasn't any starlight to splatter all over my clothes. She just evaporated. The entrance to the Mists dried up like it'd been left too long in the sun.

I sat down on the transparent tree leaves and the damp ferns.

A branch snapped off to my right. I didn't bother looking over. I knew who it was.

"I told you it was dangerous," Naji said.

"Is she gone?"

"For now." Naji paused. "Thank you."

"For what?"

He stood beside me, his sword hanging at his side. I kept my gaze down on the ground and tried not to think about tossing it off into the underbrush.

"For not telling her where to find me."

I kicked at the fallen leaves, splintering them into shards, digging a ditch in the soil with the heel of my boot. The forest noises had come back, the chittering and shaking and rustling of the rain, the crystalline chiming of the surrounding trees, but the silence between the two of us swallowed all that noise whole.

"I almost did," I said after a while.

"Almost did what?"

"Helped her find you." I couldn't look at him. "She showed me all these things that could happen if I did – amazing things. My own ship, my own crew." I stopped, not wanting to remember some future that wasn't ever gonna happen.

Naji got real still. I knew he was staring at me even though I refused to look up at his face.

"Why didn't you?"

"Cause."

"That doesn't answer the question." The hardness in his voice sliced through the liquid air of the forest. This time, I did look at him. Lines furrowed his brow. His eyes were sunk low into his face. "I can't keep doing this, Ananna, not if there's a chance you might turn me over to the Otherworld. Not if you're going to run away when I explicitly told you..." He took a deep breath. "What stopped you? Why didn't you help her?"

"Cause you're my friend," I said.

All the hardness in his features melted away. "Oh."

"I'm not going to turn you over to your enemies." I stood up, swiping the forest floor off my dress. "So you can stop fretting about that. But I'm thirsty still. That's why I left – you were in a trance and didn't bother to get water."

He didn't say nothing. I started kicking around in the underbrush, trying to find the water jar. I didn't remember dropping it, but that was probably just more Otherworld trickery.

"It's a few feet behind you," Naji said. "Beneath that tree there."

I glared at him and then fumbled around in the wet greenery until I felt the smooth cold stone of the jar. Naji waited for me, his arms crossed in front of his chest, and then we walked the rest of the way to the spring, our silence heavy with our unspoken thoughts.

The spring was waiting for us as though nothing unusual had happened. It bubbled and frothed in its usual place beneath the pine trees. I plunged the jar into the spring, and the water flooded over my hands, cold as ice and reminding me of Echo's almost-touch.

I know that Naji saw me shivering.

CHAPTER EIGHTEEN

Naji paced back and forth through the chiming forest, knocking down tree branches and those sparkling, transparent leaves. I watched him from beside the spring and waited for the thoughts to stop jangling around inside my head.

Finally I got so tired of listening to him trampling through the underbrush that I asked, "So I guess you found out where the Wizard Eirnin is, then."

"Yes." He stopped his pacing, glanced at me, and then looked away. The wind pushed through the trees, and the leaves shimmered and threw off dots of pale light, and the tree trunks bent and swayed. The chiming was everywhere.

"That's it?"

"What else is there to tell?"

I narrowed my eyes at him. He still wasn't looking at me, and I could tell he was leaving something out. He'd done it so much when we first left Lisirra I'd become a master at spotting all his omissions.

"I don't know," I said, "or else I wouldn't be asking."

"The Wizard Eirnin lives in the center of the island," Naji said. "It isn't far from here. That's all I know."

I sighed and refilled the water jar one last time. "Well," I said. "I guess we ought to go look for him." I straightened up and rested the jar against my hip.

"Are you going to take that with you?" Naji asked.

"Course I am. It's impossible to tell east from west on this damned island. Chances are we'll wind up wandering back around to the shack before we ever find the wizard."

"I tracked him," Naji said. "I know exactly where he is." His expression darkened. "Exactly how I knew where you were when the Otherworld attacked."

I shoved past him, jostling water. He didn't say nothing more about the Otherworld attack, and I let him lead me out of the chiming forest and into the darker parts of the woods. The rain had been threatening us the whole time I laid out by the spring, and now it started again in earnest. Naji plowed forward like it didn't even bother him, like he didn't even notice the rain and the gray light and the scent of soil.

We walked for a long time. The rain hazed my vision and filled the water jar to overflowing. The trees crowded in on me, looming and close, and I started wondering if it was the Mists. Echo coming back for one last fight. My hands started to shake.

And then, like that, the trees cleared out and there was this little round house built of stone sitting in the middle of a garden, smoke trickling up out of a hole in the roof.

Time seemed to stop. I forgot about the Mists and about the island: when I saw that house, there was only Naji's curse, which was also my curse. And we'd come so far across the world to get it cured.

This stone-built house hardly seemed capable of that sort of magic.

Naji was already knocking at the front door. I ran through the garden to join him. They looked like normal plants, not the weird ghost-plants Leila'd had growing in her cave. They drooped beneath the weight of the rain.

The door opened up a crack, and a sliver of a face appeared. Naji didn't say nothing. Then the door swung all the way open and this man was standing there in a rough-cut tunic and trousers. He had that look of the northern peoples, like somebody'd pricked him and all the color had drained out of his hair and skin.

"Well, look who's on my front porch," he said, speaking Empire with this odd hissing accent. "A murderer and a cross-dressing pirate."

I looked down at my clothes, ripped and shredded and covered in mud and sand and dried blood. I'd forgotten I was dressed like a boy.

"So are you here to kill me or to rob me?" the man said. "I generally don't find it useful to glow when undertaking acts of subterfuge, but then, I'm just a wizard."

You know, that pissed me off. We'd traveled half around the world to get to him, and there were monsters chasing us and Naji's curse was impossible to break, and here he was cracking jokes about our professions. I took a step forward, pushing Naji out of the way and spilling water on the porch.

"Mister," I said. "Do either of us look like we're capable of any kind of pillaging right now?"

The man looked like he wanted to laugh. "That one might," he said. "But you look halfway crossed over to Kajjil."

"How do you know that word?" Naji asked.

"What? It's not one of the secret words." The man winked. "Though I know plenty of those, too. You two come on in. I'll fix you something warm to drink, get you a change of clothes."

Naji slumped into the house, and I followed behind, setting the water pot next to the door so I wouldn't forget it on my way out.

It was nice, everything clean and tidy, with simple wooden furniture and bouquets of dried flowers hanging upside from the rafters. A sense of protection passed over me when I walked through the doorway, rum-strong like the feeling I got when I put on Naji's charm for the first time. I headed directly for the hearth, cause there was a fire smoldering in there, licks of white-hot flame. Naji sat down beside me, his hands draped over his knees. The firelight brightened his face and traced the outlines of his scars.

The man hung a kettle over the fire and pulled up a chair. I felt like a little kid again, sitting at Papa's feet while he told me stories. But the man didn't tell no stories, he just leaned forward and looked at me real hard and then at Naji. Then he stirred whatever was in the kettle.

"Are you the Wizard Eirnin?" Naji asked.

"I surely am." The man glanced over at him. "Leila let me know you were on your way. She told me about the curse." His weird pale eyes flashed. "And I've heard your name on the wind's whispers these last few days." He turned his gaze to me. "I see you emerged from your encounter with the Mists unscathed."

I looked down at my hands.

"From what Leila said about you, I wouldn't have expected it."

"What's that supposed to mean?"

Eirnin stood up. "I promised you clean clothes, didn't I? Getting dotty in my old age. Wait here." He strolled across the room and rummaged around in a dresser. I watched him. Naji watched the fire.

"Here we go." He pulled out a long pearl-colored dress, the fabric thick and warm, the edges trimmed in lace, and a gray man's coat and tossed both at me. "You can go change in the back room if you want."

It'd been awhile since I wore a proper dress, but really, having any clean clothes was a blessing from Kaol. I ducked into the back room and peeled off my old damp clothes and piled 'em up on the floor. It would've been nice to have a bath before changing into the dress, but I didn't know if I trusted a bath in a wizard's house. Still, putting on new clothes made me feel better, despite everything that had happened – warmer, too, cause these were dry.

When I came back into the main room Naji was dressed like a right gentleman, in a white shirt and dark brown trousers, no black anywhere on him. Eirnin handed me a ceramic mug filled with something warm and sweet-smelling. I knew I shoulda been more cautious, but I'd been soaked through and cold and more shaken from my encounter with the Mists than I cared to admit, so I sipped some and it washed warmth all the way down my throat. It was some kind of liquor, sweet like honey but spicy, too. I sat down next to the fire and drank and drank.

"Can you help me?" Naji asked.

Eirnin laughed. "Help you with an impossible curse?" he said. "I don't know. Tell me about it."

Naji looked down at his own mug. "What do you want to know?"

"Anything you can tell me."

The room got real quiet. All I could hear was the fire crackling in the hearth and the rain whispering across the roof.

"You know you're safe here," the Wizard Eirnin said. "I don't traffic with the Otherworld."

Naji tightened his fingers around his mug. The fire-light carved his face into blocks of darkness and light.

"I was in the north," he said. "I had an assignment. To track down the leader of a splinter group that had fled there." He sipped his drink. "It was winter. Dark, cold. I had tracked the leader to the settlement of one of the northern tribes. They'd taken him in. I wound up killing some of their tribesmen. I didn't intend to, but the leader had expected me – or someone like me…" Naji's voice trailed off.

"So which one of those, ah, accidental deaths got you the curse?" Eirnin asked.

"I don't know. They caught me – the only time I've ever been caught – and dragged me out into the snow. Everything was white. And then a woman came out of one of the tents. She looked like she was carved out of ice. And she was ancient, older than the mountains.

"She told me that someday someone would save my life. When that happened, she said, I would be indebted to them forever. I would have to protect them."

"I take it that's you?"

Eirnin's question broke the spell of Naji's voice. I jumped about a foot and spilled some of my drink down the front of my dress. Naji didn't look at neither of us, just stared into the fire.

"Yeah, it's me," I said. "I told him he didn't have to, but–"

"Well, it's a curse," Eirnin said blandly. "He can't help it." Then, to Naji: "What happens if you don't keep her safe?"

"It hurts me."

"Care to be more specific?"

"A headache, or a pain in my chest or my joints. It depends on the level of the threat."

I thought about meeting with Echo in the woods, about the cold curling mist.

Eirnin nodded.

"So can you help me?" Naji twisted around and the expression on his face was so desperate that, for a moment, my stomach twisted up in empathy.

"No," said Eirnin.

All the air went out of the room.

"What?" said Naji, and his voice was cold and dangerous, like the blade of his knife.

Eirnin didn't do nothing, though, didn't shrink back, didn't even act like he was scared. "What did you expect, Jadorr'a? It's an impossible curse. You know that. Even that one knows it." He tilted his head at me.

Naji's face twisted up with rage.

"I do know that woman, though, that ice-woman. She's quite traditional. Always casts her spells in the old northern style." Eirnin paused. His eyes flashed again. "The north is different from the hot civilized places of the world. We have different understandings of things. Of words."

No one spoke. The house pulsed twice with the manic energy of magic. I realized I was holding my breath.

"What the magicians of the Empire call an impossible curse is not what we call an impossible curse. A northern curse is not impossible in the sense that is incurable."

Naji leapt to his feet, his body hard and tense beneath his clean clothes. The sword gleamed at his side. "Then why did you say you couldn't help me?"

"It's not my place to cure your curse." Eirnin leaned back in his chair and pressed the tips of fingers together. "If you want to break one of the old north's impossible curses, you have to complete three impossible tasks."

The energy that crackled through the house like lightning died away. But Naji kept his eyes on Eirnin, his gaze strong and sure.

"Do you at least know what they are?" Naji said.

"I do. Smelled them on you the minute you walked through the door." Eirnin smiled but didn't say anything more.

Naji glared at him. "Well?" he asked. "What are they?"

"Impossible," Eirnin said.

I figured by this point it was taking all of Naji's willpower not to launch at the guy the way he had Ataño. I figured Eirnin knew it, too. You could see how he'd have gotten along with Leila.

"Perhaps you'd like to write them down," Eirnin said. "I have parchment around here–"

"No," said Naji. "I don't."

Eirnin smiled. I wanted to hit him myself. "Alright. First one: Find the princess' starstones and hold them, skin against stone."

Well. I'd no idea what a starstone was, but I didn't think that sounded too bad. Lots of princesses around. Naji just kept on staring at Eirnin, though.

"Second one. Create life out of an act of violence."

Naji's face darkened. "Are you talking about rape?"

"I'm afraid it's not that specific."

Naji pressed his hands against the side of the mug, his face all twisted up in anger. I waited for the mug to shatter.

"You want to hear the third one?" Eirnin asked.

"You know that I do."

Eirnin smiled. "The third task," he said, "is to experience true love's kiss."

"Seriously?" Naji asked.

"Quite. You'll have to find someone who loves you for who you are." He paused. "And good luck with that, murderer."

Something brightened in my heart, like the first star coming out at night. But then Naji opened his mouth.

"Leila," he said. "She's the only one..."

The light blinked out. I got real hot and looked down at my hands.

"Leila!" Eirnin roared with laughter. "That woman has never loved another human being in her entire life, and never will. I wouldn't put all my eggs in that particular basket, if I were you. Which, fortunately, I'm not."

Naji stood up and hurled his mug against the wall. I jumped at the sound of breaking porcelain and twisted my hands up in my dress. I wanted a way to get out of that house without anyone knowing why. And to get away from Naji, the Otherworld be damned.

Naji stalked out the front door and slammed it so hard the foundation shuddered.

"Looks like it's just you and me," the Wizard Eirnin said.

I stood up and straightened out my skirts. Worthless, this old man was. What a waste getting blown out here, away from civilization and people who could actually help us, to some place that used to belong to a nightmare world.

"The stories are true. This place did spawn itself from the Mists." Eirnin leaned forward. He was so pale he looked like a ghost. "They won't hurt you, you know. Not if they think you can help them. Remember that, my dear, the next time Echo comes calling. That's what she called herself today, isn't it?"

I stumbled backward at the sound of her name. "I should go." I hesitated, knowing that you never want to cross a wizard the wrong way. "Thank you for the clothes and the..." I waved my hand at the mug. "And for helping Naji. I mean, I wish you could have done more–"

"I'm sure you do." He gave me this weird knowing look that I didn't like one bit. "You be careful out there, little pirate. Things come out of those woods that know how to get at you. The Mist's not the only thing you need to worry about."

I stared at him. "I ain't little."

Eirnin grinned. That was it. I slammed out the front door.

I hadn't been walking long when Naji stepped out of the shadow of a pine tree. I shrieked so loud my voice echoed through the woods. I'd been mired in my own thoughts. Cause I was trying not to think about Echo and the mists, I thought about Naji instead, and the thing I learned in the Wizard Eirnin's house. I'd handed my heart over to him, a damned blood-magic assassin, without even realizing it.

"I told you I don't want you wandering off alone."

"Stop talking to me like I'm a little kid. You're the one who left me."

Naji fell into step beside me. "You left the water jar behind."

"Kaol and her sacred starfish!" I stopped in the

middle of the woods, whirled around in the direction of his house. "Damn it, I'm not going back there." I pushed my hair out of my eyes. "At least he gave us something to drink."

He snorted and took off into the woods, paying no mind to the snapping of branches. I trailed behind him. "So now what?" I said.

"We go to the shack," Naji said.

"That ain't what I meant." I ran up beside him. "I mean with the curse. You know a way off the island? You said the Order was protecting you – why couldn't they just bring us both back? Don't tell me it ain't possible, I know the stories."

He stopped. "How did you know?"

"Know what? About the Order?" I almost laughed. "You mean they can actually do that?"

"Of course they can." But then his expression changed. It went from hard and anger to... almost sad. "I spoke to them this morning. Magic is strong here. They'd certainly be able to send an acolyte through Kajjil."

Water dripped out of the trees and landed in dark spots on my new coat. "They aren't coming, are they?"

Naji looked at me, and then he shook his head.

I should have known it wouldn't be that easy.

He walked off, his face tilted down to the ground.

"And why not?" I called after him. "They don't want to bother with you when the Mists are on your tail? Or are you damaged goods now that you got that curse?"

He stopped. The wind rippled his hair and his new clothes. When he turned around his face was a mask.

"They wouldn't have rescued you," he said. "They wouldn't risk bringing an outsider through Kajjil."

"Guess I just ruin everything for you, don't I? Give you headaches and keep you from getting rescued–"

"I told them no," he said, "even when I thought – when I hoped – that Eirnin would have cured me."

The entire world suddenly seemed to stand still. Naji and me were statues. The forest was no longer shaking with wind and rain. Even the dripping had stopped. But my heart was still beating, pounding too fast inside my chest, threatening to break me open.

"What?" I whispered.

"Give me your hand," Naji said, and then he walked over to me and grabbed it without waiting for me to move. The shadows crowded in around us. I didn't quite understand what had happened until we were standing in the shadow of the pine trees that grew beside our shack.

"I didn't feel like walking through the woods again," Naji said, and he stalked into the shack, leaving me shaking outside.

"Hey!" I shouted. My voice disappeared on the wind. "Naji!"

He didn't come back out, and so I went in and found him staring at the fire.

"Did you mean that?" I leaned up against the doorway. "About staying with me even if you were cured–"

"Yes." He looked at me over his shoulder. "Close the door, please. The wind will blow the fire out."

I stepped inside and sat down on the floor beside him. The fire crackled in the hearth.

"It was the only decent thing to do," he said.

My heart warmed, and for a moment I thought about leaning over and kissing him on the cheek.

The first impossible task.

"Besides," he said, "the Mists would have snatched you up the moment I left. Even if you didn't give in," and he looked away from me as he said this, "even if you weren't tied to me because of the curse, they would have used you. Somehow."

The warmth in my heart froze over.

"I can take care of myself," I snapped.

Naji fed another stick into the fire.

"I bet I can get us off this island."

Naji didn't say anything.

"Any Confederation baby knows how to build a signal fire," I went on. "I would have done it sooner but I figured we should get your curse cured first."

"And we still haven't done that."

I glared at him. "You know how to do it now. It just ain't anything we can do on the island. We'll have to build a bonfire on the beach," I said. "And feed it green wood so it'll let off plenty of smoke."

"It's going to be difficult to keep a beach fire burning here," Naji said. "Because of the storms."

"Long as we keep the fire going in here, we can relight it."

"That's not very efficient." He sighed. "I know a way, but–"

"A way to what? To keep it burning?" I looked at him. "Then why haven't you done it? Why didn't you do it as soon as they told you they wouldn't rescue us?"

The look he gave me was sharp as his sword.

"Kaol," I said. "You like it here, don't you? You like cold rainy islands half out of the world. No wonder you're an assassin."

He opened his mouth. Closed it. Then he said, "Scars don't spontaneously emerge overnight, Ananna. They come from somewhere."

It took me longer than it should've to figure out what he was getting at.

"Oh," I said. "Oh, then you don't have to... I can just relight the fire–"

Naji stood up and brushed past me. He stuck a stick into the hearth and yanked it back out with a spray of ash and sparks.

"It's fine," he said, in a voice that suggested it wasn't.

"Naji–"

He walked out of the shack, and for a moment I sat there, not knowing if he wanted to be left alone. The wind picked up and knocked tree branches against the side of the shack, and I thought about how if it wasn't for me he'd be off the island right now, back in the dry fragrant heat of Lisirra. And then I wondered what exactly had happened when he got his scars, if he'd had someone to help him when it all went wrong.

I threw my coat around my shoulders and ran down to the beach.

Naji was set up a ways down from the shack. The

bit of fire was smoldering on top of the sand, and Naji was tossing driftwood into a big pile. I gathered up some pine needles from the forest's edge and added them to the driftwood.

Naji looked at me but didn't say nothing, and I didn't say nothing to him.

With the two of us working together, it didn't take long for us to get a good-sized pile. I picked the hearth-fire up off the sand. Naji jerked his head toward the woodpile, and I dumped the fire onto it. The pine needles curled up and blackened and turned to ash.

"Stand back," Naji said, his voice a surprise after us working in silence for so long.

He pulled out his knife and pushed up the sleeve of his robe. His scars glowed faintly, tracing paths up and down his arm, undercutting the glow of his skin. He closed his eyes and took to chanting and dug the knife into his skin. The fire brightened, turned a gold color I ain't never seen in fire before. I felt something tugging at the edge of my thoughts, trying to drag me closer–

Blood dripped off Naji's arm, splattered across the beach. He caught some of the drops with his free hand. His chanting sounded like it was coming from a thousand voices at once. I wanted to be closer to the fire but I knew I needed to do what he said and stay back.

And then he flung the blood into the flames and there was this noise like a sigh and the fire erupted out so hot and bright that I fell backward onto the beach. It was still bright gold, and figures were entwined in the flames, swirling and dancing, and Kaol help me but I could feel their desperation, like if they stopped dancing my whole world would end.

Naji grabbed me by the arm and yanked me to my feet. He left a smear of blood on the sleeve of my coat.

"Stay away from it," he said. "This is not a cooking fire."

"What'd you do?" I asked.

"Gave myself a headache," he snapped. "From putting you in danger."

I almost said, It's just a fire but the firelight caught on his scars and I thought better of it.

I glanced over at the fire, golden light and dancing bodies, and thought about the assassin stories Papa always told me. How there was no way to defeat them, no way to intimidate them. Funny how wrong stories can be.

Naji led me up the beach, one hand gripping my upper arm. Anytime I tried to look back at the fire he jerked me forward again. When we got far enough away from it he dropped his hand and stopped on the beach. The sea-wind blew his hair away from his face, revealing the dark lines of scars. The dark sand stirred around our feet. It was almost the same color as the sky.

"Marjani will be back for us," I said. "I know it."

Naji sighed and folded his arms over his chest. "And what does it matter?" he asked.

"It matters a whole hell of a lot–"

"For you," he said. "I'll still have this curse, whether Marjani comes for us or not. Whether anyone comes for us."

"It'll still matter to me! I'm as much cursed as you are! I have to follow you around and I can't do anything that I want to do. Can't set up shop on a pirate's island, can't work the rigging on a Confederation ship."

He didn't answer.

"And it's not really impossible anyway," I said. "Isn't that what the wizard was getting at? You just have to complete those three tasks..."

Naji turned to me, and I was expecting fury but all I got was this look of sadness that made my heart clench up. "The tasks are impossible," he said. "That's where the name comes from. Three impossible tasks, one impossible curse."

At least one of the tasks isn't impossible.

I almost said it out loud. I almost said, I'm in love with you. Even though it didn't make sense, me being in love with him, even though it pissed me off – because he treated me like a kid sometimes and he sulked around when he was in a bad mood and he hated the ocean. But I loved him and if I kissed him then it would complete one of the tasks.

And if one of the tasks was completed, then the other two could be as well.

Naji sat down on the sand, his legs stretched out in front of him. He looked so sad I didn't think I could stand it. After a few moments, I sat down beside him. The sea misted over us, and I could taste the salt in the back of my throat.

"I don't think the tasks are really impossible," I said.

"And what do you know about magic?"

I pushed the sting of that aside. "I saved your life with it."

He didn't answer. I scooted close to him and put one hand on his shoulder. He tilted his head toward me, his hair tickling the tops of my knuckles.

"Marjani will come," I said. "She'll keep her word."

"She didn't actually promise–"

"Shut up. She'll come. And then we'll get a boat, and we'll find the princess' starstones and get into battle after battle until you figure out a way to create life from fighting."

He scowled out at the horizon line. The gray northern light fell around us like rain, and the sea slammed against the underside of the island.

And in the secret spaces of my mind, I imagined true love's kiss.

Acknowledgments

I would like to foremost thank my parents, primarily for not balking when I decided to earn a graduate degree in creative writing but also for all their support over the years, and Ross Andrews, who deserves my utmost gratitude for encouraging me even when I wanted to quit and for helping me through the highs and lows of pursuing a writing career.

My beta reader Amanda Cole helped me shape this book from a mess into a story, and our discussions about reading and writing have helped me as much as any class. Bobby Mathews, one of my oldest friends, has watched me develop as a writer and given me encouragement and advice all along the way. Stephanie Denise Brown and Stephanie Scudder propped me up through the six weeks of Clarion West and proved invaluable in their critiques. To all my friends: thank you.

I would also like to thank Dr Janet Lowery, Dr Elizabeth Harris, Peter LaSalle, and my instructors at the 2010 Clarion West Writers Workshop, for sharing their knowledge, wisdom, and advice.

Finally, I would like to thank Amanda Rutter, Lee Harris, and all the rest of the team at Angry Robot, for taking a chance with their Open Door Month and giving me this opportunity. And special thanks to my agent Stacia Decker, for all the work – too much to list! – that she has done to help me.

COMING SOON :

EXPERIMENTING WITH
YOUR IMAGINATION

"BOND WEAVES A DARK AND GORGEOUS TAPESTRY FROM AMERICA'S OLDEST MYSTERY."
SCOTT WESTERFELD

BLACKWOOD

GWENDA BOND

STRANGE CHEMISTRY

"With whip-smart, instantly likable characters and a gothic small-town setting, Bond weaves a dark and gorgeous tapestry from America's oldest mystery." — *Scott Westerfeld*

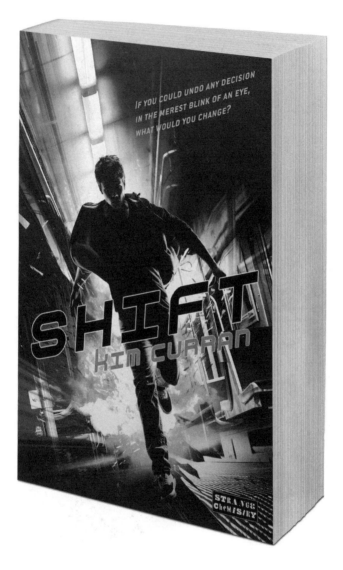

"It's like the best kind of video game: full of fun, mind-bendy ideas with high stakes, relentless action, and shocking twists!" – *E C Myers, author of* Fair Coin

"*Ghostbusters* meets *Sabrina the Teenage Witch* with a dash of *X-Files*. A magical spell with equal parts humour, adventure and surprise." — *Sara Grant, author of* Dark Parties

MORE WONDERS IN STORE FOR YOU...

- ◆ Gwenda Bond / BLACKWOOD
- ◆ Kim Curran / SHIFT
- ◆ Sean Cummings / POLTERGEEKS
- ◆ Jonathan L Howard / KATYA'S WORLD
- ◆ A E Rought / BROKEN
- ◆ Laura Lam / PANTOMIME
- ◆ Julianna Scott / THE HOLDERS
- ◆ Martha Wells / EMILIE & THE HOLLOW WORLD
- ◆ Christian Schoon / ZENN SCARLETT
- ◆ Cassandra Rose Clarke / THE PIRATE'S WISH
- ◆ Gwenda Bond / THE WOKEN GODS

STRANGE CheMISTRY

EXPERIMENTING WITH YOUR IMAGINATION

strangechemistrybooks.com
facebook.com/strangechemistry
twitter.com/strangechem